THE POET'S GAME

THE POET'S
GAME

A SPY IN MOSCOW

PAUL VIDICH

PEGASUS CRIME

NEW YORK LONDON

THE POET'S GAME

Pegasus Crime is an imprint of
Pegasus Books, Ltd.
148 West 37th Street, 13th Floor
New York, NY 10018

First Pegasus Books edition May 2025

Interior design by Maria Fernandez

Library of Congress Cataloging-in-Publication Data is available.

ISBN: 978-1-63936-885-3

10 9 8 7 6 5 4 3 2 1

Printed in the United States of America
Distributed by Simon & Schuster
www.pegasusbooks.com

For Linda

"I hate the idea of causes, and if I had to choose between betraying my country and betraying my friend, I hope I should have the guts to betray my country."

—E. M. Forster,
Two Cheers for Democracy

PART I

1

Moscow

August 2018

Alex Matthews glanced at his wristwatch, impatient for the tedious speaker to finish so he could make his way out of the crowded room and get on with some difficult business. He was on the third floor of the Hotel Baltschug Kempinski in a large soulless room facing a distant podium where a Russian speaking passable English was coming to the excruciating end of the conference's last speech. Matthews sat in the back, conscious of the short time before he was to meet an old adversary. The prospect of the six P.M. farewell cocktail hour brought a parched restlessness to the room, and a few attendees escaped to the bar.

The fierce heat of the day had begun to temper and the late afternoon sun cast long shadows on Red Square, visible to anyone in the room who preferred the view across Moscow River. Matthews had delivered the keynote speech to the Moscow trade organization, offering wisdom on how to invest without breaking securities laws. Later speakers gave advice on VAT strategies and risk management of tax loopholes, but the highlight, and the best attended talk, after his own, had been on business ethics: "Gogol's Dilemma: When a Nose Is Not a Nose."

Matthews was dressed casually in the crowd of young, impeccably attired British, French, and German attendees, having nothing to prove at his age and no one he needed to impress. He was an ordinary middle-aged man who'd left behind the vanity of youth and was comfortable being a slightly older, slightly grayer, slightly heavier version of his younger self. His hair had thinned and his waist had thickened from rich dinners with investors on his demanding travel schedule between Washington, DC, and Moscow. He preferred that age made him invisible to younger attendees, and he owed his talent for going unnoticed to his previous career in the CIA, which had trained him to slip into a restaurant without catching the waiter's eye.

Matthews took the handwritten note passed to him by his colleague. Mikhail Sorkin was his Russian lawyer and an old high school friend. He wore a bespoke Savile Row suit with a silk tie and his long silver hair was swept back on his head like an orchestra conductor. They had forged a teenage friendship during the Soviet Union's last days, drinking vodka, smoking Marlboro Reds, and reading Romantic poetry out loud as their rowboat drifted on the Moscow River. Sorkin led the Moscow practice of the London firm of Hammett & Hammett PC. His tie matched a crisp yellow pocket square, the splash of color accenting his charcoal suit. He had the firm, respectable manner of a lawyer cautioning his client.

Sorkin had written two words in bold block letters on the back of the day's program, copying them from a cell phone text: Tax

Audit. "Trinity Capital is in full compliance," Sorkin said, dismissing the concern. "We haven't bribed anyone and no one has asked for a bribe."

Sorkin said that it was a routine matter and there was no reason to be concerned, but Matthews had succeeded with his Russian investments because he was always concerned. The two men had a brief whispered conversation on how to address the matter, and then light clapping signaled the end of the speaker's remarks, and the end of the conference.

"Handle it," Matthews said. "I'll meet you in the bar in an hour. I have an errand to run."

He pushed his way through the thick exodus and escaped to a hallway decorated with plush carpets, gold mirrors, and ponderous Baroque furniture. The hall was lined with exhibitors' tables displaying colorful sales brochures and standard corporate swag. He strode purposefully past the inviting smiles of hard-eyed women whose only job was to attract questions that would be answered by older ambassadors standing just behind ready to pounce.

Matthews moved quickly down the crowded hall, but in the corner of his eye, approaching like a bullet, he saw the Russian journalist he'd avoided three hours earlier. Then she was in front of him, a tall woman blocking his way with a bright smile. She lifted her plastic conference keeper: Olga Luchaninova, *Novaya Gazeta*.

Her voice had the brisk politeness of someone about to make a rude request. When he stepped to one side, opening a way past her, she moved with him like a dance partner. She had intense eyes, flaming red hair, and an urgent expression. Her pen, he saw, was poised above a notepad like a dagger.

"A minute of your time," she said. "One question."

He knew that a minute in Russia was a notoriously inaccurate measure of time and the promise of brevity would be breached as one question begat another and another until a brusque departure ended the conversation.

"I'm sorry. I'm late. I don't have time for a question."

"Are you staying in the hotel? Perhaps drinks?" She thrust a business card. Her name in Cyrillic on one side, Roman on the other, cell phone on both. "Which room? We can meet privately later."

"Yes, later." He pointed to Sorkin, who'd come along side like a pilot fish. "Talk to him. He knows everything I said in my speech. And more."

Having offered Sorkin as his interview substitute, he made a cowardly lunge for the elevator, opening the closing doors with a quick hand.

He turned and saw Olga address Sorkin with a sour expression of distinct disinterest. Moscow was much changed from Soviet times, and different too from the early years of the Russian Federation when he'd been Moscow station chief, but *kompromat* endured. He was trained to be numb to the sad pleas of distraught women in bars and attractive reporters who offered favorable press coverage, knowing that these women were probably agents of Russia's *Federalnaya Sluzhba Bezopasnosti*.

He was alone on the short elevator ride to the lobby. He considered the possibility that the Federal Security Service was targeting him. On a different day, in a different hotel, he might have dismissed his concern as idle speculation, but that evening in the Hotel Baltschug Kempinski, he was on his way to meet a Russian asset, and whether Olga Luchaninova had targeted him was a matter of great personal concern. A man's life was at risk.

Matthews stepped into the hotel's garish lobby, furnished to appeal to Muscovites' vulgar taste for red velvet furniture and polished Italian marble. The sense of almost being in a grand hotel in Paris or Berlin was all around. He ignored the eyes of a man on the sofa who had been in the same position reading the same paper when he'd returned from a conference break earlier. The desk clerk nodded at Matthews as he passed, and the doorman in a red waistcoat and white gloves set the revolving exit door in motion so it spun slowly and deposited him outside, where another doorman offered to call him a taxi, which he declined.

He paused, looked around, and to anyone who happened to see him, Matthews would appear to be a foreign businessman enjoying the late afternoon's waning warmth near the Moscow River, watching streetlights blink on one by one. His casual appearance belied the alert eye of a man trained to spot danger. He took a measure of his surroundings, smiling at the doorman, and glanced at the river's esplanade. The ground floor patio restaurant was on his right and in front of him was a stone staircase that rose to Bolshoy Moskvoretsky Bridge, where a lively throng of tourists crossed the river to view the honor guard that goose-stepped out of the medieval fortress for its rotation at Lenin's tomb. Lights illuminated the enormous clock on Spasskaya Tower inside the Kremlin's walls.

Matthews spotted the red Toyota where he'd been told to expect it. It was ordinary and unremarkable in every respect except for its diplomatic plates. It was parked between two cars in a coveted spot, near an alley used for hotel deliveries. An old energy came back as he looked on—the nondescript car concerned him. He paused for a moment—a caution. The air was crisp with a hint of weather, and farther back toward the river it condensed into a mournful gloom that brooded over his decision. His long absence from covert work made him self-conscious and he wore caution with the calm of a man who was acutely aware of the risk he was taking. He heaved courage into his heart and stepped away from the hotel's sheltering canopy—a businessman obscure in his dark suit, his eyes checking guests by the entrance for a sign of the opposition. He was surprised how feelings from his previous career came alive, as if he'd never left that life behind.

He approached the car and slipped into the passenger seat—breathing quietly.

"You must be Alex Matthews." The driver smiled. "Simon Birch."

Matthews turned slowly to the man: mid-twenties, crew cut hair, a weightlifter's thick neck, a gray hoodie printed with a crimson "Harvard." A face eager for the night's work and unready for the danger.

"No names," Matthews said.

"Better that way."

"Yes, much better. The less I know the better."

"I was told to park here and you'd show up."

Matthews looked at him. "We've both done our part."

"What now?"

"It will happen quickly, if it happens."

"What is it?"

Matthews took a calming breath. "I get a package that I give to you. I return to the hotel and you go back to your nursery."

Matthews resisted an impulse to abandon the mission. He was stunned by the man's inexperience and appalled by the obvious license plates. He thought it was all wrong—the location, the time of day, pairing him with a rookie untested against the trained opposition of the FSB's counterintelligence service. Matthews knew the evening had been choreographed inside Russia House at Langley, vetted by the head of the CE Division, and greenlighted by the director of central intelligence. The time, location, and every turn in Birch's surveillance detection run had been assembled in advance. It was the same calcified bureaucracy he'd quit. Smart men six thousand miles away thought they needed to control what they couldn't see or touch—usurping the judgment of men on the ground. His suggestion that he meet BYRON in Moscow's quiet, outer suburbs, as they had done when Matthews recruited BYRON, was rejected in the mistaken belief that a crowded five-star hotel within sight of the Kremlin provided anonymity, but the brilliant architects of the night hadn't counted on who BYRON was—a KGB-trained intelligence officer who clung to Cold War habits.

Matthews glanced at the blue Moscow city bus that stopped on the bridge. An elderly cleaning woman in a green smock stepped off and a young couple climbed on board. Matthews could see the head and shoulders of passengers getting on and off and he looked for the familiar face.

"That's the third bus," Birch said.

"He'll come if it's safe."

"I was here early."

"There's a window. He'll come if he sees me. Only me."

"How long do we wait?"

"Until the window closes."

"We're being watched."

Matthews, too, had seen the glamorous young couple flounce out of the lobby, laughing, a little tipsy, falling into each other's arms. They had joined the short taxi queue, but they were staring now—the way Muscovites are instinctively suspicious.

Two men in a parked car talking, Matthews thought. Matthews put his hand on Birch's fingers that repeatedly tapped the steering wheel. "Relax."

"Another bus."

Off in the night, there was a bright flash of distant lightning and in a moment light rain began to fall, cooling the air. Drops hit the windshield and blurred Matthews's view of the bridge, so he put his head out to get a better view of the passengers.

"Will he know you?"

"I'll know him."

Matthews watched passengers disembark. It had been a decade since he had last seen BYRON, but there was no expiration date on rendezvous protocols. Each man's life depended on the other's diligent exercise of caution. Matthews wore a baseball cap, and so long as it stayed on his head, it signaled that it was safe for BYRON to approach.

"Why'd they pick you?"

"To make him feel safe."

"I heard you recruited him."

Matthews glanced in the direction of loud voices that came from a canopied tourist boat cruising the Moscow River spewing pop music into the evening. Rain pelted the water's dark surface and dampened the passengers' bright laughter. Matthews turned to the bus, where teenagers hopped off, and then he saw a man in a Soviet-style fedora move to the door. He instantly recognized BYRON—the stoic expression, flushed cheeks of a man who drank vodka, and vigilant eyes that surveyed the scene. He was a middle-aged man in a light raincoat, collar turned up, and he stood behind the bus driver, waiting his turn to get off. He had the studied calm of a Moscow gentleman on an evening errand.

"Hello."

Matthews saw the redhead knocking on Birch's window. Olga's shoulder-length hair had flattened in the rain and her black mascara bled, giving her a ghoulish appearance. She clutched her purse and motioned for Birch to lower his window.

"Remember me? We agreed to meet for a drink. I was waiting in the bar."

Matthews glanced at the bus.

"It's raining," she said. "Can I get in?"

"She's looking at you," Birch said. "Do you know her?"

Shit.

"What are we going to do?"

"Why don't you be a gentleman and buy her a drink?" Matthews snapped.

"Me?"

"Get her away from the car. Tell her I'll join her shortly. Tell her anything."

"Can we speak?" Olga said, tapping on the window.

She raised her plastic conference keeper at Matthews, holding it like a backstage pass.

"Just one question. Can I get in? It's raining." She touched her wet hair and pleaded her case. "Two minutes of your time, Mr. Matthews. The tax audit."

Matthews saw BYRON glance at Olga pounding on the Toyota's window. She had begun to yell, which got the attention of hotel guests in the taxi queue, and two Moscow police who sat in a blue-and-white BMW sedan parked by the river. The BMW's rotating roof lights went on and they stepped out. The officers wore black uniforms, pistols strapped to their thighs, and fluorescent yellow vests embroidered with ФСБ.

"This mission is over," Matthews said to Birch. He got out of the Toyota and took off his baseball cap, brushing back his hair, a deliberate gesture. Back in the car, he said, "Get us out of here before we're questioned."

"She's in the way."

Olga had planted herself behind the Toyota, blocking its path, and she stood defiant, arms crossed on her chest with a fierce expression.

"Back up," Matthews said.

"I'll hit her."

"Enough to pull out."

"Talk to her," Birch said. "She wants to speak with you."

Matthews lowered his window, motioning to Olga, but when she approached, he turned to Birch. "Drive now." He saw Birch's confusion. "Now," he shouted.

"She's crazy," Birch said, shifting from reverse to first gear, pulling forward. He had gone a few car lengths when they heard screams. Loud shrieks of pain mixed with pleas for help that drew a response from the two police, who hop-stepped forward.

Turning, Matthews saw the doorman join two hotel guests who had collected in a tight circle, talking in a blur of excited voices and motioning for assistance. The doorman held a wide black umbrella over Olga, who sat on the pavement holding her ankle. The doorman put his hand on her shoulder, but she threw it off, pointing at the Toyota.

Matthews stepped from the car and raised his hands in a calming gesture, using the moment to glance at the bus. BYRON's attention was distracted by something, but their eyes met in a brief acknowledgment that the operation was a bust. Voices at the scene, police asking questions of the doorman, and Matthews stood on the periphery of the chaos. The consequences of the unexpected calamity unfolded before his eyes.

For a man his age, fifty-two, remarried, and comfortable in a successful second career, he had, in his own mind, solved the problem of doing business in Russia rather well. He kept out of the scandal sheets and operated so as not to attract attention. When problems came up, as they invariably did, he knew the way through most problems was with a contrite apology and an offer of cash, and if that failed, he sought his Russian lawyer's intervention.

Matthews knelt at Olga's side, close enough to see her smudged mascara and the pain on her face. One high heel had snapped and a scraped knee showed through her torn slacks. People stared accusingly at him, so he turned his back and opened his wallet. "For a taxi home," he said. "I'll call when it's a better time."

She pushed his hand away. Her face was grave. "You are very rude."

"I'll handle this," Sorkin said, a firm hand on his client's shoulder, and he engaged with the two police officers.

Matthews stood by the car, impatient for Sorkin to finish. One officer spoke on her cell phone and the other listened impassively to Sorkin's loud protests, pointing at Olga, who now hobbled with the doorman's support. Curious passersby looked from across the street and tourists watched from the bridge.

Water streamed down Matthews's face and such was his concern that he ignored Birch's plea to get in the car. Then his old training kicked in, thinking the problem forward to anticipate what would happen next. He felt his jacket for his passport, but he remembered that he'd left it in the hotel room safe. He rehearsed what he should say—could say—about being in the car with Birch, and reminded himself: *Trust the plan*.

"The car didn't hit her," he called out. "She fell."

Sorkin stepped away from the FSB officers and approached, grim faced. "You're both under arrest."

"Nothing happened," Matthews said, agitated.

"Maybe she was hit, maybe she tripped, maybe she's lying. It doesn't matter. Once the police are involved, an arrest has to be made. That's how it works in Moscow."

2
Lubyanka Square–FSB Headquarters

Matthews was aware of unfamiliar voices close by and then they faded. At first, he thought the voices were part of a dream, but he opened his eyes and heard men in the corridor outside, and then they walked past and the sound disappeared.

He sat up on the hard bed, dropping his bare feet to the cold cement floor. He opened and closed his fists to bring sensation back to his fingers and he massaged his calves until the tingling numbness passed. He'd slept in his clothing, and his shirt smelled of sweat from his night of incarceration.

Questions and threats from the interrogating officer the night before came back to him as a puzzle of farcical absurdities, with the man's questions having nothing to do with the traffic incident. His initial blandishments had turned into a stream of shouted obscenities when Matthews kept repeating the same story about the woman, the car, the other American, while the interrogator kept returning to Trinity Capital's tax filings.

Matthews stood and stretched, moving his head one way and then the other, trying to relieve the neck pain that came from sleeping without a pillow. His mouth was parched. One small *fortochka* pane at the top of the high window was open, but no breeze entered. Dim light through the iron bars meant it was still a predawn hour.

He tried the handle of the cell's heavy wood door. He didn't think it would open, but it was a thing to do, a useless gesture of a man caught in an absurd situation. He pounded on the door and repeated what he'd said many times the night before, "I want to talk to my lawyer!"

He lay on the bed again, eyes open, listening to the silence, and in a few minutes, he drifted into groggy sleeplessness under a harsh fluorescent light that never went off.

Moscow was a bustling, modern city, but there was no sanctuary from its official criminal class for most people. The rich and agile survived its many hazards, and being both, Matthews knew how to dodge dangers without succumbing to the poison of indifference. Indifference wore him down, bled him, and kept him from understanding a predicament objectively. He'd learned the skill in the CIA and he put it to good use as an investor. There were no villains, only uncomfortable situations that required an iron will and a sense of humor.

❖

"Wake up."

Matthews was curled in a ball, hands between his legs for warmth, when he felt the poke in his ribs. He looked up into the face of an officer standing over him: clean-shaved, intelligent looking, with the fresh appearance of a man who'd just come to work. He wore a forest-green uniform and carried a high crown cap tucked under his arm. Matthews recognized the single gold star on his red epaulet: a colonel in the FSB's Sixth Service. All the things that Matthews had been trained to remember to use against the officer if the opportunity arose.

Matthews sat up, moving his feet off the bed, and saw the officer's polished black shoes and the cup of coffee he offered.

"*Koshrovo*," Matthews said, sipping. It was no worse than the shitty coffee offered by Moscow's cafes.

A lower-ranked officer stood by the cell door, hands clasped behind his back, his expression alert and deferential.

"Mr. Alexander Matthews," the colonel said.

"*Da.*"

He pointed to a table in the middle of the room with long, delicate fingers, a pianist's hand. Two battered wood chairs faced each other. "Join me."

Matthews sat and watched the colonel take the seat opposite. He placed his cap on the table and sat straight up, rigid, smiling. "You may call me Viktor Petrovich."

Wanting to be friendly, Matthews thought, giving his first name and patronymic. His last name was stitched above his breast pocket: Zhukov.

"Smoke?" Colonel Zhukov hit his pack of Primas on his arm, popping a cigarette, which he offered. When Matthews declined, Zhukov lit one and took a long pull, brightening the end. He released a lungful of smoke from the corner of his mouth and smiled.

"How are you doing, Alex? Did they treat you well last night? Have they offered you breakfast?"

"I've slept better."

"It's not the Kempinski. We don't want to make our guests comfortable."

They chatted about nothing in particular for a few minutes, pretending it was a perfectly normal conversation. Matthews listened to Colonel Zhukov go on about life in Moscow for the duration of two puffs of his cigarette.

Matthews leaned forward. "Why am I here?"

"The better question is: Why am *I* here in Lubyanka at seven in the morning?" Colonel Zhukov held the cigarette between thumb and forefinger, his elbow cocked, before balancing the cigarette on the edge of the scarred wood table. "I was informed that a terrible mistake was made last night."

"Good to hear."

"The driver of the Toyota will be held subject to further investigation, but as the passenger, you weren't involved in the injury."

"The car didn't hit her."

"Witnesses contradicted each other. The woman recanted her story, but then what people thought was a car accident turned out to be something else—serious in a different way." Colonel Zhukov leaned forward. "The doorman said you solicited the woman."

Matthews laughed.

"She pounded on the car's window pleading with you. She was overheard saying she waited for you in the bar. The police were called. A file has been opened."

Colonel Zhukov lifted his cigarette and drew on it slowly, keeping his eyes on Matthews.

"Let me give you two pieces of advice, if I may. Don't get in a car with a careless driver, because we take traffic accidents seriously. Don't let yourself be approached by a woman on the street. Prostitution is a serious matter in Moscow."

Matthews considered the advice. "Why was I brought here?"

"Here? Lubyanka?"

"Traffic accidents aren't capital crimes."

"You're not just anyone involved in a traffic incident, or just anyone who solicited a prostitute. You're a prominent capitalist."

Matthews placed his palms on the table. His voice was steady but his lips twitched indignantly to head off the false narrative of the evening. "You have it all wrong. What you think I was doing, or what someone thinks they overheard, is a mistake. That woman approached me with a question. She's a reporter for *Novaya Gazeta*."

"Drinks in your hotel room? An offer of cash?"

Matthews lurched forward. "Ask her."

"I don't need to. This matter is dismissed. Russia has many foreign investors like you, but you have one thing others don't—a good Russian lawyer."

Colonel Zhukov returned Matthews's cell phone and wallet and presented him a small color photograph that he'd found in the wallet.

"Who is the girl?"

"My daughter."

"Abide by our laws if you want to make sure you'll see her again."

"She's dead."

Colonel Zhukov frowned. "My condolences. Are you back in the spy business?"

"Business yes. Spying no. Investments."

"And this?" He held up a delicate Meissen figurine of a monkey in a drummer's uniform.

"A gift I was carrying."

"The person must be a good friend." He returned it to its bubble wrap. "A valuable collector's piece."

Matthews took the porcelain figure. "An old friend."

A dull, gray, cold September morning met Matthews when he was escorted out of FSB headquarters onto Lubyanka Square. He'd driven past the building in his old role as CIA station chief, but he'd never been inside the Neo-Baroque building. Its distinctive yellow brick façade had been cleaned of Soviet-era soot, but the ghosts of the Cheka and KGB remained, as did the hammer and sickle etched in a stone lintel above the entrance.

Mikhail Sorkin's Maybach S class Mercedes was parked nearby and he stood by the open rear door. He wore gloves and a scarf, but no overcoat. Upon seeing Matthews escorted from the building, he stepped forward, greeting his client with a reassuring hand on his shoulder and the obliging deference of a highly paid attorney.

"I'm fine. I need a shower. He wants to be friendly, which made our conversation a tedious game." Matthews pointed toward Colonel Zhukov, who had accompanied Matthews and now stood by the entrance.

"So, you're okay?"

"Yes. My basement cell had a good view. I could see all the way to Siberia."

"You know all the old jokes. I'll be back in a minute."

Matthews sat in the Mercedes's back seat and observed the two men huddled together. He was too far to overhear, but he was close enough to read their body language.

"What did he say?" Matthews asked when Sorkin slipped in the car.

"Apparatchik." He tapped his driver's shoulder and the car pulled away. Sorkin looked out at the heavy morning traffic and made his judgment. "There was the Cheka, then the NKVD, the KGB, and now the FSB. All the same scorpions."

He looked at Matthews. "Zhukov apologized for the misunderstanding. That's how things work here. They arrest you for one thing and then discover something else. In your case, it's your old job."

"I saw you arguing with him."

"It wasn't an argument."

"Just two men in front of Lubyanka shouting at each other." He looked at Sorkin. "Why would he ask me about the tax audit?"

Sorkin's eyes came off the traffic. "I asked him why he cared. A tax audit comes under Directorate K, the FSB's economic security department. Colonel Zhukov is Department M, counterintelligence."

Sorkin pondered a moment. "Be careful of Zhukov. He works for Igor Sechin, who is close to Putin. You don't want Trinity Capital to be this visible." Sorkin turned to Matthews. "Is there something you're not telling me?"

"There's a lot I don't tell you. What about the other guy? Birch."

"He'll be held while there is an investigation. He's an American who speaks no Russian, driving a car with diplomatic plates. They want to know who he is. I vouched for you, but it is best that you leave Moscow for a few weeks."

Sorkin opened the morning edition of *Komsomolskaya Pravda* to a middle page. A photo captured Matthews's raised hand blocking photographers with a caption: AMERICAN FINANCIER ARRESTED.

"She took it. Her name is Olga Luchaninova. She is a part-time editor of Russian *Vogue*, a reporter of the new generation. She sells stories where she can and she's big in the dissident crowd. Sometimes they're arrested, sometimes assassinated."

He looked at Matthews. "You need to leave Moscow to let the FSB's interest cool and you should avoid appearing in the press again. It's dangerous for a wealthy American investor in Russia to be in the tabloids."

Sorkin indicated his driver, quiet, obedient, overhearing everything. "Kirill will drive you to Sheremetyevo. I booked you on an Air France flight that leaves in five hours. You have a stopover in Paris and arrive in Washington tomorrow. I will handle the tax questions."

Sorkin showed Matthews the string of text messages on his cell phone. "Your friends are concerned." He scrolled down and presented his phone. "Anna is sick with worry."

Matthews saw half a dozen texts from his wife. It was nine A.M. in Moscow and past midnight in Washington. The texts had come in the middle of the night.

"She tried your phone but got no answer. She texted me thinking I knew where you were."

Matthews turned on his cell phone and text notices popped up and his voice mailbox had a message. "Did you answer her?"

"I did this morning. Not last night."

"Why not?"

"And say what? You'd been arrested for soliciting a prostitute?"

"That didn't happen. You know that."

"The police arrested you and charged you with solicitation. Should I lie?"

"It was a mistake. A ridiculous misunderstanding on a rainy night by an overly persistent woman."

"Mistake? Maybe. You have to be careful." He looked at Matthews. "She approached you. She was insistent. You're a wealthy American and an obvious target for *kompromat*. In Moscow, any number of people might target you."

"What she was doing and what I was doing were two very different things."

"She invited herself to your hotel room. Didn't she? I heard her."

Matthews leaned back. Lack of sleep and the exhaustion and stress of the unfolding dilemma worked its way under his skin. One small favor for a former CIA colleague—*a small thing, one meeting, you're the courier.* He could hear the director of central intelligence make his urgent plea for help.

"Directorate K can make life difficult for Trinity Capital. You operate here at the pleasure of men with their palms out." Sorkin looked at Matthews. "What were you doing in the Toyota?"

"I was meeting the son of an old friend." He added a detail to make the lie more plausible. "He's having a hard time adjusting to embassy life as a young bachelor."

Sorkin was skeptical. "You're my client, but also my friend, so let me give you some advice. That woman is an opportunist. She knows how to get what she wants."

"Don't lecture me."

"Moscow is safe, but an attractive woman can make it dangerous."

"I can handle myself."

"You have a public position with Trinity Capital. You've made friends, made money, but you've also made enemies. Your crusade for stock market transparency comes in a country where oligarchs preserve stolen wealth by hiding it." Sorkin lifted the newspaper. "The next photo of you will be with Olga Luchaninova through a telephoto lens kissing on a hotel balcony with a blackmail note offering to tear up the photo in exchange for a sum of money deposited into a Cayman Islands bank account."

Matthews said nothing. He knew a strenuous defense would deepen Sorkin's suspicion.

"I didn't mention any of this to Anna," Sorkin said. "You can give her whatever story you like. The details of your flight are here." He presented an envelope. "Once you're away from Moscow, gossip will pass. It's less likely that the newspapers will dig up the fact that you were once the CIA's top spy in Moscow."

"All that is behind me."

"It's new to someone who doesn't know."

The Mercedes pulled up in front of the Hotel Baltschug Kempinski. Sorkin leaned across the seat to Matthews as he stepped out of the car. "Kirill will pick you up in an hour and drive you to the airport." He handed Matthews a wrapped gift. "This is for your son's birthday. Give him my regards—from his uncle Mikhail. Tell Anna we'll plan a winter holiday on my yacht in St. Lucia."

Matthews watched the Mercedes drive off and he looked at his cell phone. He read his wife's texts. The first had come minutes after ten, asking if he'd be calling. While in Moscow, he called every night at ten local time to give her the news of his day and to hear her complaints about her agency interpreter's job. They were a new couple who found a way to adjust their marriage to the demands of her job and his travel. The nightly call was a way to stay in touch, talk, and share intimate details of their day.

Her texts followed at intervals of fifteen minutes and became increasingly concerned. After the fourth text around eleven o'clock Moscow time, she left a voicemail.

"Alex, is something wrong? You're not answering my texts. Call me."

PART II

3

Washington, DC

The first time Alex Matthews met Anna Kuschenko he was still getting on his feet after a boating accident that killed his wife and daughter. At the time, he was part of the CIA's Senior Intelligence Service, but he'd begun to separate himself from the agency to spend time with his son, who was the sole survivor of the accident. Well-meaning colleagues and their wives invited him to suburban barbecues and Georgetown cocktail parties to introduce him to handsome widows and single career women, but he spurned the introductions. Charm, feminine sophistication, and low-cut cerise party dresses didn't arouse Matthews. Grief and guilt were stubborn emotions and he wore his solitude like a well-tailored suit.

❖

Anna looked in on Matthews's teenage son and found David in bed asleep with headphones on. The room was dark except for moonlight that came through the window facing Chesapeake Bay. She approached quietly and lowered the iPhone's volume before removing his headphones. He was a rebellious teenager, but in sleep he had the innocence of youth. She adjusted the comforter and tucked him in.

It was Anna's great challenge to be a stepmother to a fourteen-year-old who sorely missed his mother and stubbornly resisted Anna's effort to bring a sense of family to the household. Nothing in her life had challenged her more than his resentment. She knew the unhappy boy's struggle but she didn't see it on his sleeping face. The distance between them was insurmountable, but in Matthews's absences, they ate together, spent evenings in the same house, and shared the little surprises of everyday life. They had managed to find a tolerable common ground. David had come to grudgingly appreciate her effort to be helpful and she was mindful not to try to be a substitute mother.

Anna entered the dark master bedroom and slipped under the covers. She went to place her hand on Alex's chest, but the bed was empty. She saw him standing at the window, silhouetted in silvery moonlight.

"I thought you were asleep," she said, moving to his side.

Matthews acknowledged her but turned back to his view from the bay window. Blustery wind swayed tree branches along the shore, and lights strung along the dock blinked wildly. Their dock jutted into the dark cove and the moored sailboat rose and fell on the choppy swells. Clouds passed in front of the moon and somewhere off in the night wind chimes rang.

She drew close, hand on his shoulder.

"Is David asleep?" he asked.

"He fell asleep listening to music."

"Did he miss me?"

"Of course."

"He didn't come out of his room when I arrived."

"You return every week. There is nothing special about your coming home."

Matthews turned to Anna and saw in her face the quiet, safe place that he imagined his home should be—so far removed from the drama in Moscow. He was home now, in the house that was his sanctuary and a refuge from the unforgiving demands of Trinity Capital. The cottage, as he liked to call it, was familiar and safe, and never disappointed him. He traveled to Moscow three or four times a month for a few days at a time, but he'd never had a desire to make Moscow his home. He stayed in hotels to remind him that he was there temporarily. A hotel room didn't belong to him, there were no precious familiar objects, and he collected no fond memories that were difficult to surrender when he returned to Washington. Travel to Moscow was a phase in his life that would come to an end. He kept track of the statistics of his nomadic life—another 4,898 miles added to the quarter million that he'd accumulated, and five hundred hours he'd spent in the air. It was a fraction of his life, but it weighed heavily on his marriage. He was coming to the end of that part of his life and he had no idea what he would do next.

Matthews's departure from Russia House had been traumatic, but he only came to understand the depth of his anger when he was successful with Trinity Capital. He'd joined the agency after the fall of the Berlin Wall, catching patriotism like a virus, and he embraced the agency's mission. The debacle of 9/11's intelligence failure, and the agency's subsequent efforts to help President Bush justify the Iraq invasion, appalled him, but his loss of faith came later, like a slow dusk, when he saw agency mandarins do what was necessary to regain respect in Congress, the press, and a new man in the Oval Office. Ambitious senior officers shaped intelligence assessments to be what their audience wanted to hear. Matthews spoke up. He'd risen high enough in the agency so his loud protests against the hypocrisy couldn't be ignored. There was a sharp edge of truth to his accusations that elicited caution from colleagues inside Russia House who were protective of their clubby domain. He was warned to be less vocal, but when he kept up his criticisms, ambitious colleagues worked against him. He was frozen out of key decisions, excluded from meetings, and he found himself powerless against the institutional forces that conspired against him. But it was the self-inflicted scandal of his office affair that ended his career.

The agency's moral economy operated with its own dialectic—wet work done in the name of national security was tolerated, even rewarded, but there was no room for the security risk of an open liaison between colleagues. He discovered, without knowing it at the time, that he was judged not by the quality of his faith in the agency's mission, but the quantity of his doubt in how the mission was carried out. He knew it was best for him to leave and he accepted an exit package that provided continuing health benefits through a post-term consultancy. Anna stayed in the Directorate of Operations using her language skills in support of clandestine operations. He founded Trinity Capital to make money and move on with his life.

"Come to bed," she whispered. Her hand was on his shoulder, but he stayed where he was, staring into the gloomy night. "Tell me what happened in Moscow."

It was their routine to talk about what happened during his days away from home. Sharing funny stories about daily life and the aggravations at work were a way of staying in each other's lives.

"You first," he said.

"Mostly a dull week. I worked a dinner with a delegation from the Moscow Institute of Physics and Technology. They were drinking a lot and one man hit on me. He put his hand on my knee and tried to impress me with his 'secrets,' so I didn't slap him. I kept going to the bathroom and scribbling notes until a woman in the delegation, who must have been the SVR handler, saw what was going on and confronted me in a stall. That was my excitement. Nothing to match yours."

"You heard what happened from Mikhail?"

"Tom Wallace called. He's the one I spoke to." Her voice lowered. "He said you were arrested for soliciting a prostitute."

Matthews's brow knit. "I was set up. She was a journalist wanting a story and she approached the car I was in."

He saw that she didn't believe him, or disbelieve him, but wanted to be convinced.

"She approached me and asked me about Anton Glok, which was crazy. A shot in the dark. But it happened while I was being watched. The FSB suspected something. I don't know how they knew, but they knew enough to watch me."

"What happened with BYRON?"

"It's best that I don't go into it."

"I'm in the agency."

Matthews's gaze had drifted from the window. "He was there, but he left. We aborted the meeting when the woman made a scene. I had brought a Meissen figurine, the way I used to, but it didn't happen." He looked at her. "How did Wallace know?"

"Tom's your friend. He heard there was a problem and he asked if I'd heard from you." Anna drew closer, aware that she was intruding on his thoughts. "You're looking out at the bay. Are you thinking about her?"

Matthews knew the exact spot where the sailboat had capsized and he could see it through the window near the channel island. David had been rescued. It was a long-planned family sailing excursion for David's ninth birthday, but the day before they were to sail, Matthews was called overseas on an urgent assignment, and they argued fiercely. He hated to defend himself against her claim that he put job before family, and when he said he couldn't put off the trip, she said she would go without him. She was a good sailor but the freak summer storm had been too much for her single-handed sailing skills. David was picked up in his lifejacket by a passing motor launch, but his wife and daughter were never found.

On many occasions, Matthews had wondered how things might have turned out if he had been on board. He blamed himself, but he also blamed her. She went out alone to spite him. Their marriage was fraying badly and they didn't know how to talk as they drifted apart.

"Grief never goes away," he said. "You go through it, and it becomes part of you." He had been unusually close to his daughter and her death was an open wound on the heart. The anniversary of the accident usually fell on Labor Day weekend, so the annual celebration was a reminder of their deaths.

Anna hugged him and took his arm. "Come to bed."

"In a minute."

"You're too hard on yourself."

"I should have been there."

"But you weren't. You have a son who needs you. I need you. It's not right to wallow in what you might have done. She put them at risk. Come to bed."

He followed her to bed, and once under the covers, she took his hand and kissed his fingers—one then another. She came up on her elbow. "What happened in Moscow?"

"What's the gossip you're hearing?"

She smiled and zipped her lips. "Spies are caught because of pillow talk."

"I don't work for them anymore."

"I do."

He laughed.

"Gossip?" she said. "Driscoll's getting divorced. Wallace is having another affair. This time with an English woman, attractive, married, MI6. Her husband is a gruff, crusty pillar of the British establishment and a limp dick in bed."

Matthews sat up. The idea that two intelligence officers charged with protecting national security secrets couldn't keep their infidelities private was laughably scandalous. "How does he get away with it?"

"Ask him. He's your friend."

"Does Rose know?"

"I don't know what she knows. They're coming to tomorrow's dinner party at the Cosmo Club, so you can see how they manage. We're such a small, closed community, we look to our friends for adultery. It's madness."

"It won't end well for them."

"The madness," she said. "You realize I'm fifteen years younger than you."

"That makes no difference."

"It does to David."

"He can see that I love you. He can see how well we're suited for each other."

"What happened in Moscow with that woman?"

"I told you. She wanted to interview me. She was aggressive. Asked to meet for a drink. The police thought she was a prostitute, but she wasn't. They arrested me thinking I'd solicited her. It was a misunderstanding that BYRON happened to witness."

"Have you ever slept with a woman in Moscow?"

"Oh, come on. Are you serious?"

"Have you?"

"No."

"Do you love me?"

"I just said I did. David can see it. He can see that you love me."

"Maybe I don't."

"You don't have to say it for me to know you love me. But you'll say it."

"We'll see." She smiled gamely. "You'll force me to say it. You'll waterboard me."

Matthews laughed. "I have a plan."

She pulled the sheets over their heads, making a canopy. "We're here in our make-believe world living the life we've made for ourselves. In bed sharing this."

"This?"

"Us."

He saw in her soft, lighthearted smile what had attracted him the day they met—the carefree woman in her professional shell surprising him with flirtatious behavior that made him feel younger. He deplored the pathetic examples of divorced friends who remarried much younger women, but his harsh opinion softened when he found himself a member of that club. She was intelligent, determined, witty, and passionate in bed and he no longer cared how he was judged, or even if he was judged. He'd done his service for country, fought the good fight against the intelligence bureaucracy, and made money. He could do as he pleased.

"They talk about you," she said.

"Who?"

"Wallace, Linton, Driscoll, D'Angelo. All your old colleagues. They want to know what big things go on in Alex Matthews's new life."

"What do they ask?"

"It's what they say. They resent that you're still close to the Director. You talk to the Director more than they do. Envy. Pride. Anger. Almost half the deadly sins."

"The half needed to succeed. I'm glad I left."

"So are they."

Matthews didn't have to ask the question that was on his mind.

"Driscoll wants to cut off your access to the seventh floor. He wants to shut down the favors you do for the Director—the Moscow errands."

"He's guessing."

"You've excited a lot of interest with BYRON's resurrection." She drew the tented sheet closer around them. "A cone of silence. Everything we say in here was never said."

"Will you try to fuck the truth out of me?"

"What a great idea."

Matthews felt her hand on his bare chest and looked into her blue eyes, darker in the tent, but her seductive smile was alluring. Matthews worried that his travel and time away from home put pressure on their marriage. He worried that he was too old for her and that the interests of a man his age were different from the interests of a woman fifteen years younger. He fretted that their relationship would exhaust itself and she'd find a lover closer to her own age.

"The Director called this morning," she said. "He wanted to know when you'd get home." Her voice softened when she saw his concern. "Is there anything I should know?"

His answer came quickly. "I'll talk to him tomorrow after the senator's funeral." He laid his head on the pillow and reassured her. "If it's important, I'll fill you in at our dinner party."

He had been emotionally inept when they first met. She wasn't horrified by his clumsy feelings and instead embraced the awkward moments, giving him the gift of her patience. His unconscious was cowardly, but he became brave with her teasing, her playfulness, and her eager lovemaking. It was delusional, he'd said, this thing between them—a fiction that made them happy, but why not enjoy it? The advantage of being older was that he had enough experience to know that it didn't matter—whatever happened didn't need a reason. Feelings were enough. She reminded him of no one in his former life—not sister, mother, not teenage sweetheart, college girlfriend, and not his first wife. If anything, she was the river goddess he came upon bathing in the clear waters of a forest stream.

She was asleep next to him, mysterious in the wild dominion of her dreams. He thought he knew her, but he knew only a part of her. He gently touched her shoulder, waking her. He moved closer and whispered seductive words in her ear. She stirred, rolling from one side to the other, and faced him, eyes dark and breath warm. Her moist lips met his, and she made stifled noises of desire behind the kiss. All at once he wanted her.

He placed his hand between her legs, which opened for him, and her hand slid down his stomach, taking him in a firm grasp. Their breath quickened and he saw a mischievous smile break across her face as they savored the pleasure. He felt the heat of her skin through her loose cotton top, which she threw off, and she lifted herself slightly to be on top and guided him in. Slow, patient movements hastened into grinding, and their feverish breath quickened as they dove into a warm pool of fragrant passion. His hand gripped her buttocks, and her mouth gasped for air, sucking breaths ragged in his ear.

Later, lying side by side, he pressed his face against hers. He had a clear feeling that one day she would be gone—he was older, she younger, and death would come between them. He kept his face close for a long time, holding on to the moment.

4
National Cathedral

Matthews arrived early for the funeral. He wore a charcoal-gray suit and stepped into a rear aisle of the National Cathedral after Anna, who was dignified in a black lace veil and ebony dress. Nothing on her stood out except the pinch of scarlet in her ruby pin and Matthews was comfortable in their obscurity. He picked a rear pew to avoid drawing attention, but he was conscious nevertheless of being noticed as Washington's elite moved past television cameras at the cathedral's entrance and made their way down the aisle toward reserved seats facing the black-bunted catafalque and mahogany casket.

Their quiet demeanor hid them in the crowd, yet several times he caught men and women, but particularly women, lean backward to get a better look at Anna, whose blonde hair and striking face were visible under the veil. He had wanted to come alone, but she'd said there would never be another Washington gathering like this and she pleaded to accompany him.

As he studied the printed order of service, Anna nudged his elbow. Looking up, he saw a man at his side in the aisle.

The director of the Central Intelligence Agency wore a rumpled suit with a black-and-white polka-dot bow tie, and his fleshy jowls sagged, but his right eye was alert and clear, and his left, a glass prosthesis, looked at nothing. He was a garrulous man whose bonhomie was an old spy's trick to steer conversations to harmless chitchat and in the process entice the other person to speak openly, perhaps carelessly.

"Meet me outside when this is over," he whispered to Matthews. "We need to talk about Moscow. You look like you haven't slept."

The Director smiled at Anna. "Good to see you again." His one good eye drifted to the crowd. "In this town, I'm always surprised to discover how many friends a man has when he's dead."

Matthews wasn't certain whether to laugh at the irreverence or ignore it.

The Director resumed his place in the procession of late-arriving dignitaries, politicians, media celebrities, and family members who made their way toward the deceased—Senator John McCain.

The order of service gave his age, older than Matthews thought, given his lively interactions with the man when he had sat in front of the Senate Select Committee on Intelligence, fielding the man's blunt questions. He had on occasion argued with the pugnacious senator whose well-known contempt for the president had ginned up speculation whether he would attend. Matthews, like everyone already seated, was keenly aware of who had entered the cathedral and who had not.

"Henry Kissinger," Matthews whispered to Anna. The former Nixon national security advisor seemed to have shrunk and he moved with the help of a cane and his towering wife.

"Dick Cheney," he said. The former vice president walked with his wife, moving slowly, eyes respectfully down, but with the vague smiles of a couple grateful to be on the attendee list. The secretary of defense arrived in uniform walking beside the latest White House chief of staff, and they were followed by Rudy Giuliani, who broke the unwritten rule against acknowledging his presence to the television cameras recording arrivals. Noticing the breach of etiquette, Matthews whispered to Anna, "Rude-e Rudy."

Matthews was there because he had been invited—a surprise since the invitation had come from the man in the casket, and it was only later that he learned that McCain in the last days oversaw all the details of his funeral—the music played, the invitation list, and who would speak. Matthews knew McCain hated politicians and joked at their expense. He'd heard him remark with disgust that they were scumbags, toadies, amoral reprobates, narcissistic blowhards, and no politician drew his ire more than the disinvited occupant of the Oval Office.

Arriving late, and slipping into the pew beside Anna, were Matthews's former agency colleagues. First was James Linton, head of counterintelligence, a WASPish Ivy Leaguer whose thick gray hair was combed straight back, giving prominence to his forehead. His black suit hung loosely on his tall, thin frame. He was followed by Mark Driscoll, head of the CE Division, who excused his way into the middle of the aisle. Tom Wallace, a Russia House scotch-and-cigars old-school type, whispered his excuse as he passed, "Traffic." He greeted Anna with a kiss on the cheek. "Black becomes you."

Matthews caught the compliment and her shy surprise, feeling unexpected jealousy. He turned back to the late-arriving celebrities, pointing out the president's daughter and son-in-law, who sat one pew behind two former Democratic presidents and their wives.

"It's a convocation of the political opposition," Anna said, pointing out several other prominent Democrats. The wail of the cathedral's great pipe organ filled the vaulted space, signaling the start of the service.

The two former presidents took turns offering tributes to the Republican senator they had defeated in past elections, lavishing kind praise on their former opponent's patriotic military service. Bowed heads lifted when No. 44 called upon mourners to be braver than politics, which Matthews understood, but he thought the reference oblique to many. McCain's daughter, speaking through tears, was more direct: "The America of John McCain doesn't need to be great again. It's already great."

Scattered applause, however inappropriate, filled the vast cathedral but did not mask the comment from the row behind Matthews.

"It's McCain's way of poking him in the eye."

When the service ended, Matthews and Anna escaped into the swampy Saturday weather. The early afternoon sun beat down as they took the wide stone steps with other congregants who stopped to greet acquaintances or share an observation about the funeral. He held Anna's arm when he was approached by a security officer with dark glasses and earbuds.

"Mr. Matthews?"

"Yes."

"Please follow me." He pointed to a black, customized Escalade SUV parked nearby.

Matthews handed Anna his car keys. "I'll meet you at dinner."

"Six sharp. The Cosmo Club. Seven friends are coming for our anniversary. Don't be late."

Matthews slipped into the Escalade's rear door and took a seat beside the Director and, when his eyes adjusted to the dim light coming through the tinted windows, he saw James Linton sitting opposite in a facing seat.

"I asked James to join us. It's easier to meet this way. An Alex Matthews sighting on the seventh floor would excite the paranoid imaginations of your former colleagues. This is private. No one but James knows and we'll keep it that way."

Matthews nodded at Jim Linton, taking in his expressionless face and carefully knotted tie. A man who was hard to read, he presented himself with a pleasant manner. He wore tortoiseshell eyeglasses on his angular face, and his thick hair, which had only recently begun to show hints of gray, gave him a youthfulness that added to the impression he was trustworthy. Other agency employees had followed the rest of the world and dressed casually for work, but Linton stuck to the old uniform—silk tie, starched white shirt, and an impeccably tailored suit. His hands were clasped on his lap and they had the pale look of being washed often. His lips were thin seams on his narrow face, his eyes quiet and alert.

"Sad event," Linton said. "Anna was striking."

The Director stuffed his bow tie in his pocket. "I hate this thing. I have just one and it's getting too much use. At our age we don't need to be reminded of what's next. At least his daughter was blunt."

The Director looked at Matthews as the SUV pulled away. "Your wife's name?"

"Anna." Matthews noticed a Scottish terrier curled on the Director's lap, and he did his best to ignore it, but the dog lifted its attentive eyes and wagged its tail.

"He's my wife's, but she's out of town and he demands company, so he rides with me to the office. I don't like pets and never had one as a boy, but Pooch doesn't bark in meetings and he lets me know when he's got to pee." The Director affectionately petted the old terrier with his thick-knuckled hand and turned back to Matthews.

"James reminded me that Anna works for us. A language specialist. So, in my mind you're still in the family."

Matthews said nothing because the comment didn't require an answer.

The Director fixed his one good eye on Matthews. "Fill me in on Moscow."

Matthews had spent the long flight home and the days since considering the details of the busted rendezvous, trying to arrive at a plausible explanation. The easy conclusion was that chance intervened in the form of the female reporter whose actions caused the unforeseen events that followed, but that explanation didn't feel right. Didn't satisfy his doubt and it didn't account for BYRON's last glance. He was trained to be a skeptic and not to reward an adversary's clever deceptions by excusing failure as the convenient working of chance.

"Well?"

"BYRON was late. The embassy driver was nervous. A woman drew police attention and I had no choice but to abort."

"Was BYRON there? Did he show?"

"He was there, but he never got off the bus."

"But he was there. He was willing to meet."

"He was there. I had to end it when the woman crashed the party. She prevented a disaster." Matthews looked to both men. "BYRON saw something. He was looking down the street, away from me."

"Compromised?"

"The FSB was waiting. He saw the trap. We were saved by the random act of a crazy reporter who wanted to interview me."

The Director considered the news. "BYRON was always the smartest one, which is why he is the only one still in place."

"KEATS, SHELLEY, BLAKE?" Matthews asked.

"Gone," Linton said. "BYRON is the last one in your poets' network."

"What happened to the rookie driver?"

"Birch is being held," Linton said. "It should be a diplomatic flap. Declared persona non grata, expelled. But they're holding him to trade—maybe for Anton Glok, but that won't happen. Birch is a throwaway and Glok is Putin's arms merchant. Was there a choice?"

Matthews stared hard at Linton, voice lowering. "They took me, they took Birch. Birch can be exchanged, but if BYRON were caught, he'd be imprisoned or turn up dead. He's smart, but he's tired."

Matthews looked from Linton to the Director, voice with a hard edge. "Agency planning was terrible. A clean slot rookie dressed like a kid on spring break. Inexcusable. Meeting outside a five-star hotel a short walk from the Kremlin. Irresponsible." Matthews's voice rose to an indignant tenor. "Incompetence all around."

"Or a leak," Linton said.

The suggestion created an awkward silence in the car. *Traitor* was a word that never appeared in memos and it went unsaid in meetings, but it was James Linton's mission as head of counterintelligence to be vigilant against the possibility of a security breach. Agency employees were regularly approached by foreign nationals, and lie detector tests were a part of internal security protocols, but Linton knew the precautions were inadequate. It was naïve, he liked to say, to believe that there were no penetration agents among the thousands of agency employees.

"A few senior officers knew the details of the meeting," Linton said.

"A few too many?" Matthews snapped. "I don't work for the agency. You put me at risk."

"Do I know you were compromised?" Linton said. "No, I don't, but it would be irresponsible to ignore the possibility—the probability—given who BYRON is. Someone in the group of men who knew about this is working for the Russians."

Linton clasped his hands tightly in his lap like a priest who'd completed an exorcism.

"It's your job to think that way, James," the Director said. "But I don't want this operation to be hostage to your paranoia." He looked at Linton. "You do what you need to. Follow the stink. But I won't have this operation held up while you perform your colonoscopy. I need what BYRON has." The Director added, "Is that clear?"

Matthews and Linton were contemporaries, having joined the agency the same year from the same Ivy League college, but their careers had diverged and advanced on parallel tracks. Matthews had moved overseas with tours in the Balkans, Lebanon, and Russia, while Linton had stayed in headquarters—the solitary man who spent long nights and weekends assessing anomalous data that were the first clues to treason—intelligence officers spending beyond their known income, erratic behavior, excessive drinking, and unreported romantic relationships. His work didn't build friendships in the agency, but it generated respect and fear among every intelligence officer who inadvertently failed to file a contact report or scratched a lie detector test. Matthews was an exception. They had become friends during training.

Linton turned to Matthews. "Who knew you were meeting BYRON?"

"Wallace, Driscoll, D'Angelo, Birch. The three of us."

"Who chose the spot?"

"Whoever wrote the script."

The Director raised his hand abruptly to pause Linton's questions. "I said this is a different meeting."

"We've lost two assets in the past year. More are at risk."

"Yes, yes. I know. You'll investigate, but not in this car." He leaned toward Matthews and studied him with his good eye. "I need you to try again."

"You asked for one favor. I did it."

"But it's not over."

"It's over for me."

"You go back and forth to Moscow for business. It's all very normal, shuttling here and there." He petted the dog when it became nervous with the raised voices. "No one will suspect your non-official cover."

"I was arrested. Trinity Capital is being put at risk. I didn't sign up for this shit."

"You recruited him." The Director patted Matthews's knee, like an understanding coach comforting a star player after a well-played loss. "I don't want to sound sentimental, but he risked his life to come forward. Do you trust him?"

"No. No. I do not. What I have are investors who put their trust in me."

"You left us, but your oath doesn't have an expiration date. We defend this country from enemies foreign and domestic."

Matthews's eyes came back from the light Saturday morning traffic on Wisconsin Avenue. The Director's last word had fallen with his tone of voice, emphasizing "domestic." He looked for a hint of the Director's meaning, but saw only fleshy jowls, rangy eyebrows, and his glass eye.

They had known each other for a decade and their bond was forged on the anvil of Washington's brutal politics. They had both left the agency, Matthews with an embarrassing shove, and the

Director for a higher-paying private sector job. But in the working of the capital's revolving door, he'd come back as DCI. He was a scholar of threat and his view of the world was shaped by the enemies he'd encountered.

Matthews looked at the Director. "What does BYRON have?"

"That's a question I hoped you wouldn't ask. But, if I'm asking you to stick your neck out—as a favor to me, another favor—I owe you the courtesy of an answer. But let me be clear. I am asking you, and it has to be you, because BYRON requested you."

The Director looked at Linton. "Are you okay with this?"

"I work for you."

The Director smiled grimly. "That's the problem with this job. I have to make the hard choices." He turned to Matthews with a sober expression.

"There is a person. We'll call him TOPCAT. He hired me and I owe him that, but I have watched him stew in a combustible mix of grievance and ambition. He is a cynic about human nature and is relentlessly suspicious and always tuned to vulnerabilities that he can exploit. He is not a big believer in the better angels of the human spirit, but he can be persuaded with praise."

The Director paused. "Indulge me. I'm going on a tangent for a purpose, to answer your question. I will stipulate that you've been read in so I can talk openly. TOPCAT believes in getting even and he is a master of payback. I say this because in my view these qualities have hardened in the past two years as his grip on power has tightened and his circle of advisors narrowed. It increases the risk he will act irrationally and dangerously. There are fewer people who will challenge him. He's surrounded himself with crackpot lawyers and advisors who tell him what his itching ears want to hear. None of his views are more questionable, his judgment more suspect, than on Russia. And Putin."

The Director paused, pondering.

"This conversation stays with us. James knows my views and now you know. But no one else does."

He continued in a grave tone. "He's ignored the intelligence I've given him on Putin's interest in Ukraine and he's said he wants to move cautiously. I have presented evidence that Putin will claim Ukraine as part of the greater Russia, but TOPCAT wants to move slowly. To accommodate."

The Director drew in a deep, troubled breath. "Do I know this to be true? Have I warned him? Yes. What I get back is crazy silence. I worry—and I stress this is only one man's suspicion—that he is playing against cards that Putin holds. If that is true, then the worst case is that our national interests are in the hands of a man whose hunger to stay in power is at the mercy of *kompromat*."

The Director's eyebrow arched and his eye settled on Matthews. "I work for him. He hired me and I am grateful for that, but I didn't pledge loyalty to him. If I suspect something, I need to investigate."

A fatigued breath heaved from his chest and he sank deep into the seat, a man grievously challenged by what he knew. "Decisions could go one way or the other, but one confronts Putin and the other appeases. One is in our national interest and the other doesn't appear to be against our interest, but clearly benefits Russia. The difference between the choices is subtle, but one may be disastrous in the long run. That's my nightmare."

The Director stared out the window, silent for a long moment.

"I like the man. He can be charming, funny, a hail-fellow-well-met, especially after two bourbons." He turned back to Matthews. "But I can't ignore the evidence. It goes back to August 2013 when he visited Moscow for the IAAF World Championships. Then in June this year he met alone in the Oval Office with the

Russian foreign minister and Ambassador Kozlov. We didn't have advance notice and never got a readout.

"Then there was the July meeting with Putin in Oslo. He took the interpreter's simultaneous notes so we have no record of what was said. If it was only these instances, I'd be concerned, not alarmed, but we know he keeps things from us."

The Director looked at Matthews. "BYRON was dormant for ten years. Then last month he contacted Moscow station following the protocol you set up, using an old code book. A dead drop in a church. He wrote that he has the FSB's *kompromat* file on TOPCAT."

"What does he want?"

"He asked to meet with you. It's been ten years. He doesn't know anyone else and he won't trust anyone but you."

"There's got to be other sources—better sources—than BYRON."

"He's not the only one we're looking into. The investigation into Russian interference in the election has uncovered other threats—men close to the White House with Russian business connections."

"Who?" Matthews saw the Director's face tense with reluctance at the thought of sharing names.

"It's not important."

"It's important to me. I work with Americans who do business in Moscow." Matthews listened to the Director vent about the danger of sharing classified information, but Matthews didn't relent, and then in the face of Matthews's intransigence, the names came out. Matthews didn't personally know two of the men, but he'd read news reports that connected General Michael Taylor and Paul Mercer to dirty money. He'd had drinks with James Dowd and he was aware of Dowd's advisory work for Gazprom. A slippery man with dubious business dealings who Matthews didn't trust.

"They are on our list, so BYRON isn't our only angle, but he's the one you can help with." The Director paused. "Go back to Moscow, make contact through whatever arrangements you previously used. Bring me what he has."

Matthews considered the full scope of what he'd heard. "He asked for me because I'm the only name he's got. You have a dozen competent Russian-speaking case officers. All good. All know how to run an asset in Moscow. Why me?"

"You're not in the agency, that's why. An official agency action in Moscow would provoke questions on the seventh floor and the White House. TOPCAT has spies inside the agency, of that I am certain. How long before I'm called to the Oval Office like a truant summoned to the principal's office and he demands to know what's going on in Moscow? It's not in the national interest, or my career interests, to confirm that we're looking into *kompromat* on him. Imagine that conversation." A beat of silence. "I need plausible deniability."

"Why would I take the risk?"

The Director gazed out the SUV at Lincoln's Cottage near Rock Creek Cemetery, which they were passing in the meandering route the driver chose for the long conversation.

"Lincoln went there during the Civil War to get away from the pressures of the White House, the war, and Congress. George Mueller went there when he was DCI to clear his mind and think straight about the job's burdens. I started to visit last year. You might say it's a tradition. I escape the seventh floor's insular thinking and reflect on my terrible choices."

He turned to Matthews. "Presidents come and go, but our job remains the same." His forehead creased. "There are people in the agency who haven't forgiven you, but frankly some of them should have left instead."

Matthews thought it remarkable—even grotesque—that a man with the Director's malleable principles would openly question the motives of the president of the United States. That he would undertake a covert mission to buttress a criminal case against the man was breathtaking. In his thirty years of professional life, he'd never found himself in a position to profoundly influence the course of political affairs, and joining the conspiracy felt treasonous.

The Director added, "Lincoln struggled with lonely choices when he visited the cottage and I can only imagine what went through his mind with the war raging. He knew that our 'noble experiment' in self-government is unique among nations. We don't take an oath to a man, a king, a government, or a religion, but to a document. A scrap of paper. Lincoln knew we could defeat foreign enemies, but he saw that we are defenseless against ourselves." The Director paused. "Today's battle is different. We fight against falsehoods that stoke violence and we're ill served by men who put self-interest above the common good. The hot rash of narcissism in the White House threatens to scorch this country."

He smiled grimly. "I sound preachy, but that's how I feel. TOPCAT has gotten in front of an angry crowd and he leads it forward. My blood stirs at the thought of all his crap."

Having vented his feelings, the Director sat back, but his eyes fixed on Matthews. "James will start an investigation into the leak. He will chair a working group to assess the failure in Moscow, but that will take time, which we don't have. I need someone outside the agency to move quickly. You recruited BYRON. He knows you. He trusts you. It has to be you."

Matthews was vexed by conflicting emotions. He resented the Director's request to rise up and do his duty, saying he was a good man. It was cheap flattery offered like an ersatz gift, and with it, he felt the satisfying power of his ability to disappoint them. But beneath that he also felt the attraction of his old work. The purposefulness. The adrenaline. The fear. None of the challenges of making money satisfied him in the same way.

"If I do this," Matthews said, "I don't want help from the inside."

"You'll need support."

"If I fail, I don't want it to be because I trusted a Cassius."

"You're still angry."

"Wouldn't you be?"

"James has arranged your flight to Moscow Friday."

"My son's birthday is on the weekend. The trip will wait a week."

"You'll tell no one."

"Anna has to know."

"Make up a story. She works with Wallace and Driscoll. They're on Linton's list."

5

A Private Party

Anna was beside herself.

She had planned the dinner party trying to think about everything needed to make her fifth wedding anniversary a memorable occasion, but she had not foreseen that dinner in a private room at the Cosmos Club would fall on the same evening as the annual White Russian Washington gala. In the corridor, older men in tuxedos and dignified women in gowns laughed and greeted each other, enjoying the evening's spectacle. Then as the gala got underway, the music rose. A string ensemble rendered a Stravinsky with a syrupy rhythm and the distant relatives of Tsarist Russians commemorated their permanent exile with song, dance, and laughter.

"Excuse me," Anna said, closing the ballroom's door, and returned to her guests across the hall, firmly shutting the second door.

Anna enjoyed being a hostess in Washington's close-knit intelligence community. Secrets were the currency of power in

Washington and invitations to the city's military balls, theater benefits, and political cocktail parties went to insiders who were cleared to have secrets and knew how to respect them.

She resumed her place at the end of the table facing her husband. She had seated her seven guests to avoid the dull conversation that comes from seating wife next to husband, Democrat next to Democrat, and Republican next to Republican. She arranged their friends to ensure a lively evening in celebration of her marriage in her favorite private dining room. A large teardrop chandelier provided light for the guests at the table; velvet curtains were tied with gold cord, and replicas of Hudson Valley landscapes gave the room Victorian warmth. A waiter hovered just to one side, filling wineglasses when he saw them empty.

Anna caught her husband's eye and he acknowledged her ingenious solution to the raucous White Russians. He toasted her, she smiled back, and she looked around the table, happy to have pulled off a private evening among friends.

Mark Driscoll, CE Division head, and his wife, Jean, sat across from each other. Tom Wallace complimented Anna's bravery with a friendly smile, raising a glass of the first growth Bordeaux he'd brought for the occasion. A morose James Linton sat next to Wallace's quiet wife, Rose, and Linton's wife, Margaret, beamed with flushed cheeks as she clapped politely at Anna's performance. Chris D'Angelo, Moscow station chief, smiled from the end of the table. He was in Washington for a briefing and came alone.

Jean Driscoll commanded attention in the middle of the table with her husky voice. Side conversations paused and guests turned as she discussed a personal dilemma.

"But you're so good at event planning," Anna said. "Why would you stop?"

"I've done it. I need another challenge."

"It's not easy to be good at anything. It takes time to establish yourself and who knows if you'll succeed at a different thing."

Anna used the second person singular unthinkingly, but the grammatical form of her comment implied the familiarity of an old friend, which Jean was not. They circled each other, curious about the other's secret past. Anna knew that Jean had once served in Brussels as non-official cover in the United Nations.

"Washington parties all feel the same to me," Jean said, looking around the table for an objection. "Don't they?"

"Does that include tonight?" Wallace asked.

"I'm talking about political parties and diplomatic receptions, not one of Anna's dinner parties. I'm hired to do events. No matter how charming or loud, the big gatherings always have a put-on feeling. They were splendid at first: the cocktails were new, the food abundant, and the diplomats, generals, celebrities, and Republican donors carried on as if they were enjoying themselves. But the parties have all blended together: the same faces, the same drinks, the same scraps of sushi, and the same tiny hors d'oeuvres served by interns. The same feeling that everyone is there to make a connection, hustle money, or get laid. It's disgusting. I get paid well but I no longer enjoy renting out my relationships in this town to men and women who hope to buy their way to respectability."

Jean looked at her quiet dinner companions.

"But it's what you do," Wallace said. "And you're good at it. Not many of us have good careers after leaving the agency." Wallace looked around. "What? It's not a secret, is it? There was a big flap at the time. You were pregnant. Now you've got a new career and a husband."

"You've had too much to drink," Driscoll said, defending his wife.

"Enough," Anna intervened. "It's my anniversary."

Jean gave Wallace a vicious look, but then a brisk smile painted her face. "It's not a secret. I'm proud of my time in the agency, but I prefer working for myself." Her smile softened as she looked at the guests. "I can say this because we're all friends, but I wouldn't say this to anyone else. People come to Washington, take what they want, play the game, and go home when they're voted out of office. Some stay, craving power."

Jean shrugged. "I do get paid well, but I feel dirty. I'm looking for another challenge now that my kids are growing up. Don't we all want a fresh challenge?"

Jean waited for one of the others to answer, but no one did. "I've thought of doing a cable talk show. I already know the delicious secrets." She turned to Anna. "Who would you put on the show? Speaker of the House? Majority Whip?"

The lively conversation that followed was filled with gossip about journalists, senators, and lobbyists, and then the loud trumpet and an accompanying piano from the gala across the hall briefly interrupted before quieting again.

"White Russians still remember," Anna said. "It's been one hundred years but they still remember. It gives them something to dream about." Her sarcasm drew glances from the others. "Prince Oblonsky, whose grandfather served the tsar, came to the gala every year until he died. He was a distant relative. Our families escaped the Bolsheviks and ended up in adjoining villas in the same Tuscan town. Russians hate the 'state' but love the motherland so, once a year, we dress up, dance, and feed on caviar and hope."

Russia had been raised and the conversation inevitably turned to politics. Jean said that the Mueller investigation hadn't gone far enough and it was obvious the Kremlin interfered in the last election. She looked around the table at the intelligence officers who hoarded their opinions, but then settled on Anna.

"What do you think?"

"Me?" Anna said. "I think it's probably true. True in some way. He—"

"Who?"

"You know who I mean. He's smitten with Putin. It may not be for the obvious reason, but you can see it in his behavior. Everyone sees it. I don't believe it's all about his admiration for dictators—wishing he could act like one. I think it's worse than we think. There is no normal explanation for what he does. But it's all endless speculation. None of us knows what's going on, or how to stop it."

Wallace looked at Matthews. "You just got back from Moscow. What do you think?"

"About Russia?"

"Yes, we're talking about Putin."

"I thought we were talking about POTUS."

Matthews saw Linton's admonishing head shake, a signal. "It's an ugly topic," he said. "Like climate change."

"You're a big player there, Alex. Take a shot. What have you heard?"

"Things haven't changed," he said, deflecting the question. "You've never heard of the Russian philosopher Peter Chaadayev. He said Russia is a separate world submissive to the caprice of a single man. He wrote that in 1854." He looked around the table. "Things haven't changed. Stalin, Brezhnev, Putin. All strong leaders."

"He's unhinged."

"They're both unhinged."

Women laughed and husbands shook their heads. Waiters quietly filled empty wineglasses.

"He's the president, for God's sake," Driscoll shouted. "Come on."

"Enough," Anna interrupted, tapping her wineglass with his knife to get the group's attention and in the process breaking it, spilling scarlet wine on the white linen.

"It's fine," Anna said, and took a new glass from the waiter who suddenly appeared. "Once we talk politics the conversation becomes depressing and I break a glass. Let's change the topic so we don't turn on each other."

"To what?"

Anna looked at Tom Wallace and his wife, Rose, who had been quiet most of the dinner. "It's our anniversary dinner. Let's talk about ourselves. How did you meet?"

"Meet?"

"Yes, fall in love. I find it interesting to hear a couple's origin story. How did you meet?"

Rose looked at her husband. "Shall I tell the story?"

"Go ahead. You'll make it sound interesting."

Rose looked at him. "You don't remember, do you?"

"Of course I do."

She turned to the others, laughing. "I wasn't his first choice. We lived a few doors from each other and every morning I saw him walk his dog and he saw me walk mine. We never had much to say to each other except we discussed our dogs and their poop. I found him attractive but he was seeing another woman and I was married. At the time, I was getting divorced, but he didn't know it. He moved away and one year later we found ourselves sitting next to each other on the Acela going to New York. He remembered me and had met my father, who is a big shot lawyer. We struck up a conversation that led to books, music, movies, travel, and we never mentioned our dogs. In the course of things, he said he'd stopped seeing the other woman. I think I flinched. He invited me to dinner when we arrived at Penn Station. We had dinner the next night at Balthazar and one thing led to another. That's it."

Everyone smiled.

"What about you?" Anna looked at D'Angelo.

"I'm alone. I get a pass."

She smiled at Linton and Margaret. "Your turn."

"Is this a parlor game?" Linton asked.

"Go ahead," Margaret said. "Embarrass us."

"Come on," Matthews said, motioning for wineglasses to be refilled. "Let's hear it."

Linton waved off the encouragement. A man who wore his privacy like a bespoke suit was visibly uncomfortable, but colleagues around the table who knew only his work persona were eager to hear.

"I'll tell the story," Margaret said. "You won't get a peep out of him." She smiled at the others. "I was just about to graduate from college and had no interest in following my older brother in the family investment banking business. Wealth didn't interest me, probably because I already had it."

"How did you meet?"

"I was in Harvard's library reading a poetry journal and I happened to pick up a *Village Voice* book review and I came across a name I've never forgotten: Katz Meow. The review was of a book about names by a man named Train. I laughed out loud. Katz Meow, Brandy Whine, Mary Pantzaroff.

"The man sitting next to me asked what was so funny. I showed him the names. Names interested him and they interested me. We started a conversation and traded addresses. I stayed in Cambridge a few months, but then, in the fall of 1986, after I had graduated, I heard from him. He invited me to visit him in New York City. I made my way to Manhattan and the Lower East Side. I had a romantic idea of what it was to be a poet that was shaped by reading Dylan Thomas and Allen Ginsberg. I was vaguely familiar with the literary scene in the city and the literary brat pack of McInerney, Janowitz, and Ellis. They claimed to be the voice of their generation, but they treated writing like banking—bright lights and big advances. For me, they were the symbol of cultural decline—self-indulgent, destructively liberal ideas. Decay, vice, greed."

She smiled. "Maybe not that bad. Back to the story. I found the apartment in the East Village, but when I arrived, the man wasn't there. His roommate let me in. We did a lot of talking, and because it was getting late, we went to a restaurant. We talked about rent and poetry. He had come to New York a few months earlier and he was disenchanted with the divine decadents, as he called them. We walked to Times Square, which was a spectacle of squalor, and back to the East Village, which was safe only if you were friendly with the Hells Angels on Third Street. I slept on the couch that night."

She paused. "I guess what brought us together was that I had come to visit one man I hardly knew and instead met his roommate." She looked at Linton. "Did I leave anything out?"

"Some things are best left out."

Laughter rose, glasses clinked, and when the room settled, Anna turned to Margaret. "What happened to the man who wasn't home?"

"He's right there." She pointed at Matthews.

Anna was shocked. "I never heard that story. Were the two of you a thing?"

Matthews raised a hand in protest. "It was a long time ago. I gave up poetry and followed James into the agency."

"What about you, Anna? How did you and Alex meet?"

Matthews turned to Driscoll, who'd put an innocent gloss on the question, but he knew that Driscoll had been among the senior staff who'd used the office affair to push for his dismissal. "I don't think we should get into that."

"Of course we should," Jean coaxed. "It's your anniversary we're celebrating. Talk as dessert comes."

Anna met Matthews's eye. "Should I tell it?"

"Go ahead. I have my version, which some of you might know, but let's start with the fictional version."

"We met in Vienna," Anna said, "the city of chocolate and Strauss music. We noticed each other during a NATO conference, where I was an interpreter and he was meeting his counterparts from intelligence services in Estonia, Latvia, and Ukraine. I think he was done with grief and was open to romance."

"Probably best if I tell the story," Matthews interrupted. "I was assigned a pool interpreter fluent in Russian. Meetings were often in English and my Russian was good, but I requested an interpreter so I didn't misunderstand language nuances. It was also convenient to let them assume that I didn't know Russian.

"Anna presented herself but didn't give her name. She was organized. Brisk, perfunctory, and all business. A little cold, I thought. I remember she wore black pants and her hair was knotted in a bun. I was impressed with her efficient interpreting of the rapid-fire back-and-forth conversations, whispering in my ear what they said. She did a good job of shading their comments to lessen the hostility. When the meetings ended, I told her that and she was offended. 'You tricked me,' she said. 'You didn't need me. Your Russian is good enough.' She walked out and I ran after to apologize. That's basically it."

"Come on," Linton said. "There's more."

"There's always more, but it's not for this room."

"Don't hold back, Alex."

Matthews reluctantly continued. "I liked that she was indifferent to my status. She treated me as a conference attendee and not the conference honoree. We had dinner in a restaurant on the last night of the event. She arrived in a scarlet gown, pearl necklace, and hair down to her shoulders. I stood up. She approached and said, 'Don't you recognize me?' She was gorgeous and I said something stupid, like, 'You're dressed differently.'"

"When was the conference?" Driscoll asked.

"After his wife's accident," Anna broke in, answering before Matthews could impeach himself. "He was a grieving man who buried himself in work and I found him sympathetic."

Matthews had been offended by some colleagues' efforts to date their affair to months before his wife's death, but the old rumor lived on. "After dinner we went to the bar for a drink. When she saw that the pianist was on break, she played a Chopin nocturne and asked me to join her. She said, 'I know you also play.' I did but I didn't know that she knew. We played a duet.

"She's modest about being a trained classical pianist. I was shocked when she launched into a Madonna song. She performed one, then another, then a third. Everyone in the bar clapped and whistled. Her hair was Madonna's; she moved like Madonna. Her voice was lower, slightly darker, and she played the piano, which Madonna doesn't, but she projected like Madonna, her expression a young Madonna's. She didn't just sing like Madonna. She was Madonna."

"Show us," Jean said.

"No. Not tonight." Anna waved off the pleas, but her refusal made them insist.

"There is the piano waiting for you." Jean, slightly drunk, pointed to a glistening black baby grand Steinway at the end of the room. "After that story, we need to witness your talent."

Anna stood reluctantly, setting aside her embarrassment, and made herself comfortable on the piano bench. Guests gathered around holding a drink, crowding in, looking. She tested the keys, fingers moving in a glissando, and then struck several chords. Her fingers danced spectrally over the yellow ivories and her voice rose, but stopped.

"That is what I played." She smiled bravely. "It's been a while."

"Go on. Don't tease us."

Her fingers confirmed the piano's tone and then her hand came down in a bright chord. Madonna's pop verses sprang from her soprano voice—strong, perfectly pitched. Her blonde hair moved as she looked from one guest to the other, and her fingers played confidently. The group was mesmerized. Linton leaned into Matthews. "She is a young Madonna."

Anna finished one song and was loudly encouraged to sing another, and as she parried their demands, Linton took Matthews aside.

"Come with me to the bar. I need to discuss our conversation with the Director."

"First, the bathroom."

Matthews returned in a moment, but Linton was gone and Anna was no longer at the piano. Jean talked with D'Angelo, and he saw Anna was in the small garden outside the French doors, speaking with Rose Wallace. He went to join them, but stopped when he saw Rose grip Anna's arm in a hostile way and speak angrily. Matthews stopped. He was deeply curious, but instinct and politeness kept him from entering the garden.

"Coming?" Linton appeared at Matthews's side. "One drink. A short conversation."

Matthews looked away from the women and met Linton's eager expression. "Let's go."

6

The Poets' Network

Matthews's thoughts were clotted in the minutes after he witnessed the two women arguing. He didn't know what to make of Anna's measured reaction to Rose forcefully taking her arm and he struggled for a plausible explanation. He was curious, but not so distracted that he couldn't put on a good front for Linton, who sat with him in the dark bar away from the mirrored wall of liquor bottles. Dim light from wall sconces darkened the clubbish bar atmosphere, and his eyes wandered to the other drinkers, but turned back to Linton, who sipped his mahogany scotch. They sat in stiff, high-back chairs separated by a side table.

"He is an extinct species," Linton said.

"Who?"

"The Director. I was talking about the DCI. You're not listening."

In the short conversation that followed, Linton made it clear that he wanted to make sense of what Matthews knew, what he didn't know, and whether he had a reasonable basis to suspect that a traitor was responsible for the catastrophe in Moscow. In the course of his meandering comments, he shifted again to the Director.

"He's making a dangerous call keeping this from the White House. Maybe it's the right call, but I worry what happens if it gets out. What do you think?"

"I'm not clairvoyant."

"What would you do if you were him? Your instinct?"

Matthews recognized Linton's subtle goading. Instinct served Matthews well when his training failed, but the layered hypocrisy of Washington's politics was a tricky shadow world that made instinct unreliable.

"He knows what he's doing. He's served four presidents."

"Fair enough."

Linton rubbed the edge of his empty glass, setting it down, and licked the liquor dregs from his finger. His hands formed a steeple and he spoke in a grave tone. "He made his career dealing with the existential threat of the Soviet Union's nuclear arsenal, but that doesn't qualify him to understand today's Russia. You understand the new Russia. You've made a tidy fortune playing the markets there. He still sees Russia and Putin as adversaries, and of course they are, but not in the same way. The game has changed."

Matthews sipped his drink. "How?"

"Anton Glok, for example, if you need a case in point. Glok runs old Soviet arms to African thugs and we prop up weak, popularly elected leaders thinking those poor shits have a use for democracy. God, did we fuck up in Iraq. We're fighting proxy wars, not wars measured in megatons of mutually assured destruction."

Matthews looked at Linton's sober face for a hint of where the conversation was going. He had the unsettling feeling that he was being set up, his views tested by Linton's Jesuitical interrogation. He had left the agency to escape the professional suspicions that lay beneath each disingenuous smile and every watchful gaze.

Matthews knew Linton, or thought he did. The bookish undergraduate poet who applied the heuristics of poetry to the allusiveness of intelligence gathering, looking for meaning in the unsaid. The solitary, inward thinker who looked for patterns in the firehose of anomalous data. Matthews suspected Linton had thrown out a rebuttable proposition as a way to test his loyalty to the Director. Everyone in the agency was a Cassius circling his Caesar.

"He has values," Matthews said. "He's not a weathervane."

"Thank God for that." Linton took his new glass of scotch, that had appeared silently from the hand of a discreet waiter, and swirled the ice with his finger. "Which brings me to you, Alex, and your poets' network. Is there just BYRON? No one else left?"

"All gone as far as I know. I've been cut off since I left. Dormant? Executed? I never heard. It was a difficult time."

"It was the year you married Anna?"

"Where are you taking this?"

"Driscoll raised it. Just curious."

"I resent the question. It's the double standard that makes me angry." He set down his glass and looked directly at Linton. "Am I under suspicion?"

"No, no, no." Linton touched his ear, a nervous tic. He waved off the suggestion with a theatrical flourish. "I don't want to open old wounds, but with BYRON active again I need to know the historical context to understand the present danger—to protect you. When did Anna join us?"

"I saw her store facts in her head without taking notes while interpreting back-and-forth conversations. She was remarkable, so after Vienna I recommended her. She passed the background tests."

"I like her." Linton leaned back in his chair, pondering, and changed the subject without skipping a beat. "I liked your crypt-onyms. We don't give ourselves our names. Our parents make that choice and we live with it, and that's how it works with our assets—we give them names from a sterile list, but you got to name the men in your network. How did you get away with that?"

"Isn't it obvious?"

"I wouldn't ask if it was obvious."

"If you were FSB counterintelligence and you came across a network of traitors named after English poets you might think they were related in some way—a nested grouping. The same directorate, same field of expertise, or men grouped by having been turned in London or Vienna."

"Ah, but they weren't, were they?" Linton smiled, pleased with himself. "Nothing in common. No thread to pull that would unravel the whole tapestry of deceit. Nothing in common except the man who recruited them." Linton paused. "You're the Rosetta Stone. Clever."

"Not clever enough, apparently."

"They figured it out, did they? And they're targeting you. Looking for BYRON, knowing he'd want to meet you?"

Linton folded his long fingers together. Nothing was said between the two men for a moment. Linton looked affectionately at Matthews. "You were a great loss to the agency. I was sorry to see you leave. Now your old enemies are jealous of your success. They would have been happier if you'd retired to a start-up consultancy with deadbeat clients."

Matthews had the indifferent smile of a man who knew he was being played.

"The agency has changed since you left. We are inundated with data from satellites, social media, and signal intercepts, and random noise overwhelms us. I am out of tune with the chorus of hackers inside the agency. Algorithms are smarter, but the flood of disinformation makes it hard—impossible—to know what is true, what is false, and who gains from the confusion." Linton paused. "Which brings me back to you, Alex, and your HUMINT network. Everything comes back to you. To what BYRON has that will save us from Apocalypse 45."

Linton spoke in a measured tone. "Who knew you were meeting BYRON?"

"We went over that."

"Just so I have it right. There's Birch, Driscoll, Wallace, D'Angelo, the Director. Anna. Anyone else?"

"She didn't know."

"Any others? Armstrong? Pierce?"

The names were familiar to Matthews. Senior intelligence officers in Russia House protective of their domain. "I don't know. I'm outside the bubble. You're in a better position to create the Venn diagram of possible compromising conversations. There is also you and me."

"I think we can eliminate you as the source, and I'll stipulate that it's not me. If it were me, the agency would have a bigger problem. Let's start with Wallace."

"Is this a good place to get into it? The others are waiting for us."

"A few minutes. They'll come looking if we're missed. Better here than in Langley or an SUV." He raised his glass. "We can drink, talk, speculate. Two former colleagues ripping a mutual acquaintance over scotch." Linton leaned forward, eyebrow arched. "I start with Wallace because he suggested Birch. Birch will get an Exceptional Performance Award to make a public show of his bravery, but he was a terrible choice. He failed polygraph tests for alcohol and drugs, and he admitted taking cash from a woman's purse on a flight to Paris. He was supposed to be a clean-slate rookie who would clear FSB surveillance from the embassy, but he was miscast. Wallace knew his background, but he assigned him anyway."

"Birch was incompetent."

"Why did Wallace pick him? I've started asking questions but a great amnesia has set in around the mission's planning. No one wrote up what was said in the planning sessions, no one recorded who received a briefing or who signed off. So there is no record and senior men are stonewalling, keeping me out. The failure has become an orphan—lost to poor record keeping. From what I know, the playbook was written by Wallace, as Armstrong's deputy; Driscoll vetted the script and D'Angelo coordinated resources in Moscow. Wallace was Birch's mentor. He knew Birch's demerits, but no one wanted to shitcan him. Too much time and effort are put into recruiting and training and we go to great lengths to have a young officer find his way. We're hard on our enemies—soft on our staff."

Linton paused. "We get close to a colleague. We work with their problems, but friendship blinds us. A man drinks too much and we excuse it. Why not? He's a friend. He has the office next to yours. You know his wife. Go to his son's christening or bar mitzvah."

Linton looked directly at Matthews. "How well do you know Wallace? A good friend?"

"Friendly."

"You saved his life."

"He won't admit that."

"Trust him?"

"He was angry when he was passed over for the job I got. I don't think he ever forgave me. He's ambitious, but so are you. What would his motive be?"

Matthews didn't share all that he thought about Tom Wallace—that he was a mediocre talent who'd risen as far as his talents permitted, who liked to think of himself as being part of the agency's upper tier. Who liked to brag of his family connections to William Casey, who'd brought him into the agency on the advice of a New York lawyer who knew Wallace's father. He knew that Tom Wallace wanted to be thought of as another Wild Bill Donovan of the agency's Golden Age. What he lacked in talent, he made up for with self-esteem. Matthews thought him a sad case. For members of the agency's Georgetown set, there was something dilettantish about Wallace. He didn't get invited to lunch with the DCI at the Metropolitan Club or play tennis with the national security advisor at the Chevy Chase Club. Wallace, like others of his ilk, was tolerated, used, led on, but they did not become part of the inner circle. Matthews didn't say any of that to Linton. He listened in an unusually reserved way and he understood what it meant to say nothing against Linton's accusative line of questioning. He was inclined to reserve his judgment, a habit that came naturally to him, and at times it made him an object of suspicion. He knew that silence was no defense against a friend's incrimination and could lead to the accusation that he was nothing more than a politician.

"He's always been the outsider," Matthews said. "The poor kid who hoped his Ivy League friends' fathers would help him get a good job."

"Is he honorable?"

Matthews thought it an odd word choice—code for loyal. "He has the appetite for honor."

"There are three rules here. You take lie detector tests. Report your sanctioned contacts with foreign nationals. Report your romantic relationships. We think he's failed the last one."

"Who?"

"I won't get into that."

"Poor Rose."

"Wallace is on my list. I got a printout of his entering and exiting headquarters. He rarely arrives on time, often leaves early, and never works on Saturdays. He takes cigarette breaks throughout the day. I have requested three years of his Performance Appraisal Reports and I've got his financial profile. He seems to have money and I'm looking into that." Linton paused. "But I don't think it's him. He's too obvious, too clumsy, and too eager to fit in."

"He resents his treatment."

"A successful penetration agent survives by mastering the art of obscurity. Unless, of course, the clever act of standing out is a subterfuge."

Matthews saw Linton relish the complexity of the problem he posed for himself, a man whose legendary ability to think and rethink a problem enhanced the stories that circled around his talent for finding coherent patterns in misleading data.

"Who is top of your list?" Matthews asked.

"I don't have a number one. All are equally suspect." Linton stood.

"Find out who suggested the Kempinski. It was crazy to meet there. Public, police nearby. Ludicrous. Maybe it was an incompetent choice, or it was a deliberate trap."

Matthews signaled the bartender for the tab.

"I'll pay," Linton said.

"They don't accept cash. It's on Anna's membership. Her treat."

As they walked down the hall toward the sound of the gala, Linton said without any urgency in his voice, "I've convened an internal investigation—a formal Committee of Inquiry—because the White House is asking questions. You'll be called to testify when you return from Moscow."

Linton added, "I don't think Wallace would mind if you never came back from Moscow."

7

At Home

Jealousy was not an emotion that Matthews felt often. His conscious act of forbearance helped him suspend his suspicion that Anna was having an affair. He banished the image of the garden encounter, but the memory of her retreat from Rose's anger stayed with him like a stubborn cold. Linton's reference to Wallace and his refusal to give a name combined in his mind as corrosive doubt. His jealousy was not based on any specific evidence, but the reason he was drawn to Anna made her attractive to others. She was lively, gracious, professional, and he worried that his frequent travel helped her lose interest in him. The only comforting thought was that Wallace was a blowhard and a narcissist, and he, too, was middle-aged, but he seemed to have a talent with women, and women liked him. It was the thing about Wallace that Matthews never understood, but he observed it, so it didn't matter that he didn't understand how women found him attractive.

Matthews knew his wife well, but he also understood that he only saw what she allowed him to see—and there were things in her past that she never discussed. Where did she learn to sing like Madonna? Her answer: "Every little girl lip-synchs in front of a mirror."

Her passion in bed was as lusty as ever: hot laughter, warm body, coaxing romance, and a pleasantly transparent smile. Perhaps too transparent. If he let himself drink the poison of suspicion, he saw a woman with a secret—confident that she was free of her husband's suspicion and carefree in the way that she kept him talking about himself. He had been trained by the agency to read other people's minds, but the danger of looking at the world through the lens of doubt was that sometimes he saw guilt where there was innocence. Making that mistake at work could be corrected, but in a marriage it was disastrous.

❖

They made love that night. Sex had always come easily to them, desire from one met willingness from the other.

Anna slipped into bed naked, the fresh smell of a bath scenting her body, and she turned off the bedside lamp. Their difference in age vanished in the blind darkness under the soft comforter.

The first night they'd slept together in Vienna, he'd felt a mix of emotions. They'd returned from a long walk along the Donaukanal, talking in the enthusiastic way people do when they're attracted to each other. When they returned to the hotel, they went to the hotel bar and drank and talked about everything and nothing, intoxicated by each other's company. He knew it was a special moment as he lived it and he wished it wouldn't end.

His grief was still green then and he felt a twinge of betrayal, but he was a practical man as well as a lonely man, and he knew he had to move on from his wife's death. He woke the next morning pleased to find her beside him.

Anna was both more private and more gregarious than his wife. After the first months together, he stopped comparing them, and his wife slipped into the part of his mind that contained his forgotten past. He was happy with Anna. Her enthusiasm and spirit were a salve for his regret and he was glad to be able to love again.

They argued, as couples do, but they found ways to move beyond their differences. Their arguments were a part of the warp and woof of an affectionate couple managing the demands of marriage, work, and family.

Matthews stood at the kitchen sink and looked out at the bay. Anna had drifted off with her back to him, but he'd been unable to sleep. When his restless thoughts became too much, he rose quietly and went downstairs to the refrigerator for a glass of water. He needed to clear his mind of what he'd found when he'd grabbed a condom from the drawer of her bedside table. BLT Prime Bar and Restaurant matches were there beside a pack of cigarettes. He hadn't thought anything of it in the excitement of the moment, but afterward, lying in bed, he came back to the book of matches. He had an urge to ask where she'd gotten them, but he didn't want to seem petty, jealous, or controlling. They led active lives and he didn't feel a need to question her about what she did while he was away. He trusted her—he wanted to trust her.

Light of the full moon illuminated the calm water of the bay and silvered his pale skin, giving him a cold appearance. Houses along the shore were dark and the late hour brought a gloomy peace to the cove. A container ship's running lights marked its slow movement down the channel to the Atlantic. So much had happened in his life, so much was changed, and now he felt that he had another thing to contend with.

"Are you okay? I felt you get out of bed." She was at his side at the sink. She addressed the concern on his face with a kind hand on his shoulder. "What's wrong?"

He looked at her and wondered about the matches, but didn't ask about them. He knew he'd feel terrible when she gave a perfectly innocent explanation. Her face was bleary with sleep and full of trust. She'd thrown on a kimono and her arms hung at her side in flowered butterfly sleeves, her eyes curious.

"I couldn't sleep. Too much on my mind."

She moved closer. "What did James want? The two of you disappeared for half an hour. I had to play hostess to the group, and they wanted to know where you'd gone off to. Tom asked about you before he had to leave."

"We went to the bar. James asked about Moscow."

"What did happen?"

"I was doing a favor for the Director and there was a problem."

"Birch?"

He turned to her, surprised.

"Tom used the name. He said Birch was the wrong one to send." She looked at him. "You don't have to do this. You don't work for them anymore."

"The Director thinks he has a claim on me."

"Does he?"

"In his mind, you never stop being a part of the club. I left, but you're inside, so I'm still a part of their world."

"Come to bed."

They lay side by side under the comforter watching the moonlight dance on the ceiling, the light shifting through the leafed trees. They were quiet, unable to sleep, each with concerns, and silence was a chasm between them.

Anna sat up. She leaned over to look into his eyes, dark and awake. "I never heard the story about you and Margaret. How could you keep that from me?"

"It never came up."

"Did you sleep with her?"

"When?"

"Ever?"

"Years ago."

"Were you married at the time?"

"No."

"Was she?"

"They were engaged. We both had too much to drink at a Christmas party. We just fell into it."

"You don't just 'fall into it.' Where did it happen?"

"Someone's home in Georgetown. I don't remember. We bumped into each other going to the bathroom and she kissed me. It meant nothing. We both knew it was a stupid, drunken mistake."

"Does James know?"

"He might. Sometimes I think he does because he seems to resent me. I don't know if it's because I left the agency, or because I've made money, or because Margaret confessed."

He suddenly sat up, drawing her surprise. "I saw you talking with Rose in the garden. She looked upset. Is there anything I should know?"

"She is unhappy with Tom."

"She grabbed your arm."

"It was a private conversation. Were you watching?"

"I happened to pass the open door and saw the two of you arguing."

"She is having a problem with Tom. It's a private matter. She thinks he is having an affair with me, which is not true, but she confronted me. Please don't raise this with him."

Matthews listened for the lie in Anna's voice and looked for a dissembling expression. "I'm sure it must be hard on her."

"Yes." She looked at him, forehead knitting. "This world of ours, the world you have tried to leave, that I'm still in, claims us. Everywhere we turn we look for something that is different from what we see. Always looking for the lie or the subtext. But sometimes a shoe is just a shoe, a smile is just a smile. Sometimes, and this may be one of those times, the thing you're looking at is just what you're looking at."

Anna placed her hand on his chest. "We'll be with them tomorrow on the boat. Please be civil. Don't bring this up."

8

Chesapeake Bay

Blustery September weather swept clouds from the sky and turned the bay into a festival of color. Dedicated sailors from local marinas harnessed the wind in billowing spinnakers, and their sailboats cut zigzag patterns through the whitecaps.

Matthews stood next to Tom Wallace, who steered his thirty-one-foot sloop toward a spit of land on the eastern shore. Mark Driscoll and his wife, Jean, stood to one side, hands holding onto a stay, wearing windbreakers against cold spray, as the bow cut through choppy water. The humidity of summer was gone and the season seemed to have changed overnight with the arrival of Labor Day weekend. The bright sun was high on the horizon and its warmth was pleasant against the cold air.

Matthews felt Driscoll move closer and saw his dark glasses glint in the sun.

"I never heard the story about Margaret," Driscoll said. "You bonded on a common interest in the name Mary Pantzaroff?"

"We were young. What was funny then is silly now. What's on your mind?"

"I heard that James has questions about Wallace."

They were standing a short way from Wallace at the sloop's wheel, but the blowing wind kept their conversation confidential.

"Who told you that?"

"Some things I pick up. It's in the air, like mold."

Testing, Matthews thought. "You should ask him." He nodded toward Wallace.

Driscoll shook his head. "He insulted Jean at the dinner party. I'll let him apologize." He looked off at the many sailboats. "It's a fine tradition that you've got. Better to celebrate loved ones you've lost than to be grim and solemn. It's the right way to remember her."

Jean joined them. Her hair was held in place with a scarf whose ends flapped wildly, and she steadied herself at their side. She wore white-framed dark glasses and her free hand held a bottle of beer.

"What are you drinking?" Matthews asked.

"Stella."

"I'll grab one. How is your celebrity gossip cable channel getting on?"

"Plenty of Gulf money looking for a home."

"Anna said she'll quit the agency to join you."

Matthews returned to the stern, where Wallace was in his element, confidently steering the sloop at an angle to the wind for maximum speed. Matthews felt spray on his face and the excitement of the blustery weather held him in its grip. He looked at the bow, where his son sat with his legs dangling over. Anna stood at his side, talking in a serious way. She wore a pale-green, cable knit sweater and white shorts. It was very casual, but the snug fit of the clothing on her winsome figure made the outfit look graceful and elegant.

Wallace had lit a cigarette, cupping his hands over the match, and turned away from Anna. "Rose hates my smoking. This is the only place I smoke anymore." He looked at Matthews. "Anna was a good catch. For a man your age."

"You think so? Maybe it was my age."

Wallace laughed, looking at his head of thinning gray hair. "A widower with a young son. It wasn't your sense of humor." He nodded at the sloop's bow. "She's good for David. They seem to get along."

"She doesn't try to be a substitute mother."

"You're lucky."

"How so?"

"She's faithful to you."

Matthews was surprised by his comment—so gratuitous, so casually put out there, as if it was a concern that he should be aware of.

"I never heard the story of how you met in Vienna. Chocolate and Strauss music." Wallace took up his beer in his cigarette hand and tilted it to his lips, a short pull. He motioned toward a spot on the water near the end of the approaching island.

"We'll be there in a moment."

"Thanks for doing this," Matthews said. "Is that the Russian compound?" Matthews pointed toward a channel that entered the bay.

"You can't see it from here. It's in Centerville on the other side of the preserve. Upper Chester River. Six or seven miles that way. On a weekend like this they'll have FBI spotter boats offshore with telephoto lenses."

"How long have you had the sloop?"

"Ten years. Rose hates to sail. I do it alone." His arm made a wide arc across the bay. "It can be treacherous if you don't know the currents and the sandbars. She is equipped for single-handed sailing, with all the navigation and radio equipment to sail to the Caribbean."

"Who named it?"

"The *Red Queen*? You like it? We get to name our children, our assets, and our boats."

"Where's the beer?" Matthews asked.

"Down below. Cooler cabinet."

Matthews found locked cabinets in the cabin below deck. He tried one and then a second, which was also locked, and when he tried the third, he found two shelves stocked with bottles of scotch, gin, whiskey, vodka, and tequila. Most half-empty. Matthews knew that Wallace drank but he was still surprised to see the evidence of his habit.

The fourth cabinet was also locked, but the latch didn't fit and he opened it with a slight tug. He saw a 9 mm Glock in its snap-on holster. Beside it, he saw stacked electronic gear and he recognized a burst radio transmitter. He'd used one when he parachuted behind Serbian lines in the Balkan war. Burst radio transmitters sent compressed packets of encrypted messages in short sequences that were hard to detect with wave frequency triangulation techniques, hard to intercept, and difficult to decrypt.

Matthews emerged from below deck with a cold Stella, moving toward Wallace with questions about the equipment, but Anna motioned wildly at him.

"We're here," Anna said, and pointed to a spot off the island.

Matthews moved purposefully forward toward the bow, holding on to the guardrail against the sloop's rise and fall. There was something in his cautious walk that expressed what was on his mind. He was careful and used his hand to steady himself.

It was the same way he'd moved through his agency career—a clear-eyed intelligence officer who balanced risk with purpose, open to the use of covert action to solve a problem. But for all his challenges in the Balkans, Iraq, Lebanon, and Russia, no challenge was greater than suspicion of a friend's betrayal.

"The flowers," David shouted, pointing to a large cardboard box on the deck, tethered to the mast. Peeking over the top was a colorful bouquet of lilies, dahlias, daisies, violets, and Queen Anne's lace. David had picked flowers from the abundant beds his mother had planted years before, adding to the florist's bouquet.

Wallace released the main sail, letting it flutter in the wind so the boat lost speed and drifted toward gray-blue water a short distance from a sandbar. High winds clipped the tops of cirrus clouds, flattening them like anvils.

Matthews was at his son's side. The boat was off the main channel roughly equidistant from Cove Point and the island. Their cottage was visible in the distance.

"Here," Matthews said, handing the bouquet to David. They stood on the sloop's starboard side, sun at their backs. The annual ceremony honoring the accident always coincided with David's birthday and cast a shadow over the day's festivities.

His wife had once talked about cremation and sea burial, but he had not been able to honor her wish. The bodies had never been recovered. The Coast Guard abandoned their search a week after the boat capsized. A body was tangible evidence of death and without their bodies he'd had to come to grips with what it meant that they were missing. Dead and missing were not the same, even if a missing person was declared dead, as his wife and daughter had been. The state of death was concrete, the corpse a physical manifestation of the end of life. But a missing person was like a sentence without a period. It continued on, waiting to be finished.

To honor their deaths, Matthews and David sailed into the bay on the accident's anniversary, stopping in the general area where the sailboat had gone down. There was no cemetery to visit, but they had a set of coordinates that described the watery grave.

Matthews was not a conventional Catholic, but he had deeply personal spiritual beliefs and nothing challenged him more than his daughter's death. Her anorexia had developed during his travel-heavy agency years. He knew that his long absences and the stress it placed on his children and marriage contributed to her illness.

Matthews was at his son's side. David took one red rose from the bouquet and threw it out to the water. He took several Queen Anne's lace and dropped them overboard and he did that twice more, letting the act of releasing the flowers salve his pain and bring comfort to the moment. He sent the rest of the flowers into the bay with a gentle underhanded toss. Father and son watched the flowers drift in the water and one by one they sank below the choppy surface.

Matthews wanted to put his arm around his son's shoulder, but he didn't want to risk rejection. He was aware of his son's pensive mood and he saw tears on his cheek. *It never gets easier*, he thought. He waited at David's side for the grief to pass.

On many occasions, Matthews had considered how differently things would have turned out if he had been on board. He had never talked to David about the problems in the marriage, but he knew that children always saw everything, heard the arguments, and were wise to their parents' strife. He wanted to be honest with David, but there had never come a moment where honesty felt right or appropriate. Nothing he could say would change what had happened.

"I miss them," he said.

"Why weren't you with us?"

Another urgent call to go overseas, another crisis that wasn't a crisis, but he'd answered the call to go. Demands of work that he didn't have the will, or courage, to resist.

"I was told to be on a flight. I didn't have a choice. We've talked about this. Many times."

"You always have a choice."

"I'm not sure you understand."

"You don't think you're responsible, but you are. You drove her to go out on the boat alone with us because it was all agreed. It was planned. But you had to go off somewhere. Where? I don't even know. Beirut? Cairo? Moscow?"

"Kiev."

"Oh, great, now I know. What was so important in Kiev? What?"

"Your mother was a good sailor."

"Not good enough." David stared at him. "Were you and Mom getting divorced?"

He shook his head. "There were problems between us, but we were committed to the family. I miss them terribly. You know that."

"Liz couldn't handle your arguments. It was always better when you were away. She suffered when you were home and we heard you fight. We looked forward to your trips."

"I'm sorry you feel that way."

"It's the truth."

"I quit the agency to change that."

"You quit the agency. I didn't even know that you worked at the CIA until you said you'd left." David turned to his father and his face flushed crimson with anger. "Then you started Trinity Capital and you're in Moscow all the time. Nothing has changed."

David turned back to the view of the gray water. He plucked petals from the last flower in his hand and threw them aggressively into the water one at a time, and then he tossed the deflowered stalk as far as he could.

Anna appeared at their side. Sensing tension between father and son, she smiled bravely. "It's a shame to spoil the event with unhappy faces. Let's enjoy the beautiful day. It's still early and I brought lunch. We can anchor in the cove."

She looked from father to son. "I brought our bathing suits. The water in the cove will be warm. I brought champagne and you can dig for oysters."

"Fine with me." David moved to the boat's stern.

Matthews looked at Anna, already in her two-piece bikini, her blonde hair in a ponytail.

"What did you talk about?"

"It's the same conversation. He's still angry."

"Of course he is. He lost his mother and sister and he has me in his life."

Matthews was matter-of-fact when he spoke, and there was little he ever said that he didn't consider first. "He's told me that you're gone a lot."

She turned to him. "I'm sorry. What do you mean to imply, that 'I'm gone a lot'? You know what agency work is like. I don't travel as much as you, but it they need me in London or Brussels I get on a plane. If there is a late meeting, I stay in the office."

Matthews heard her indignation and he wasn't comforted by her explanation. The day's stress tugged at his emotion. His eyes came off the cove and he spoke in a softer voice. "I thought things would change when I left the agency." He put his arm around her shoulder with as much feeling as he could summon.

"It's all coming from inside you." She allowed herself to be drawn close, but then she pulled away. "The Director would take you back in a minute. You've made money. Go back and make a difference. You brighten up when you talk about the favors you do for him."

9
Langley Headquarters

Without great fuss, an internal investigation looking into the circumstances surrounding the arrest of Simon Birch in Moscow was convened by James Linton. A man comfortable in his official anonymity, Linton was annoyed by the public display of Simon Birch in Moscow's Khamovniki District Court, which brought American press attention to the case, and with it, urgent demands for an explanation from Washington's intelligence community. Reluctantly, Linton appeared before the Senate Intelligence Committee and answered questions in closed session, and he provided sanitized details of the catastrophe to the FBI and the national security advisor.

Linton was a master of false transparency and skilled in the art of obfuscation, so it came as no surprise that he merged his investigation with a long-standing joint FBI/CIA task force charged with investigating security threats. Four trusted members of the task force convened in a windowless conference room on headquarters' second floor and began conducting interviews to establish what went wrong in Moscow, identify a list of possible "leaks," and quietly get to the bottom of things.

A large wall chart with cross-coded intelligence losses going back several years was the task force's blueprint. Different pinned notecards identified dates, agency contacts, and known locations of each compromise. Red string became arrows that drew links to photographs of confirmed dead Russian assets, while yellow string connected data to men whose fate was unknown—the missing assets: KEATS and BLAKE. FBI evidence was overlayed against interactions between each asset and CIA personnel. The chart depicted a grim history. Photographs of executed or disappeared Russians made it a gruesome reminder of the dangers of treason. It was Linton's masterpiece. He sat in front of the wall chart late at night and pondered the complex array of connections hoping the data would provoke an inspiration. Burton Smythe, the FBI supervisory agent, was officially in charge, and Linton graciously deferred to his authority because that was the way Washington's bureaucracy worked, but Linton kept the wall chart in headquarters. Smythe was quick, a pragmatic thinker, a cooperative agent, but Linton wasn't ready to be fully open about the scope of the agency's problem, and he didn't trust the FBI to withhold information from the White House.

Alone at night, Linton placed a celluloid overlay onto the wall chart that drew links of his uncorroborated personal suspicions. He sat in his chair with a scotch and meditated on the mystery with the deep concentration of a priest seeking spiritual guidance.

❖

Matthews waited in the underground garage. His fingers fidgeted with his cell phone, turning it over to look at the screen, and he checked the time again. He paced between his parked Volvo and another sedan, and then back again, repeating the pattern until he lost track of time and checked the screen again. He was tempted to call, but he'd been warned not to make contact with his phone. He was alert to sounds in the quiet garage and he was conscious of being in a place where drivers came and went and no one had a good reason to hang around. Harsh fluorescent lights on the low ceiling made him feel exposed. The underground space was hardly vented and Matthews caught the faint hint of peppermint.

"How did it go today?"

Matthews turned abruptly to the voice and saw the Director emerge from behind a thick column, unwrapping a stick of chewing gum that he put in his mouth.

"How long have you been here?"

"Long enough." He pointed at the Escalade SUV that was parked inconspicuously among a dozen other black cars. "I waited until I was sure you were alone."

Suddenly, a car engine came alive somewhere in the garage and tire rubber squealed on the smooth concrete road surface. The two men stepped behind the column and watched as a silver Mercedes drove slowly toward the exit ramp.

"What you don't know," the Director said, turning away from the car, "is that someone at McCain's funeral saw you join me in my SUV. TOPCAT's chief of staff called that afternoon wanting to know why we met. I told him you once worked for us, but he kept probing." The Director looked at Matthews. "He asked questions about you, about what we discussed, so we have to be careful how we meet." He nodded at the underground garage and turned back to Matthews. "How did it go with Linton?"

"He put on a good show."

"Who else was there?"

"Two others, a man and a woman. Louis Kind and Margaret Savage, so I suspect they're FBI or agency aliases. I was there two hours and James didn't let me say much."

"By design. That's his job. They're not FBI or CIA. The national security advisor requested that they be there. Whatever comes out of this investigation will find its way to the Oval Office. We'll redact what we can, and we'll limit what is discovered, but we're in an intelligence vortex. POTUS goes behind our backs with his own sources, and the Russians see their opportunity." The Director was visibly frustrated. "There is no map for this. All we can do is shine a light into the darkness."

The Director nodded at his driver. "We got you a seat on a flight to Moscow tomorrow. Linton will know when you're back and I'll arrange for us to meet like this, somewhere private."

The Director looked around the garage, shifting his eyes with the alert instincts of a man trained to wear caution. "Be careful in Moscow. Stay away from the embassy. After Linton interviewed you, he questioned D'Angelo about problems in Moscow Station. We learned that D'Angelo suggested you meet BYRON by the Kempinski Hotel so Linton has his eye on him. Linton also met with Wallace. He thinks Wallace might be our problem. I know he's your friend."

"Everyone says that." Matthews leaned forward. "I won't defend him, but tell me, what's his motive?"

"He resents us. He resents me. There are people in the agency, and he is one of them, who want to use the Moscow catastrophe against me. They see me as a wounded beast."

The Director heaved an exhausted sigh. "We've lost two assets in Moscow in the past year under D'Angelo's watch. In February, a Russian Ministry of Foreign Affairs staffer committed suicide during his interrogation in Lubyanka Prison with the cyanide pill that his CIA handler had supplied him. The other, a GRU colonel, died in a suspicious fall from his balcony. D'Angelo hasn't solved the problem in Moscow Station and I was urged to remove him when it came out that he was friendly with James Dowd."

Matthews waited for the Director to go on.

"It's not your problem," he continued, "but you should be aware of my concerns. For your safety, steer clear of the Moscow embassy. You should also avoid Dowd. I have back-channel intelligence that Russians close to the Kremlin used him to funnel laundered cash into golf resorts."

The Director paused. "I'm prattling on about things you don't need to know." He popped two strips of gum into his mouth, chewing hard. "One of these days I will say 'fuck it' and smoke again. Giving up smoking has been the hardest thing I've ever done." He thumped his chest with a closed fist.

"I gave it up because my granddaughter can't stand cigars. Abstinence is one of life's cruelest pleasures. And secrets. It was easier when I smoked." He held up his government-issued cell phone and then his personal cell phone. "I don't trust these. There are too many people in Washington who'd like to know who I talk to and what's on my mind. It's Mossad, MI6, the FSB, but it's also the FBI, DOD, and the White House. There is no topic of greater interest than Russian interference."

His voice lowered, his eyebrow arched, and he looked directly at Matthews. "What I am going to say is extremely sensitive, in the realm of a beheading offense. Understand?"

Matthews nodded.

"I visited the Oval Office yesterday. I had briefed the Gang of Eight on the Moscow incident two days ago and the conversation turned to Anton Glok. Putin wants him back. He's in a federal penitentiary awaiting charges for selling weapons that killed several of our assets in Sudan. He's also run money-laundering operations in Cyprus.

"The White House got word of my briefing. My assistant pulled me out of a meeting with the secretary of defense and said TOPCAT wanted to see me. I was summoned like a truant to the principal's office. I've been there many times, but this time it was a different routine. I got out of my car at the little portico by the West Wing, which is how I always arrive for meetings in the situation room. A Secret Service officer made a phone call and before long the president's personal bodyguard came to escort me.

"You have to understand how unusual this was. His bodyguard took me directly to the Oval Office for an unscheduled meeting. He was behind the Resolute Desk when I entered and he came around to greet me.

"I'm a big man, but he is taller and heavier and he moves like a man of bulk without weight. He never walks. Everything is a stride. As he approached me, I saw his expression—part menace, part welcoming. I know how to read politicians as well as anyone who's run this agency, but he is a tough case.

"We shook hands and then he was behind the desk again, leaning forward, elbows on the desk, hands clasped. He had me sit in an armchair in front of him. His chief of staff was there on one side of me and the White House counsel on the other, but he ignored them. He started by saying:

"'We forced out the FBI director. People are happy that we finally got rid of him. People in the FBI are glad he's out. A lot of them are happy. We had to do it because he mishandled the Clinton email problem. Really mishandled it. He had to go because of that and a lot of other reasons, like the terrible Steele Dossier.'"

The Director's eye turned to Matthews. "That's how he started the meeting. He asked if I wanted the FBI job. He said it was a promotion—not a lateral move. I told him I was happy at the agency. He said 'You've done a great job. Fabulous. Fabulous.'

"You know him. He has a way of not complimenting you when he's complimenting you. He went down a list of people in the administration, disparaging them. The attorney general is a pussy; the secretary of state a loser; Madam Speaker a dumb broad. He saved his most poisonous vitriol for the FBI director, who he called a nightmare. 'Disloyal, ignorant, pathologically incompetent, a total loser.' His words."

The Director paused. "Then he looked right at me and said, 'People are telling me that I should get rid of you.' He asked if he should fire me. I asked, 'On what grounds?'

"'You lost a man in Moscow. Everyone tells me it was a stupid operation. A botched job. Bad planning. Terrible work. But no one can tell me what it was about.'

"He looked at me like a cat teasing a mouse and he leaned forward. 'What was so important in Moscow that you geniuses ran an operation that risked one of your best officers? I'm told he's bright. Young. Promising. You call yourselves intelligence officers but there is nothing intelligent about getting caught. Losers get caught.'"

The Director's expression was gloomy. He added two sticks of gum to his mouth and he looked off at nothing, ruminating.

"It's not a pretty sight when a politician loses power. He wilts, crumbles, and clings to the vestiges of office. He mourns his vanished perks and the entourage. He doesn't accept that his day in the sun is over. One moment he's on the world stage and the next he's a bit player doing regional theater. It's terrible to see. Some men go gracefully. Some do whatever it takes to stay."

The Director turned back to Matthews. "At the end of the meeting he asked his chief of staff and the general counsel to leave. He stood and paced the room, his brow knit, disparaging the two men he'd just dismissed, and then he sat behind the desk again. He looked at me and asked if we should trade Anton Glok for Simon Birch. I said it wasn't an even trade.

"'I hear Glok is innocent. He's a harmless businessman who happens to sell guns. That's what I hear.'

"I replied that Glok's guns were used to kill half a dozen of our assets. I said Birch is a throwaway rookie and Glok an arms merchant. He said, 'Think about it. Think about the promotion I've offered.'"

The Director shook his head in sad disbelief and looked right at Matthews. "You need to work quickly in Moscow or you'll find another person in my job." His voice deepened. "Glok isn't a harmless businessman. Putin is the only one who could have put that bunk in his head."

PART III

10

Sheremetyevo Airport

Dense early morning fog laid a false peace on the remote airstair where the Air France jet had parked. Matthews stepped onto the bus, groggy from the long overnight flight. He gave up his seat to an older woman and, as he stood, his cell phone vibrated as it connected to a local wireless carrier. Planes were ghosts in the mist that covered the tarmac in impenetrable gray that had moved in after his plane landed. The weather made the bus ride quiet and gloomy, and the texts that filled his phone added to his unsettled mood. Too many texts from people who shouldn't be messaging that early.

Terminal F appeared in a few minutes. The brutalist architecture of the old international arrivals building was meant to celebrate the Soviet Union's grandeur, but now at forty-five years, it was an appalling reminder of Communism's failures. A recent cosmetic facelift for Russia's hosting of the World Cup did little to improve the grim façade.

Moscow was out of his mind when he was away, but memories returned as he entered the terminal, hearing the voices, smelling the air, taking in the familiar setting. How many times had he been there, that exact spot? There was something illusory about time and space. Past visits washed over him as he joined the throng of passengers lining up to clear passport control. In the crowd, looking around at security, his instincts for operating safely in Russia returned.

Matthews bypassed the passport control queue and opened a door that led to the VIP lounge, where a brisk young woman in a crimson-and-gold uniform took his documents.

"Welcome back, Mr. Matthews."

Matthews forced a smile. She always remembered his name and always wore the same uniform with ruby heels, black hair cut short, and the same bright confident smile of the well-paid concierge class. She took his documents, adding them to others she'd collected from passengers in the lounge who had the money to pay for an immigration expediting service. She presented the stack of documents to the border control officer at the counter.

Matthews sat in a leather lounge chair and looked at his phone. It was midnight in Washington and Anna's text had come through a little earlier.

Everything okay?

He texted back. *Just landed.*

Has Sorkin reached you?

Matthews looked through the text string and saw two from Trinity Capital's office manager, but he didn't see one from his lawyer. The office manager's text had come in early that morning. They were disjointed and clipped, even in the cryptic syntax of text messaging, but by his third reading of the thread he determined that police from the FSB's Directorate K had arrived at their offices in Tverskoy District with a search warrant, and they'd broken into the office's locked file cabinets.

He texted Sorkin, *I'm at the airport. What happened at the office?* The answer came back quickly. *Talk in person.*

Matthews pondered the message and whether Sorkin feared his phone was compromised, or whether the topic couldn't be properly addressed in texting's shorthand. Directorate K was the economic counterintelligence unit of the FSB's Fourth Service that supervised banking. Matthews considered the possibilities. His shareholder activism approach to investing in Russia had made him wealthy, but it also threatened the convenient alliance between government regulators and the oligarchs who controlled most of Russia's private sector. He arbitraged free market forces against the limited floats of dozens of companies on the Moscow stock exchange, making good returns by finding companies whose stock prices didn't represent their underlying asset values. He'd openly taken calculated risks, but he hadn't counted on attracting unwanted attention.

He called Sorkin but got voicemail.

Matthews grew impatient. He looked for the document expediter, but she was gone. He picked up the morning's *Komsomolskaya* and flipped through the pages, and then did the same with another. Celebrity gossip and adulterous romance were popular features in many Moscow tabloids. The rich were fair game for editors and he looked to see if he knew any of the men caught leaving a Moscow strip joint or pricy restaurant. In Moscow, you could pay a small fee to avoid the passport queue, but the price to avoid public scandal was high.

Again, Matthews looked up to see if the border control officer had completed processing his documents, but the man was gone, as was the expediter. Two passengers who he recognized from his flight were already processed and had left the lounge.

Matthews leaned over the counter and looked for the missing officer. "Hello." There was no one. He looked at his watch and was surprised to see that he'd been in the lounge thirty minutes.

"Mr. Matthews."

He saw the expediter enter from the corridor with a concerned expression.

"There is a problem," she said.

"What problem?"

"The officer left with your documents. You will have to wait."

Ten minutes later his cell phone vibrated and Sorkin's number came up.

"Where are you?"

"I haven't cleared passport control."

"What's wrong?"

"I don't know. A mix-up." The border control officer returned. "The officer is here. Stay on the line."

Matthews stepped to the counter and held the line open so Sorkin could listen in and intercede if necessary. The border control officer's previous pleasant efficiency was gone, replaced by brisk impatience.

"There is a visa problem. You will be escorted."

The officer brusquely waved Matthews to the side, taking the next person in the queue.

"Did you hear that?" Matthews said to Sorkin, speaking into his phone.

"You've never had a visa problem. Something isn't right. I'll call D'Angelo."

"The embassy doesn't need to know I'm here. This will get resolved. I'll call when I'm in the hotel."

Matthews slumped on the lounge chair, fretting the inconvenience, trying not to give in to dark suspicions. He stood up like a jack-in-the-box when two FSB officers approached. They wore high-peaked caps with black visors and hard-eyed expressions that discomfited Matthews. The taller one had a hatchet face and held Matthews's passport and visa; the shorter officer was older, heavier, and spoke curtly.

"*Dobroyeutro.* Follow us."

Matthews saw the indifference of glum authority in their faces. He recognized their forest-green uniforms and insignia patches—one of the FSB's many branches. The tall officer took Matthews's bag and his partner led him from the lounge into the crowded arrivals hall. Passengers loaded with suitcases were greeted loudly by waiting families and above the din came the booming public address announcements of planes' arrival statuses and gate changes. Groups of stranded passengers sat on bags, given over to the vagaries of travel.

Matthews was moving past the gauntlet of chauffeurs holding placards with passengers' names when he saw his driver.

"We have your ride," the shorter officer said, holding his arm.

Revolving glass doors sent them onto the sidewalk's pick-up zone. Matthews was directed to a boxy Mercedes SUV parked illegally. One officer put his roll-on bag in the rear compartment and the other opened the front passenger door.

"He will drive you," the officer said, nodding at the driver, who at that moment looked to his left so Matthews saw only the back of his head, but he knew the blue epaulet with a single gold star of a lieutenant colonel, and he recognized the uniform of an officer in the FSB's Sixth Service.

"What is this about?" Matthews said angrily to the driver.

"Look irritated," the driver said, facing Matthews. "Don't let them think that we know each other."

Matthews blanched, recovered, and stared at BYRON. He hadn't been this close in a decade and what he remembered of the younger BYRON's face merged into the face of the man beside him. Slightly older, slightly heavier, paler, but still with the careless caution of a man exhilarated by risk. He was clean-shaven and his thinning gray hair was combed back on his forehead; a garroting tie swelled his neck, and his eyes looked past Matthews at the officer.

"*Spasibo.*"

The officer snapped a brisk salute and left.

BYRON pulled the SUV into traffic and spoke without looking at Matthews. "This isn't how you expected to meet me, but this is the safest way, for now. It's good to see your surprise."

Matthews glanced at Lieutenant Colonel Dmitry Grigoryev— BYRON.

"You have attracted attention. Too much attention. I'm here because you need me as much as I need you."

Matthews looked in the side mirror.

"The silver Volga is from Department K of the Fourth Service. They're looking into tax irregularities at Trinity Capital. The red Fiat behind them is my branch in the Sixth Service. I drive you, Department K follows us, and my Sixth Service colleagues follow them. We are friendly collaborators, like the CIA and FBI." He laughed. "We get along if we need to."

Matthews ignored Grigoryev's bravado explanation. "Why are you here?"

"Me here? Driving you?" He looked back at the road. "Colonel Zhukov knew Directorate K ordered border control to flag your entry. He appealed to a senior officer arguing that your bogus tax issue is less important than your usefulness in uncovering the traitor BYRON. I offered to help. He was skeptical, but I convinced him that you would feel safe if I met you."

Matthews stared at Grigoryev. "He doesn't suspect you?"

"Of course not." He glanced in the rearview mirror. "Meeting you here is a risk, but less risky than getting off a bus on Bolshoy Moskvoretsky Bridge. They were there. You didn't see them. In the alley by the dumpster with garbage slopping over the top. FSB units sitting among the rats."

A curse fell from Grigoryev's lips. "Someone on your side is working to have me caught. Many things have changed in Russia, but one hasn't. Traitors are taken to a basement cell in Lefortovo, made to kneel, a bullet fired into the base of the head. Brezhnev abolished the death penalty, so now there are only prison 'suicides.' Viktoria won't know what happened to me until a death notice appears in the mailbox. I'll be buried in an unmarked grave in an unknown location. Death is hard on a traitor but worse for the ones left behind."

Matthews looked directly at Grigoryev. "What's the problem in Washington?"

Grigoryev was quiet for a short time, hands clenching the steering wheel. "Colonel Zhukov knew you were arriving. He had your assigned seat, your flight number, and arrival date. That is how I know the problem is in Washington."

Grigoryev looked at Matthews. "I am driving you to Colonel Zhukov. We can talk until we arrive. It's not enough time, but it's what we have, so you can spare me small talk about your life."

"What happened?" Matthews asked. "It's been ten years." He nodded at the trailing vehicles. "Why risk this?"

"I have my reasons."

"What?"

"What!" He cursed.

"You're putting me at risk."

"Finally, we're equals."

"I don't work for them anymore. Let's get this over with."

"You think it will be that easy. It is different now. Worse."

"I wouldn't be in this car if you didn't trust me."

"It's not that simple. We're not teenagers smoking Marlboro Reds, drinking vodka with Sorkin, and reading shitty poetry while we float on the river. Those sunny days are gone and now I'm in a meat grinder."

Matthews knew that the world had changed in the past decade, but he recognized his old friend's bluster. "I was told you have a package for me."

"I am the package."

"I was told it was *kompromat*."

"*Yob tvoyu!*" He shook his head. "I have what you want, but it leaves Russia with me."

"What is it?"

"You're bargaining."

"I want to know if it's worth risking what I've built here."

"You've already risked it." He nodded at the silver Volga two cars back. "You can't trade one risk for another. They add up. Look back. Now there is another car, the BMW. See how important you are."

Matthews confirmed that a blue-and-white police car had joined the procession. He was comfortable moving in the shadows of a conference, away from the scrutiny of curious strangers. He was appalled by the surveillance, appalled by Grigoryev's casual indifference to the situation, and in spite of an effort to remain calm, his neck muscles tightened.

"Traffic is slow," Grigoryev said. "Maybe you'll be arrested like the American kid they grabbed at the hotel." Grigoryev laughed. "Or maybe not. It's been ten years, so a lot has happened." He shook his head. "Ten years. Here's what I can say, what you may not remember. My father was proud of me when I earned a master's degree at the KGB Academy. You remember him. Big, intolerant opinions. It was his choice that I join the KGB, not mine. He called it the family business. My grandfather was a colonel in the NKVD, my great-grandfather served in the Cheka. My two cousins are big shots in the FSB.

"My father and I never had a normal relationship. There were two opinions at home: his and wrong. Even going to high school at the Anglo-American School was training to get to know foreigners. Learn to laugh at your shitty jokes. Think how you thought. We were friends but I studied you. My father tested me every week on what I learned."

Grigoryev glanced at Matthews. "You're surprised. Almost as surprised as being in this car with me. You, me, and Sorkin rowed on the Moscow River reading Pushkin, smoking, drinking. I would describe our outings to my father, leaving out the drinking and the smoking, and he'd be happy with my reports."

Grigoryev shrugged. "You need to know all of this to write up a convincing report. 'Oh, yes,' you'll say, 'I learned things I never knew. La la, la la.'" Grigoryev gripped the wheel. "After I was commissioned second lieutenant, I learned that you had returned to Moscow as a commercial officer in the embassy, and it served my career to recruit you. I allowed you to think you'd recruited me to your poets' network."

"I did recruit you."

"I let you think that, but I told my supervisor it was the other way around. I recruited you. Both our careers advanced. I gave you obsolete ballistic missile drawings and you gave me gossip about Pershing missile deployments that were already in the press that I passed along as classified intelligence. I wrote reports on our meetings and my boss would call me into his office. He'd say, 'Good job, Dmitry.' I was promoted. They were convinced I'd recruited you. That was 1992 or 1993. The new Russia struggled after the collapse of the Soviet Union and the FSB was happy to claim my counterintelligence coup."

Matthews considered the whole fraught history of courtship, recruitment, clandestine meetings in Vvedenskoye Cemetery, the money, and the motive, now refracted through the lens of Grigoryev's crazy confession. He knew it was good to pause before he took one of Grigoryev's claims at face value. "Did it earn you a handful of medals?"

Grigoryev laughed. "Sometimes you didn't gossip and I had to make up fake intelligence."

He looked in the rearview mirror. "I'm here driving you to Colonel Zhukov because he wants me to find out who BYRON is."

Matthews stared and said nothing.

"Imagine. I should walk into his office and give myself up." He coughed his sarcasm. "He's a toady who thinks he's cleverer than he is. He plays Chopin on the piano and his wife cooks nouvelle cuisine. They are the new bourgeoisie."

Grigoryev shook his head. "My father was proud of me. I had recruited my high school friend, the son of a big shot foreign correspondent. He complimented himself on the hard work he put into my training."

His voice deepened with anger. "He was a difficult man. You never saw that side of him. He was proud, polite, boastful. He and I argued and then made up, but our relationship ruptured over my marriage to a woman outside the FSB family. He planned for me to go into foreign intelligence, which is why I was sent to the Anglo-American School, but there was no talk of that after my marriage. Viktoria was an outsider, not to be trusted, and my career suffered. You can imagine what it was like to live with a wife and father who hated each other."

Grigoryev paused. "There was never a reason to tell you this, but it is part of why I contacted the CIA. I need your help. There is a trade I want to make."

"What trade?"

"I am exfiltrated and you get the *kompromat*."

"What about your wife?"

"She's already left Moscow and is staying in our home in Montenegro. But I am on a restricted travel list." Grigoryev honked at a car that cut him off. "Idiot," he said, gesturing at the driver. "So now the whole story comes out." He looked at Matthews. "You haven't spoken."

"I'm listening."

"Maybe you see comedy in my misery."

"Why did she leave?"

"I was moved to Department M in the Sixth Service, which is the new police of the police, and we do things we can get away with. I was assigned to the financial crimes unit investigating money laundering and foreign businessmen who come to Russia to make money. So, I know what they've got on you, and we have things on other foreigners—one in particular."

He lifted a small USB drive. "The FSB doesn't have the German precision of Stasi record keeping, but we have a big network of intelligence. The case files have everything. Thousands of pages. Transcripts of cell conversations, hours of hotel video footage. Agent surveillance reports. Things like, 'In the evening, the subject left his hotel for dinner with two women. At 11:10 P.M. a black Volga picked him up at a bar with such and such escort.' Very detailed reports. It is all there. Personal lapses described in the sterile language of surveillance.

"The early years of his visits involve money, oil and gas negotiations, and a sports franchise. Later, files were linked to election influence. For years, the FSB has targeted promising young Americans offering favors, and when their success comes, we call in our Faustian bargain."

Grigoryev lifted the thumb drive. "Such a record exists for the leader of the so-called Free World." He rounded the vowels of the last words to deepen his sarcasm and then he looked at Matthews. "Evil is everywhere. Russia has no monopoly on it, but we are expert at knowing how to make it useful. I am trading what I have."

Grigoryev glanced back nervously at the three surveillance cars trailing the SUV. "Traffic is heavy today but we'll be there soon enough. Things became dangerous for Viktoria and me two months ago. To advance in Department M, I played the game and took bribes from corrupt bankers. I saw oligarchs laundering rubles into euros and dollars through a network of subsidiary banks and shell companies in Malta, Cyprus, Estonia, and the Cayman Islands. Money left Russia circumventing foreign exchange rules in mirror transactions. Cash came in and it went out—dirty cash became clean. The basic fee was 10 percent. My team took a cut. Our principal job was to look the other way. We gave our supervisors half. It's the way the Sixth Service under Sechin works. His relationship to Putin goes back to St. Petersburg in the 1990s when he was Putin's deputy.

"In time, we were making thousands of euros a week. Viktoria spent money on a new lifestyle and people took notice. I gave explanations that no one questioned because in Moscow you don't ask where someone gets his money. If Viktoria wanted to buy a new coat, I'd give her what she needed. One hundred thousand rubles. Two hundred thousand. I peeled notes from a thick wad.

"The whole operation was complicated and illegal but, for us, it was business. Oligarchs stole state assets and my team taxed the corruption. Once in the game you don't get out. You are a risk to the ones who stay in. You are either *nash*—one of us—or you are *chuzhoy*—one of them. Money became easy, but of course we became too greedy and we drew attention.

"My father learned of our work. He's an old Communist who dedicated his life to the Soviet cause and then when the Soviet Union fell, he sank into saccharine revisionist nostalgia, longing for the old days of Stalin. He forgot the abuses, the betrayals, the starvation, and the gulags. He blamed the new corruption on the collapse of Soviet ethics."

Grigoryev shook his head. "He lived in his own unreality. Anyway, when he found out what I was doing, he tried to ignore it for a long time. But then Viktoria's spending got too extravagant and he confronted me." He made an expression of disbelief. "We had so much money—wild fantasies of wealth filled our heads. We felt like no one could touch us. No one could stop us, but then our greed blinded us to danger. We asked for double the fee on one big deal and the bank, with the consent of Sechin, moved against us. My bank account was frozen. Threats came to the house. My father, who was in his late seventies, found out. His advice? Shoot myself."

A bead of sweat formed on Grigoryev's upper lip. "Viktoria flew to Montenegro, but as I said, my name is on a restricted travel list. I can't leave Russia as Dmitry Grigoryev. I need false documents—a new birth certificate, new domestic identity card, and a transborder passport." Grigoryev looked at Matthews. "There is always a quid pro quo in our work."

Grigoryev continued in a relaxed voice as if everything he had just said was perfectly normal between two old acquaintances. "Viktoria is not well. Stress, worry, nights of not sleeping. Threats to our lives. All the money was a new toy, but now we have no peace of mind. She traveled to Montenegro a month ago for the Mediterranean climate. I was able to reassure neighbors that Moscow's weather aggravated her asthma. That story stopped questions for a few weeks, but I am watched when I leave my apartment block. I don't know who they are. Chechen thugs, Russian mafia hired by the bank, the Fourth Service?

"I am still useful to Colonel Zhukov because he thinks you're my asset and he needs me to uncover BYRON. So, we're meeting in my car, and later I'll write up a report for him that will be false but adequately believable."

He looked at Matthews. "The trade is simple. I leave Russia with false papers, and when I'm across the border you get the thumb drive. Colonel Zhukov will protect you from Department K as long as he thinks you can lead him to BYRON. We must move quickly. Colonel Zhukov will be pleasant when you meet him, but he is a *chekist*."

"How will you leave Russia?"

"By car with you. Overland border crossings are less risky."

"Which border?"

"Probably west to Estonia across the Friendship Bridge. South through Ukraine is what they'd expect. North to Finland is possible."

"How good is the *kompromat*?"

Grigoryev's forehead darkened. "That is a stupid question. The man outside a brothel doesn't ask how good she is. He asks how much she costs." He looked back at the heavy traffic on the Ring Road. "My new documents have to be professionally done with all the new digital security. I can't buy them on the black market, but your technical services department can make what I need: an internal passport, *Pasport Grazhdanina Rossiyskoy Federatsii*, with everything inside correct—place of birth, names of relatives, home addresses since childhood, list of employers. The man I will become died two weeks ago in a village in Irkutsk. His death will find its way to the FSB's records in a month. Dmitry Grigoryev will stay in Russia, and engineer Oleg Borodin will cross the border. The transborder passport for international travel must have an issue date of July 2010 so your technician can match the watermarks in use then."

"How do I get the information?"

"From me. I will contact you. A surprise, like today. The less you know in advance, the safer for both of us. We can meet openly because I am handling you. Your cell phone is probably monitored. It is important the passport has the right watermarks. It's critical."

Grigoryev paused. "If we need to meet, use the old system. The tobacco kiosk by Novokuznetskaya Metro Station. Two chalk marks means you need to meet. Three means I need to meet. We'll use the same place, the Orthodox church on Mayakovsky Street."

Matthews saw they'd entered another street and he recognized the yellow-brick, Neo-Baroque façade of FSB headquarters. As he got out of the SUV, he felt Grigoryev's hand on his arm.

"Be careful of Zhukov. A scorpion with a smile." He held on to Matthews's arm and added gravely, "There is no time. They watch me. They'll watch you."

11

Lubyanka Headquarters

olonel Viktor Petrovich Zhukov sat at his uncluttered desk on
the fifth floor of FSB headquarters looking at the two documents he'd place side by side in front of him. The deputy head of
counterintelligence was a career officer whose dedication to his job
had earned him the departmental award for meritorious service
issued under Order 415, but he was also skilled at navigating the
FSB's complex bureaucracy, and his controlled demeanor disguised
a ruthless political infighter. He had earned the nickname Caligula.
He knew how to be humble, but it was his choice, and he didn't let
himself be treated humbly. Nothing irritated him more than to be
surprised by activities in the FSB's sprawling security apparatus
that impinged on his domain.

Both documents were stamped "confidential" and bore his
name on the routing slip, and earlier recipients had made a mark
showing they'd seen the paper. He was senior, but last on the list,
and he could see from the date that it had taken five days for the

first document to reach him. Both reports had the same subject: Alexander Matthews.

The first document summarized Department K's investigation into Trinity Capital's portfolio companies' potential for VAT recovery. Colonel Zhukov was not a tax specialist but he was familiar with Department K's schemes to target vulnerable companies and put money in the hands of Kremlin allies. He didn't condone the official corruption that was linked to powerful men with close ties to the president of the Russian Federation, but neither did it serve his interests to speak up.

Trinity Capital's success had been regularly reported in memos from Department K, and a decision had now been made to "tax" the success. The case was laid out. A lawsuit had been filed in Novosibirsk District Court 3,500 kilometers from Moscow to claim a large debt against Trinity Capital's largest portfolio company. A local lawyer fraudulently claiming to represent Trinity Capital had been hired by Department K. He had lost Trinity Capital's defense of the lawsuit, and the portfolio company's assets had been awarded to satisfy the debt, which was expected as the appeal was denied. Meanwhile, the company's claim for VAT tax refunds would be investigated to implicate the owner of Trinity Capital in tax fraud. It recommended that an arrest warrant be issued for Alexander Matthews.

Colonel Zhukov dropped the report on his desk and considered its grave implications for his work. The second piece of paper was labeled File 912018ÈPF, addressed to a cryptonym used for secure communications that came from Washington. He recognized the code identifying the report as a transcribed burst radio transmission received by the *rezident* in the Washington embassy. It contained the details of Matthews's arrival in Moscow and reported that he would attempt a second meeting with the man the Americans called BYRON.

Colonel Zhukov rose from his desk, leaving his cup of black tea and sugar-dusted *ponchiki* untouched, and he moved to his window that overlooked Dzerzhinsky Square. He lit the first of his day's quota of cigarettes and drew on it.

"*Ublyudki.*" Bastards.

The curse slipped from his lips. He had a deep contempt for the men in Department K, whose plans to enrich themselves by taking down the American Matthews would threaten his operation. Without thinking, he clenched and unclenched his fist. He faced the well-tended beds of late summer flowers across the street in the square, but he saw only the difficult challenge of the task ahead. Early morning fog that had greeted him when he arrived in the office at dawn dispersed, but the day was gray and with it had come a drizzle.

The desk telephone rang. When he answered it, his assistant said that the American he was expecting had arrived.

❖

"We meet again."

Matthews was gazing from the sparsely furnished waiting room's window when he heard the voice. He turned to the open door, surprised not to have heard Colonel Zhukov enter. The FSB officer's uniform was a trim fit on his athletic form and his high-crown hat was propped under his arm. He had a flat expression that brightened with a false smile as he crossed the room, stopping a meter away.

"Do you remember our first meeting?"

"I prefer this view."

"The old joke again." He pointed at the square across the street, where a small group of dissidents with placards looked up at the façade of FSB headquarters. "They come to protest. Sometimes tourists on tour buses stop to look at the former KGB headquarters. We considered removing the hammer and sickle above the door, but it required that we put in temporary supports and new yellow brick, which you can't get anymore, so we left the Communist symbol in place." He looked at Matthews. "Things change but the old jokes stay. Have a seat."

"I prefer to stand."

Colonel Zhukov took out his pack of Primas. "Smoke? Oh, yes, I forgot you don't smoke." He lit his own. "I limit myself to six a day. This is my fourth and it is not yet nine o'clock." He looked at Matthews. "How did you stop?"

"I never started."

Colonel Zhukov smiled. "That is the answer to all our sins: envy, pride, lust, and the one popular among Moscow's oligarchs—greed. The rich want to be richer. In Soviet times you were rich with one old Lada and a dacha with two square meters of garden. Today, you're not rich unless you have six homes and a monstrous yacht."

Colonel Zhukov cocked his head. "Can I offer you coffee after your long flight?"

"I had some on the plane."

"You're back in Moscow sooner than I expected."

"My business is here. Some things can't be done by phone or email."

Colonel Zhukov held his cigarette as he had in their last meeting, elbow cocked. "I interviewed the woman from the car incident outside the Hotel Baltschug Kempinski. She confirmed your story that it was an unfortunate misunderstanding." He drew on the Prima and released smoke from the corner of his mouth.

"She is a well-regarded journalist and the widow of a prominent dissident. You should be careful of associating with her. She is Russian intelligentsia—*chuzhoy.*"

"Is that why I'm here, to get your advice?"

He frowned. "You're here because we have a mutual acquaintance, my colleague, Lieutenant Colonel Dmitry Grigoryev."

Matthews hesitated too long.

"The man who drove you here."

"I know who you mean."

"You were uncertain for a moment, so I thought he might not have introduced himself."

"I hesitated because I'm not sure why you're asking."

"He says that you once worked for us."

Matthews nodded noncommittally, conscious how his body language was being watched, and careful to answer the question in a way that satisfied the colonel.

"Is that not true?"

"I work for myself."

"You worked for the CIA."

"I left. Now I work for myself."

"And you worked for us at one point. I've seen the records."

Colonel Zhukov removed an envelope from his tunic and laid out photographs on the waiting room's wood table. The photographs were taken with a telephoto lens and there was little depth of field. The first showed two men walking along the Moscow River in winter with long coats and snow on the ground. He recognized himself, and the man he was with matched Grigoryev's height and shape, and wore his Soviet-style fedora. They were younger in the photograph. By the make of a parked car, he guessed the photograph was taken in the early 1990s.

Matthews looked up and met the colonel's eyes. "Photographs don't lie, but they don't tell the whole truth. We knew each other from high school. We met socially and we sometimes did business together."

"Social chit chat between two covert intelligence officers."

Matthews heard the sarcasm in Colonel Zhukov's voice, but he knew that it would be a mistake to tell him what he wanted to hear. An ambiguous answer left room for doubt, while agreement closed down uncertainty. The photograph confirmed what the colonel wanted to believe. A man with a firm conviction didn't look for contrary evidence.

"Why am I here?" Matthews asked.

"You are the subject of a tax fraud investigation. You have substantial holdings in Russian publicly traded companies. The investigation that has been opened against you puts Trinity Capital, and you personally, at risk." Colonel Zhukov turned to the window, gazing out, but in a moment, he looked directly at Matthews with a cold expression.

"We are loyal to our friends, loyal to our families, loyal to job and country, but the test for each of us is: Are you brave enough to be loyal to your country when your livelihood is at risk?" He paused. "We are like your old employer, the CIA: the airing of suspicion without evidence can ruin an innocent man's career. *D'accord?*"

Colonel Zhukov smiled. "My grandparents were Francophile Tsarists and I learned French as a very young boy. I am the only FSB officer who speaks Russian with a slight French accent."

He gazed out the window at a clutch of assembling protestors, who faced off against arriving riot police.

"Moscow is an old city that is testing its many freedoms, but the average Russian prefers a strong leader. Moscow is a safe city, but it can be a dangerous place to do business."

He turned to Matthews. "I understand that you know the identity of a man the CIA calls BYRON. I can be helpful with Department K's tax investigation if you help me identify the man." He looked at Matthews. "You should consider the offer."

12

Hotel Baltschug Kempinski

Matthews's thoughts were tangled and unsettled. It was unlikely that Colonel Zhukov knew Grigoryev was BYRON, but it was also likely that he had a short list of suspects and Grigoryev was among them. It was also possible that he was in the dark, and the threat against Trinity Capital was a ploy to pressure him.

He lay on the bed fully clothed. He was back in the sepulchral city, beautiful on the outside, but dangerous at its core. He knew there was only one way forward. Follow the plan. He hadn't counted on the threat to Trinity Capital, and even so, his only choice was to proceed. Unforeseen things happened, but the mission remained the same. Linton needed to have Technical Services recreate security watermarks in use in 2010. A border control officer might not pick up a wrong personal detail in an identity document, but he would be alert to counterfeit watermarks.

Matthews looked at the ceiling, thinking. He knew the room's internet access was monitored and he didn't want to risk using a computer in the business center. He had to communicate with Linton on a secure channel or risk a misstep that might lead to his arrest. His old fear of dying in a Russian jail returned. He had once conquered the fear, and there was even a time when he had thought he would welcome death as an escape from the burdens he'd brought on himself. It was a dusk coming as certain as night follows day and he had tried to find ways to become familiar with his eternity. His agnostic Catholic faith had provided no comfort, only the pleasant rituals of Sunday mass and the occasional guidance of prayer. At times, he had wondered if there was an afterlife, and then he had hoped that there wasn't because it would take energy, and in his final days as Moscow station chief he had none to give. The failures of his life—his first marriage, his daughter's death, his shallow faith—were there to depress him. When he met Anna in Vienna and his pact with death vanished, the familiar fear returned.

Matthews removed his cell phone battery, disabling the signal, but remembered there was probably a hidden camera observing him preparing to begin a surveillance detection run. He juggled the phone like a toy, to confuse whoever was watching. A crazy stunt. A man with nothing on his mind. He took his raincoat, but then reconsidered, and left it on his bed so it wouldn't be apparent that he was leaving the hotel.

He ate dinner in the hotel's restaurant, ordering a light meal of grilled trout and asparagus. He engaged with the waiter and said a few things about the entrée and the quality of the burgundy, sharing innocent gossip about life in Moscow that he knew the waiter would be asked to describe when the FSB later questioned him. He commented on the inclement night, saying he didn't want to miss the changing of the guards at Lenin's Tomb. He left a big tip so the waiter would remember him.

Matthews took the umbrella offered by the solicitous doorman, saying that he was going out for a short walk to stretch his legs. Leaving his coat in his room but taking an umbrella, he was a man acting on impulse after a good dinner, not an organized man with a deliberate plan. Matthews was glad to be out in the cool evening air and away from the confinement of his room. There was a lonely sameness to five-star hotels.

Leaving the hotel's awning, he set out on a meandering surveillance detection run. As he walked, he felt fear come alive—and he understood how much he missed his old work. He climbed Bolshoy Moskvoretsky Bridge's stone steps and at the top he asked for directions from a policeman, but he used the moment to look back at the hotel. He noticed a heavyset man in a tight bomber jacket and short black hair. He was certain that he'd been there earlier that evening with a partner. *Surveillance.*

He pondered where he was going, the route he would take, and the number of men who might be assigned to follow him. It was still early. He had two hours to make his way to the Arbat District.

Matthews enjoyed the cool, misting breeze as he walked under the wide black umbrella. He was just another foreign tourist willing to brave the weather to visit Red Square and take in the beauty of candy-striped St. Basil's Cathedral. A single man in Moscow on business out strolling after an exhausting day of meetings. He had always found walking a reliable way to gather his thoughts and prepare himself for what he had to do. To think, to ponder, to weigh his choices. *God, how had it come to this?* he thought. His five years of building a new career made him a target. And Grigoryev. Revealing himself at the airport, hiding his treason in plain sight. He could only imagine the complex lies he was living.

Part of Matthews wanted to believe Grigoryev's story about his father and his wife, but part of him knew that Grigoryev had always been a fabulist—liking the idea of being important and enjoying his cleverness. The story he'd told about recruiting him was so improbable and also so like him—the life story that he wanted to claim. And now Matthews had to ponder how to exfiltrate him. Several of his poets had disappeared after he left the agency, but he had never lost an asset on his watch. Grigoryev put his life in Matthews's hands and he had a duty to protect him.

Red Square was before him. He crossed the vast open space, strolling clockwise around the medieval walls enclosing the Kremlin. His eyes rose to Spasskaya Tower's enormous clock where low clouds obscured the spire's red star. He'd been there many times before, under difference circumstances, and the memories came back, time playing tricks with his mind. He was station chief during the last year of Yeltsin's presidency and he was in the official American delegation at Yeltsin's funeral, joining Clinton and Bush, meeting Vladimir Putin. Their eyes had met—two cautious spies judging each other. He'd returned to Red Square when he started Trinity Capital. The same spot. A similar night. He remembered standing there as a businessman; he'd been startled and unsettled to be alone. Without surveillance. No longer of interest to them.

Now, he glanced back. *Make fear your ally*, he reminded himself. The square was full of voices trapped under the cobblestones that echoed off the Kremlin's walls. As he walked, he thought he heard footsteps just behind him matching the rhythm of his stride. He heard things. Laughter. Old laughter. Cries from his narrow escape years ago and voices calling out. *Halt. Halt.* He heard all these things in his mind. They weren't real, he reminded himself.

Then, in the corner of his eye, a dark shape standing beside the monument to Minin and Pozharsky in front of St. Basil's. He let his eyes drift off the tall man in a gray mackintosh, reading his newspaper in the drizzle. Matthews had gone a short distance when he saw the man walk a parallel course. *More surveillance.*

Two black vans entered the corner of Red Square by the GUM department store and they stopped near a tight clutch of protestors who shouted slogans, carried placards, and raised their fists. The vans' doors burst open and a squad of riot police in black body armor and balaclavas jumped out. Cries, shouts, and a flash bang explosion. Protestors were thrown to the ground, struck, and dragged to the vans. It was over in a moment. The vans sped off and rumors passed like wildfire among startled tourists and Muscovites. A bomb? Chechen separatists? The muffled terror of a nervous city waking from its dream of normalcy.

Matthews hopped on a blue line city bus in the midst of the incident, and from the window he saw the tall man urgently looking around, realizing he'd lost his target. Matthews rode the bus two stops, boarded a bus going in the opposite direction for ten minutes, and then exited at a Metro station. He took an escalator at one end, exited the station at the other end, and strolled casually through the Arbat shopping district. An hour later, he ducked into an alley, looking back to confirm he was alone. *Black*, he thought. He was in a clandestine dimension that put him off the grid. The comfortable darkness of night closed around him and he became a solitary man in a foreign city who moved without catching a stranger's eye. Unseen, but seeing, his senses were alert to sounds, smells, movement on the street, and he felt the exhilaration of his former work.

He entered the Diskont Internet Café on Tverskaya Street, dropping his newspaper into a wastebasket. Teenagers sat in front of large monitors playing video games with intense concentration. He went unnoticed by players whose faces reflected the greenish glow of the screens.

Matthews paid for an hour of internet time and found a computer station in the rear of the café, not visible from the street. He opened the Tor dark web browser and navigated to a Ukrainian wedding site, clicking through the menu going down two levels to a backdoor. A password and username took him to a proxy server inside the agency's firewall and he addressed his email to one of Linton's aliases.

Codespeak was obvious, but only someone who understood the context would make sense of the message. *Contact with our friend made. He lost his passport and he needs a new one with the same issue date of July 15, 2010. I'll bring his personal details when I fly back, but he wants to know the security features are correct. He'll bring his gift for the bride when we cross the border together.*

Matthews was back in his hotel room half an hour later. He glanced at his watch, a dual-time-zone Hermès, a birthday gift from Anna. One time zone was set for Moscow and one for Washington so even when he was away, he knew what hour it was at home—always a reminder of where he was and where he wasn't. He put the battery in his cell phone and saw a string of text messages pop up. Anna's was first. *I never heard back. Everything okay?*

It was ten P.M. in Moscow and late afternoon in Washington. She'd still be in the office, and her part of the agency didn't permit cell phones in secure office space. He texted an answer on a secure Telegram account that she would see when she was driving home. Her response appeared immediately on his cell.

There has been a problem with Wallace.

What type of problem?

He's missing. He didn't show up in the office today. Rose hasn't seen him.

How does a senior intelligence officer go missing? he thought.

Security is involved. What's happening in Moscow?

We shouldn't do this on text. I'll call tomorrow.

Matthews lay on his bed in his clothes. He resisted undressing. He was aggravated by the idea of being undressed in front of a hidden video camera. It made the muscles in the back of his neck twitch, but he also knew that it was unwise to appear to know that he was being surveilled. Even a casual apprehension would be noted with interest and the surveillance routines would shift, become more sophisticated, and more dangerous.

He brushed his teeth in his boxer shorts as usual and turned off the light as he lay on the bed. The news about Wallace deeply unsettled him, and it bothered him that he was cut off from whatever was happening in Washington. He closed his eyes, pushing aside the news, and concentrated on what he had to do in the morning.

His phone rang. He lifted his cell on the fourth ring, grabbing his eyeglasses.

"Hello."

"You know Trinity Capital's offices were searched."

Matthews recognized Sorkin's voice. "I tried to call you."

"There's nothing we can do at this hour. I'll see you in the morning."

Matthews shut down his phone and lay back on his pillow, feeling the quickening dread of what he would learn in the morning.

13

Trinity Capital's Offices

Who did this?"

Matthews was next to Sorkin in front of Trinity Capital's small suite of offices on the third floor of a Neo-Classical building, but he directed his question to a young woman who stood by the shattered glass entrance. Anastasia's face was drawn with deep worry and she was obviously distraught, mixing English with Russian.

Glass shards were scattered in the hallway but the door latch was still in place. Whoever entered had stepped through the broken glass door. Inside the lobby, filing cabinets were ransacked and drawers hung out like parched tongues; documents covered the floor. Everywhere a scene of violation. Matthews had rented office space in an older building in Tverskoy District to be within walking distance of the Metropol, where a lunch table was regularly reserved for him. He had opted for convenience over the practical benefits of a modern building with twenty-four-hour security in the ground floor lobby.

Anastasia was talking, but not answering his question, and she was making little sense. She was close to tears, her pale face flushed crimson. She gave off the impression that she was somehow responsible.

"Calm yourself," Matthews said. He put his arm around Anastasia's shoulder, comforting her. "It's not your fault."

"It happened yesterday," Sorkin said, stepping over the glass, and entered. "I got a call from the security monitoring service. We were kept away until this morning."

"Who were they?" Matthews looked at Anastasia. "Do you know?"

Anastasia led Matthews and Sorkin to the firm's small server room, where a young employee had retrieved CCTV footage from the office security camera. Its position high in a corner of the room recorded the arrival of six men in black uniforms wearing balaclavas. Low resolution black-and-white video showed the men approaching the glass doors at 5:12 A.M. Two swung a heavy metal battering ram, shattering the glass. The time stamp read 5:18 when the four men with automatic weapons stepped through the broken glass and one of them forced open a filing cabinet with a crowbar. When the man turned away from the camera, ФСБ in bright yellow letters was visible on his back. A second security camera captured footage from the hallway and from the server room, but the images gave few clues to the object of their search.

"FSB," Sorkin said. "Unannounced searches usually come late in the day, but they came in the early morning hours."

"What does that mean?"

"I have no idea. Maybe it means nothing. Or maybe they knew you arrive late for work and they wanted to be done with their search before you showed up."

"What did they take?" Matthews asked.

Anastasia didn't know. The files had been ransacked and it was impossible to establish what was missing until the vandalized files were inventoried. Anastasia explained that important files containing confidential bank account records and account information for various holding companies were on servers, which had not been breached.

"It's a warrant," Sorkin said, examining a document taped to the wall.

Matthews paused in the doorway of his corner office when he saw the chaos left behind. Files lay scattered on the floor and furniture was turned over. Numb to the violation, he thought he should try to put his files together again, but then stopped. It was useless. He returned framed family photographs to his credenza, but his daughter's picture frame had cracked, so he removed the photograph and put it in his jacket. A glass vase that Gorbachev had given his father after he'd written a flattering profile was smashed beyond repair. His computer hadn't been touched. He'd made his office into an inviting place to spend time while away from home and the vandalism was deeply offensive.

Matthews felt Sorkin's hand on his arm.

"Better to talk in a place without walls," Sorkin said.

Sorkin's Mercedes was parked outside. His driver opened the rear door for Sorkin and then hop-stepped around and obliged Matthews.

"They are from the Fourth Service." He flipped through the pages of the warrant. "This is a notice for Trinity Capital to appear in court to answer questions from Department K's economic crimes unit about its tax practices. There is no innocent explanation for this." He read a few more pages. "This claims irregularities in one of Trinity Capital's subsidiary's VAT filings."

Sorkin put down the paper. "Anton Karpov runs Department K. He is close to Sechin, who runs the Sixth Service. Karpov is a bureaucrat with political ambitions and you've become a target. Who knows what they want—money, the satisfaction of ruining you." He looked at Matthews. "You need to hire a good lawyer."

"I don't need a lawyer. I already have one."

Sorkin's voice deepened and became circumspect. "We are old friends. I can consider the case but you know how Moscow's courts work. I can argue the facts, I can invoke the law, and I can raise my voice in your defense, but if the prosecutor and the judge are against you, I can't succeed. If the judge has been told to convict you, my defense will fail."

Sorkin looked out the window at well-dressed Muscovites making their way to work in the brisk morning air and he looked back at Matthews, his mood solemn. "I know situations where the case was decided before the trial began. Lawyers don't want to work against a corrupt system. I am not one of those lawyers, but I have a good track record of victories because I know which cases not to take." He raised his hand, dismissing Matthews's protest. "Everyone is entitled to defense, but not everyone is entitled to my defense."

"Is this my friend talking or my lawyer?"

"Both."

"When did you become so cynical?"

"Cynical? No. Realistic. Do you know the difference? There is an old joke. A realistic man in Russia is a man who is happy with his one moldy potato because that is all the shopkeeper has to sell. The cynic looks at the one moldy potato and curses the shopkeeper for hoarding his potatoes to sell on the black market."

"We're not living in Soviet times."

"Some things in Russia haven't changed. We have money, vacation homes in Croatia, four-star restaurants with French chefs, and so-called free elections. But everyone in Russia is a cynic—wary of too much happiness. Waiting for peril to strike. I'm not one of them. I'm happy with my one potato."

Sorkin looked directly at Matthews. "My advice to you? Be happy with your one potato. Liquidate Trinity Capital's assets and find a way to move the money out of Russia. Cash out your success and leave before corrupt investigators find a way to extort you."

The crumpled warrant he presented still had duct tape attached. "Tax fraud can bankrupt you. It can land you in jail. I can delay things, but you are being targeted. Liquidate and declare victory. Better to be a free poor man than a jailed fat cat."

"Foreign exchange restrictions prohibit currency exports."

"There are ways. The Russian mafia does it, so do oligarchs." He looked at Matthews. "Whoever set this in motion wants to ruin you. You made the unforgiveable mistake of being a successful American financier in a country that remains deeply, profoundly suspicious of the West."

"I'm not the West. I'm one man with a family."

"A wealthy man with an American passport." Sorkin put his hand on Matthews's knee, patting it, and his tone of voice became conciliatory. "Anna would like you home more. You should spend time with your son. You've made a lot of money. Now you have to make sure that you keep it."

Sorkin paused. "You pay me well for my advice, and my advice is liquidate the assets, launder the money to get it out of Russia, and spend time at home. Save your marriage."

Matthews met Sorkin's gaze. "Why do you think my marriage needs saving?"

"She's younger than you. You're gone too much. What does she do when you're in Moscow?"

For several moments, Matthews held the accusation in his mind and wanted to argue with Sorkin, but instead he felt the working of their friendship. Sorkin could tell him anything, if it was important enough.

"Look," Sorkin said. "I don't know anything, so don't look at me like that. I know Russian women. I have been married to three. One of them twice."

He lifted the document and waved it at the steel-and-glass skyscrapers rising on the Moscow skyline. "It's money. That's all. Money disappears and when it's gone you work hard to get it back. But when love is gone, you don't get it back." He smiled. "Time's work turns flesh to dust. You lost your first wife. Don't lose Anna. I say this as a friend. She's been good for you and good for your son. She's an attractive woman and you're getting to be an old man."

Silence settled between them. He knew everything came to an end and he also believed that it was best to choose the time of an ending, and not suffer heroically waiting for a better outcome. He'd seen smart men fall on the sword of hope.

"Talk to Grigoryev if you're still in touch with him. He's flaky, but he knows how to move dirty money."

"Why him?" Matthews looked up. "You had a falling out?"

"That's a kind way to put it." Sorkin paused. "He always liked you and admired you, so maybe he'll help. I know how to contact him." Sorkin shook his head with a private thought. "We had good times together on the Moscow River. I brought the poetry, he brought vodka stolen from his old man. The world was crap then, but we enjoyed a few hours getting drunk and contemplating our depressing futures."

Sorkin turned away from the view out the car's window. "I know he moves money out of Russia through Angstbank. His unit investigates expatriation of funds. As an old friend, he might help. If he does, he'll ask for a percentage, but that is how things are done. I will invite him to meet us in a restaurant, using some pretext, which he'll probably see through, but if he comes, he'll know we want something from him."

"He's FSB," Matthews said, testing.

"He's an old high school acquaintance. He has his own troubles. If he refuses, you're no worse off. But you'll enjoy a good meal and we can tell old stories. No cigarettes. No poetry. Just vodka and a few jokes."

Sorkin pointed down Tverskaya Street as they passed the intersection. "Over there is where we climbed out of the sewer before graduation. My interest in the underground and his recklessness got me arrested."

It was always shared danger that created a bond—exhilarating adventure in the face of possible arrest pursued without regard to the jeopardy placed on their futures. It had been the spring of their last year at the Anglo-American School, and they were excited by Sorkin's suggestion they explore Moscow's notorious underground tunnel system. They'd emerged at night after two hours exploring the maze of dark tunnels built under the Bolshoy Theater and Red Square and expanded by Stalin to accommodate the Metro. Plainclothes KGB had spotted them climbing from a sewer cover.

"I'll never forget." Sorkin lifted his hand to show his crooked ring finger. "There was always exaggeration and conceit in his stories and I made the mistake of believing him. I was the one who was beaten and arrested, which put a black mark on my record and kept me in school another year. The two of you ran in one direction and he told me to run the opposite way, which took me into the arms of the police. He thought it was a wild joke at my expense."

Matthews heard something frayed in Sorkin's voice—an old bond broken by an unsettled resentment. He felt a little storm burst over Sorkin and then pass away. The friendship among them was more complex and fragile than he'd imagined, like a spiderweb.

They were different: Sorkin the careful thinker who measured his words and Grigoryev all bluster and bluff.

"I was chased through traffic and beaten when caught." He clenched a partial fist, then again, demonstrating his handicap. "He's conveniently forgotten, but this reminds me every day."

Matthews thought he'd known his friend well, as well as any teenager can know another, but he'd been surprised when Sorkin claimed to be an expert spelunker and suggested they enter the tunnels. Sorkin surprised Matthews again in the early 1990s when he returned to Moscow as a consular officer in the American embassy. He'd reconnected with Sorkin and they spent an evening catching up over brandy. Sorkin confessed that after the collapse of the Soviet Union he engorged on the literature that had been prohibited under the old regime—Kafka, Solzhenitsyn, Orwell—and his particular interest, English spy novels.

He'd had a romantic idea that he would go to Paris, sit in a café, smoke Gauloises, and return to a small desk in a garret that overlooked a courtyard to write a long, difficult, and ambitious novel about the Cold War from the Soviet perspective. He had discovered that there was no Russian le Carré. He thought such a writer must exist—in jail, or in a cemetery—but there were no serious Russian spy novels and no political novels of any kind from the Cold War era—only Yulian Semyonov's wildly popular Stierlitz adventure stories.

Matthews had encouraged him to write, but then without any explanation or excuse, Sorkin took up a career in law, representing Russians who bought up state assets. He still read poetry, still smoked Gauloises, although less often, and he remained an avid reader. Matthews asked him what happened to his ambition, and Sorkin replied cryptically, "We all have dreams and then we wake up."

14

Café Dr. Zhivago

Matthews hesitated by the maître d' and glanced through the garishly lit restaurant, looking to see if any diners had lifted their eyes toward him. He knew the difference between the casual excitement of a person spotting a celebrity and the hard-eyed glance of plainclothes police taking an interest in the arriving customer.

"Mikhail Sorkin," Matthews said to the statuesque maître d' whose loop earrings swung as she turned to face him with a well-drilled smile.

"This way. He's expecting you."

Matthews was led through the crowded main dining room where couples huddled intimately, holding hands in candlelight, and elsewhere large raucous groups lost in their own enjoyment paid no heed as he passed. He was taken to an adequately quiet corner away from the main dining area, taking the seat the maître d' pulled out. Across the table, Sorkin sat, menu in hand.

"You're late," he said.

"I'm here before Grigoryev."

"He's not coming. He backed out when I said you'd be here. He asked if I was trying to get him arrested." Sorkin shrugged. "I said, 'For what?' For being in a nice restaurant with two old high school friends." Sorkin shook his head. "You know how he gets. Always looking for a reason to be suspicious. He doesn't trust me."

Sorkin nodded at a place setting where a purse strap hung over the back of the chair. "I invited someone else who might be able to help you."

Matthews had picked up his menu when Sorkin stood to greet the guest. The woman towered over Matthews when he looked up. Her red hair was pinned in a bun on the top of her head, revealing abundant freckles on her neck, and her green eyes met his, startling him.

"You don't remember me."

Matthews turned to Sorkin, confused, and then he stared at her, uncertain how to respond. She sat and put forward her hand.

"Olga Luchaninova."

"I remember," he said.

She shook his hand with one forceful motion and then withdrew, sitting back and unfolded a napkin in her lap. "You look surprised," Olga said. "Should I leave and make another entrance?"

"Stay," Sorkin said.

"And you?" she asked Matthews. "Our last meeting was an unfortunate experience for both of us, but I understand that you spent only one night in jail. One night for rudeness."

Matthews nodded. "It all worked out," he said. In the weeks that followed the incident at the hotel, he understood that her obstreperousness act had helped save BYRON from a savage trap. He might have thanked her, but that required that he explain, and that was out of the question. "I was rude. I apologize."

She laughed, taking her menu. "Don't apologize. I wanted an interview and you had other things on your mind. I never expected my performance to attract the police." She turned toward him with a sly smile. "I saw you in a car alone with a handsome young man, and I thought, 'Who am I to judge the tastes of a married man.' You were impolite and now I know why."

Matthews dismissed her comment with a wave of his hand. "I know his father and he asked me to give his son advice on Moscow life." Matthews looked at her. "What question was so important that night?"

Sorkin leaned forward and spoke in a low voice. "I spoke with Olga earlier today and explained that Trinity Capital will be liquidating assets and hoarding cash for a hostile acquisition."

"You've talked?" Matthews took in the implications that there were things that had been said before he arrived.

"I am familiar with your predicament," she said. "You seem to have several predicaments."

The conversation was interrupted by the maître d', who arrived with a bottle of champagne. With one arm behind her back, she tilted the bottle into flutes placed by a waiter. "Good to see you again, Mikhail Abramovich. And your guests. Old friends?"

"Friends," he said. He looked at Olga. "Would you excuse me a moment? I need to use the men's room. Alex, why don't you join me?"

Matthews followed Sorkin to the men's room. They stood at the porcelain sink by the large mirror. Sorkin looked under the stalls, confirming they were alone, and he opened the hot and cold taps, running water, and turned to Matthews. "She writes an important financial column. Liquidating your positions will become obvious in the market. I told her we would benefit from hearing her views on possible targets. So don't make me sound like an idiot. A respectable journalist speculating about takeover candidates is a smart diversion."

Sorkin drew two paper towels from the dispenser and wiped his hands vigorously. "Be polite. She can be helpful if she takes up your cause."

Olga looked up from her menu when the two men returned and looked from one to the other. "I hope you said nice things about me."

Matthews put his napkin in his lap. "He warned me to be polite. He said you were an important journalist who could help my cause." Matthews smiled. "What companies do you suggest? What would be a good target?" His voice deepened with sarcasm. "Lukoil? Sherbank? Magnet?"

"You have that much money?"

Sorkin put his hand on Matthews's arm. "Olga was kind enough to join us. Don't make me regret this dinner."

Matthews looked at her, judging her, and he saw in her face the brisk curiosity of a skeptical mind. He met her eyes. They looked at each other and, in that moment, she was no longer the sassy journalist throwing herself in his path, pen poised like a dagger, but a useful ally.

"I apologize for being impolite. There is money to put to work, and if I sound abrupt it's because I'm uncomfortable acknowledging what I really feel."

Her eyes widened. "You don't look like a man who is uncomfortable with anything."

Matthews heard sarcasm in her voice and he understood that she was mocking him; he wasn't sure what to make of her. He turned to Sorkin and changed the subject. "Why didn't Veronica join us tonight?"

"She is back in St. Petersburg. She doesn't like Moscow for more than a few days at a time. We spend weekends together in St. Petersburg and I take the overnight train back to Moscow. It's a good arrangement. It keeps us attracted to each other. I don't ask about her lovers and she doesn't ask about the criminals I defend."

"You're joking," Olga gasped.

"I like a good joke," Sorkin said, "but yes, that is how we've organized our lives."

Matthews had stopped making judgments about others. Indiscretions, adultery, moral lapses. The full range of human frailty that he had witnessed was no longer a thing he felt he had a responsibility to condemn or condone.

The waiter arrived for their orders and Matthews was happy to shift the conversation away from Sorkin, but at the same time, he saw Olga observe a young couple two tables away.

"They're listening to us," she said. "They might be wondering who we are, or they might know who we are and are pretending not to know." She sipped her champagne. "What is it like to be young, Russian, and newly wealthy? Look around. They weren't born when Gorbachev resigned and handed the nuclear codes to Yeltsin. They aren't old enough to have lived in the Soviet Union."

Olga was curious about the couple, and she continued to hazard every sort of guess about their status in the new social order. She pretended to be casually interested, but Matthews saw that she looked at the entire restaurant scene as if it were a thrilling play.

She pointed to a young man in sports jacket and open shirt collar arguing with the maître d' to have his party of five seated. "He can see that the restaurant is fully booked, but he arrives with his entourage, without a reservation, and expects to be seated. The rich are inconsiderate here, as they are everywhere."

"Who is he?"

"Vladislav Chuikov. He got his start as a soldier in the Red Army assigned to the elite unit that guards Lenin's Tomb. He joined McDonald's when it opened its first location and rose from floor sweeper to store manager after attending Hamburger University in Chicago. Two years later he opened his own chain of Starbuck's-style coffee shops in Moscow—a revolutionary enterprise in a city where coffee was always undrinkable. He spends his days visiting his stores and telling baristas to "smile, smile, smile."

Olga turned back to Matthews. "He's worth one hundred million euros. He thinks he can get a table like this." She snapped her fingers. She added, "I interviewed him. He is a typical Russian entrepreneur. Arrogant. Rich. Obnoxious." She judged Matthews. "Some of your qualities. You'd also make a good interview, but for different reasons."

Olga sipped her champagne and pointed to a big man with a thick neck and shiny bald head standing at the bar. His gut folded over a cinched belt and he stood beside two companions who talked with the false purpose of men pretending to be occupied.

"His name is Yakiv. He's Ukrainian. He once asked me to dinner and presumed that his great wealth would impress me. He dictated how I should write a complimentary profile. Then at dessert, he offered me the privilege of sleeping with him."

Olga laughed her judgment. "I declined his invitation, and when the critical profile came out, I enjoyed his ire. Now he harasses me with nasty insults and death threats."

She turned her back on him. "He is worth ninety billion rubles. He says he's helped bring order to post-Communist Russia's chaos. He'll tell you the Russian Federation is in its Wild West stage. See his cowboy boots. He boasts they're made of rattlesnake skin.

"For men with money, everything is for sale. For those in government without money, the law has a price. Mikhail knows that. Men like Yakiv bribe their way to the right judges, and because they drive luxury cars and own mansions in London, they think they are immune from prosecution."

"He's looking at you."

She glanced over her shoulder, scoffing, and turned to Matthews. "He thinks he's charismatic." She lowered her voice to an exaggerated baritone, mocking him. "To be charismatic you must speak slowly in a deep voice and meet their eye. A charismatic man is a good talker, a better listener, and above all he must never smile." She coughed her disdain.

"He's staring. He knows you're mocking him."

"Let him look." She lifted her pinkie. "His charisma."

Dinner was delivered by three waiters who lifted serving covers simultaneously, revealing the entrées. With the food, the conversation shifted to lighter topics, moving to the Bolshoi's latest artistic scandal, to Putin's fear of flying, and the armored train he used for travel to Sochi. Olga leaned toward Matthews.

"I did some research on your case. When Misha invited me to dinner with the American who'd insulted me, I asked myself, 'Do they think I'm a stupid cupcake?' Perhaps, like Yakiv, the narcissist at the bar, he thought I'd be happy to write a glowing profile just because he asked."

She paused. "What did I find? There is a tax fraud case that has been brought against Trinity Capital. Of course, you know that, but you might wonder how I know. I'm a journalist. Everyone has enemies and they give me confidential information, and in return I ask questions and get answers. Secrets are good bargaining currency here."

Olga looked skeptically at Matthews. "Tax fraud is always about something else, and it's used to put a person in prison and bankrupt his company. Do you really think I would believe that you are liquidating assets to mount a hostile takeover on the Moscow exchange?"

There was a long silence at the table. Matthews fidgeted and glanced at Sorkin. He had the calm of a highly paid lawyer who could tell the most audacious lies with a straight face.

"I didn't know that he invited you," Matthews said.

"Is that an excuse?" She leaned forward. "None of this would be happening to Trinity Capital unless Igor Sechin approved. And if Sechin approved, he went to Putin first." Olga raised her arms theatrically. "Look at who you are. Former CIA Moscow station chief. Wealthy American investor advocating for shareholder transparency in a country that hides wealth and the corruption it breeds."

"Why are you here?"

She glanced over her shoulder at the bar where Yakiv was watching her. "I have my enemies. Sometimes it is good to have friends."

"Why would you do this?" he asked.

"I haven't said I would do anything."

"Why did you come, then?"

"Question for question." She looked at Sorkin and then turned to Matthews. "I could leave now and write up the story I discovered. It would make an interesting article and I'd be rewarded." She looked at Matthews fiercely, but then softened. "But there is a more interesting article. It is the one I'll write after you've left Russia with your money and I can describe the corrupt system you fled. That is the better article. Writing about your crime and arrest would exonerate the wrong people."

Olga poured herself a large glass of the burgundy Sorkin had ordered and drank half. "I will help you because I have my own reasons to dislike the men working against you." She looked at the two men. "Unless you don't want my help."

"We'll take the help," Sorkin said.

"I know what to write. Now you need a way to get your cash out of Russia." She smiled. "I suspect it's too much for a suitcase."

15

A Desolate Street

Matthews and Olga lingered at the table after Sorkin excused himself, saying that it was late and he had an early morning court appearance. Dinner had lifted Matthews's spirits, and not merely because he thought he'd found an ally for his cause. He was also surprised to find Olga oddly entertaining—her caustic wit, snide observations, and complete indifference to the power of money. She hadn't yet agreed to help, but as he settled the bill, she asked questions that signaled her interest in his case.

Their conversation continued as they moved to the restaurant's exit. He threw out a few company names as he helped her with her coat, before taking his own from the coat check. He mentioned an undervalued oil company on the Moscow Exchange that was run by a political hack, and Olga agreed that it was vulnerable. She suggested a quote to accompany her article, but he objected, saying that her words made him sound mercenary. "That's the point," she snapped. She needed to demonize him as an American financier extorting Russian companies. It was what her readers would believe and it was better to satisfy their expectations with a lie than challenge their skepticism with the truth.

"The truth can get you in trouble. No one is interested in the truth."

They stepped from the warm, loud restaurant into the chilly night. A rainstorm had blown through, leaving the street slick with moisture and remnant water pooled by a clogged gutter. Rain and dark buildings along the wide sidewalk brought gloom to the street. Even the lurking paparazzi were gone from the corner where they regularly waited for celebrities to leave the restaurant. One black Mercedes taxi sped past, ignoring Olga's wild wave with her handbag.

"It's late," she said, stopping abruptly at the curb. "We drank too much and stayed too long." She glanced at her watch. "The Metro is closed."

It was at that moment that Matthews heard loud voices from the restaurant, where someone had thrown open the door. Yakiv and his two companions emerged onto the sidewalk.

What Matthews first noticed about them was their obvious show of malicious intent. They watched Olga, but pretended to look away when Matthews glanced back, a clumsy effort to appear not to take an interest in her. Yakiv was heavyset with a neck so thick it seemed that he had no neck at all. He tossed his cigarette to the sidewalk and ground it with his heel. He pulled leather gloves over his stubby fingers, making a great show of clenching his fists. His tall companion was rail thin with a hatchet face and he wrapped a thick scarf around his hand.

Matthews thought there was something almost comical in their behavior, but he knew not to underestimate their potential for violence. He stood at the corner of Tverskaya Street and the

Ring Road, and across the street, beyond the groomed gardens, the Kremlin was brightly lit. He turned to Olga, but his voice was drowned out by a street sweeper that rumbled past with a deafening mechanical clatter. He met her eyes and nodded at Yakiv.

"Mr. Charisma," she said, pulling her fur collar tight around her neck.

"What does he want?"

"At this hour with his two goons? It's not to say hello."

She put her arm in his and pulled him along the sidewalk. "I don't live far. They won't be nasty if you're with me. Walk normally, but quickly."

They walked briskly arm in arm along the wide sidewalk, but coming to the street corner, Matthews looked back. They were being followed. He searched the street for sanctuary—a shop still open, people on the street who they could approach, but the brightly lit boulevard was empty, and their path back to the restaurant was blocked.

Yakiv began to whistle a tune that floated in the cold night air. He stood under a streetlamp and the notes came across the avenue, bright and clear. The tall man moved further along across the street, while the third man crossed in a flanking movement. The whistling stopped and there was only the sound of approaching footsteps.

"Hurry," she said.

Matthews knew that they couldn't outrun the men—Olga wore high heels and he was a little drunk. He looked around, evaluating the empty street, and eliminated the obvious choices.

"This way," she said. They were passing the Moscow Art Theater, dark and brooding at that hour. She kicked off her heels and sprinted ahead, rapidly turning the building's corner. Matthews followed her, and as he turned, he passed a narrow alley, a slit at the end of the old Baroque building, and felt himself pulled into the dark recess. They stood side by side, breathing rapidly, absolutely still, listening. Matthews wrinkled his nose at the pungent smell of urine.

Footfalls slowed and stopped. Matthews could hear their voices nearby and he felt Olga clasp his hand. Silence rang loud in his ears. One curse, another, anger between them. Then the men moved past the alley and their voices became distant as they raced off.

Street light stopped at their feet, but in the other direction at the far end of the narrow alley, he saw a slit of light—the next street.

"My apartment is this way. Not far." She added, sarcastically, "You've done this before."

They stayed close to the buildings and away from the wide arc of streetlights, and in time, Matthews knew that they were out of danger. He moved quickly, occasionally glancing back to see whether they were being followed. They turned one corner and the air was thick with CS gas and they heard far-off sirens. She checked her cell phone. "Protests closed bridges across the river. You won't get back to the Kempinski tonight. You'll stay with me."

The small square they entered was surrounded by Beaux Arts apartment buildings and dominated by an equestrian statue. The end of the rain brought out couples who sat on the narrow benches indifferent to the cold. Doorways were dark and there were only quiet whispers from young lovers.

"Look. Those two men, pretending to be lovers." Olga walked past the stiff, hand-holding couple, who looked up, eyes alert. Olga nodded, acknowledging them, and a few steps further on, whispered, "Police waiting to grab gay couples making out."

She stopped at the square's huge equestrian statue—a proud figure astride a bronze horse, arm triumphantly raised.

"My husband and I would come here on a night like this. We'd look at the statue of Yuriy Dolgorukiy and feel good about being Russian."

She pointed to the street corner. "Two women were killed there protesting against the Afghan war. My husband and I joined the dissident movement to honor their murders. We conducted a tour for foreign journalists of the city's assassination sites that we called the martyrs' tour. From here we went to the House of Unions, where ten men were condemned in the first of Stalin's show trials, taken to prison, and shot in a basement cell. Anna Pelitkovskaya was gunned down in the elevator of her apartment block. Her articles criticized Putin, and now she is buried in Troyekurovskaye Cemetery with poets, writers, and a former head of the KGB. Three years ago, on Bolshoy Moskvoretsky Bridge, Boris Nemtsov was shot seven or eight times. A year later, my husband was murdered on the same bridge."

Matthews abruptly turned to her.

She waved off his concern. "Dissent is a bad impulse to have in Russia. In the thirties, there were great show trials and everyone was convicted and executed. Today, there are no show trials, but dissidents are murdered anyway." She looked at him. "Pyotr was a prominent journalist who wrote about FSB corruption and the bribe economy of the courts. For that, he was assassinated. Men approached him on the bridge by the Kempinski Hotel. He was shot twice in the head. Putin went on television and announced that he was personally overseeing the investigation. It's been two years and no one has been arrested."

From her handbag, she pulled handwritten notes she'd taken during dinner. "I am doing this for him—to honor him. To fight for what he cared about." She paused. "Now I do the martyrs' tour alone. The last stop is where he was shot."

Matthews heard her voice crack.

She wiped a tear from her eye. "It's nothing. A drop of rain."

They continued through the park and pointed to the other side of the square toward the wrought iron entrance of a graceful, five-story apartment building. "I live there." She explained that her father made money after the collapse of the Soviet Union and he'd bought a pied-à-terre in a good building. He'd given it to her as a wedding gift, and she and her husband had hired an Orthodox priest to rid it of the ghosts of her father's trysts. She described her father as a conservative Russian who disagreed with her rebellious behavior.

"I would have been surprised if he'd approved of my liberal politics. My parents were good citizens and casual intellectuals, but the extent of their dissent was to trade *samizdat*. They found a way to live with the system they disagreed with."

16

Olga's Apartment

Olga's finger was on her lips. "Shhhh. My neighbor. Be quiet."

She inserted her key in the door and quietly turned the dead-bolt lock, pushing the heavy wooden door to reveal a dark apartment. Matthews glanced back down the graceful marble stairwell and heard shuffling footsteps one floor below. The stairwell was quiet but light from an open door illuminated the far wall. Olga drew him into the apartment and closed the door.

"She pretends to be deaf when you ask a question, but her ears are good enough to hear tiptoeing up the stairs. Her son is FSB and she tells him everything she sees in the building, most of which she makes up." She pointed. "Your shoes."

She turned on a wall switch, illuminating the apartment, and a grand living room opened before him. Four casement windows looked out to the neighborhood and soft light from a Venetian chandelier illuminated a bulky display cabinet—a *shkaf*. It dominated one wall and loomed over a worn, clawed-footed sofa and two unmatched bergère armchairs that sat on either side of a glass coffee table. The furniture was old, but not antique—random pieces collected from relatives, secondhand shops, or found on weekend excursions to the countryside. The room's mix-and-match aesthetic didn't belong to a particular era or style but was one person's eclectic design choice.

"My home."

Floor-to-ceiling bookcases occupied the wall opposite the *shkaf*, and nestled among the volumes, he saw a Chinese vase, dolls, and Incan bowls. The third wall had abstract expressionist paintings mixed with nineteenth-century Romantic landscapes, arranged like a salon, art rising to the ceiling. Matthews moved to the *shkaf* and looked at the photograph of a man standing on a T-52 tank outside the Russian Parliament.

"My husband. It was his favorite picture. He was a twenty-six-year-old standing with Yeltsin against the coup. It was how he thought of himself—standing against *zhulikov i vorov*—swindlers and thieves."

She pointed to a second photograph on the shelf. A young Soviet Army officer sat by the turret of a tank among a group of rugged enlisted men with ammunition bandoliers draped around their necks, arms raised high with Kalashnikovs, poised over three kneeling Mujahedeen prisoners.

"He volunteered for the Afghan war and then became disillusioned. He was changed by what he saw—the brutality, corruption, senseless death, and stupid generals blind to what was happening on the front. He saw things that he wouldn't talk about, but I didn't need to hear the stories to see how the war changed him."

Olga moved to a glass breakfront and lifted a corked bottle. "Plum brandy?"

Matthews took the drink and contemplated the two photos—same man, same face, both on a T-72 tank. Matthews moved to the bookcase and its large collection of literature. Russian books dominated, but he saw small groupings of English, French, and Arabic works. He was surprised to find a set of Edgar Allan Poe's collected works and Winston Churchill's six-volume history of the Second World War. It was his belief that knowing what people read opened a window into their minds.

Olga sat on the sofa and stretched her legs on the coffee table.

"*Na zdorovie.*" She sipped her brandy. "He liked to be photographed, but six months ago I removed most. I also kept his captain's uniform, but the rest . . ." Her hand flicked dismissively. "I woke one day and felt I was a prisoner of my old life with him—a prisoner of my grief. We lived together, shared friends, and then he was gone. It took me a long time to discover myself again—who I was before we were a couple."

Matthews sat across from her and smelled the brandy's nose.

"Pyotr was a prominent journalist, so his murder was a big political scandal. No one was accused, and his unrepentant criticisms of Putin made him enemies in the FSB and among the men who owe their wealth to the regime." She raised her glass. "Do you like the brandy?"

"Very pleasant."

"My uncle makes his own and gives me several bottles at Christmas."

"In Moscow, everyone has an uncle who makes his own brandy."

She laughed. "You know Moscow well." She stood abruptly. "It is late. I will show you your bedroom."

He followed her down a short hall with doorways on either side. "This is your room." He saw a small bedroom with walls painted in bright pink and blue balloons. A crib sat unpacked in a cardboard carton and a single bed sat by a bay window.

"Do you have a child?" he asked.

"This is why it is dangerous to get ahead of your future. I was pregnant when Pyotr was murdered. I lost the child that winter and now I have a crib I don't need."

She lifted a pair of baby mittens. "I got rid of Pyotr's photographs and next I will find a home for these."

Olga indicated the narrow bed. "This is where you will sleep. Sheets are there. The pillow is on the bed and the bathroom is at the end of the hall. It's not a five-star hotel but it is better than a park bench."

He noticed her gazing at a newborn's clothing folded on the dresser, and he saw sadness overcome her. "Grief comes to everyone," he said.

She waved off his concern. "It's no comfort to know other people grieve. You don't console a sad friend by reminding her she was once happy." She looked at him. "Are you an expert on grief?" Her eyes were cold.

"I'm familiar with it."

She contemplated him. "That makes you more interesting. A wealthy man with tender feelings." Her expression was indifferent. "Forgive me for being difficult. You are a guest. Are you married? Do you have children?"

"A son. My first wife and daughter died in an accident. I remarried."

"I am sorry to hear that, but you've found a way to have another woman. That must be a comfort."

Matthews hesitated too long before he answered, and she said abruptly, "I don't mean to pry. Every marriage has its problems. Sometimes I think it is better to be alone without sharing the problems of another person, when I have my own." She raised her hands to dismiss the conversation. "It is late, but the brandy doesn't make me sleepy. There is a roof garden and it has a good view of Moscow. It is always more interesting to talk under the stars."

Matthews followed her up a narrow flight that ended at a bulkhead door, which she unlocked, and they passed into the evening's darkness. He joined her at a wrought iron railing in the cool air and light breeze. The garden perimeter had topiary and unweeded planters of dying summer flowers. They stood side by side and looked toward the panorama of central Moscow. A luminous glow rose from the city into the dark night and ghost clouds left from the earlier storm were vague shapes. St. Basil's Cathedral and the red star on Spasskaya Tower were beacons in the night. Traffic had quieted but floodlights still illuminated remnant police activity in the distance. Far away was the sound of a siren, but below, in the street, was the carefree laughter of two lovers.

"It's an old city enjoying its rebirth," she said. "Young people are happy. They weren't alive in the old terror, so they have no memory of the suffering." She pinched a dry flower she'd taken from the overgrown planter. "Pyotr and I came up here on pleasant evenings like this. We sat over there and enjoyed a glass of wine, talking about our lives, about our writing, about our frustrations. Now I am here with you. A man I hardly know. Time plays tricks on us. New moments push out the old." She turned to him. "You are a good companion to have when there is danger on the street. A man with many secrets."

She sipped her brandy, but when he didn't respond, she turned away. She looked into the night when she spoke. "I don't need to know your hurt to see it. It is on your face. I read it like a map."

She looked at him. "One day you will tell me your story." She put her hand on her chest. "Sometimes it is good to talk, to share your burdens with another person."

Matthews was surprised when she patted his hand. He met her eyes and tried to look into her mind, but he only saw her curious gaze. He moved his hand away, pointing toward Kudrinskaya Square's barely visible tall buildings that were an iconic reminder of Stalin's ambitions of empire. A thought came to him, but it died before he found his voice. The humbling night was more interesting than his feeble thought.

Evening winds blew away the faint hint of tear gas, and shifting clouds revealed a full moon that bathed the city in silver light. Matthews wasn't from Moscow, but he was of Moscow, and it was the city that had drawn him to her warm bosom. It had embraced him and comforted him in his childhood years, and then it became a dramatic stage in his first years as a young case officer, moving in its dark alleys and underground cafés. And now he was in Moscow as a private citizen and investor. He was drawn to the city's foreignness. It remained mysteriously unapproachable like a brightly lit Christmas tree in a store display window that could only be appreciated from the street. He never tired of its history and contradictions, and contemplating it gave him an often irrational attachment to what he imagined about it.

Standing beside Olga, he was keenly aware that his days in Moscow were numbered.

They stood close to each other on the iron balcony cloaked in erotic darkness. Olga wrapped her arms around her chest, seemingly lost in her thoughts.

"The old Communists had dreams," she said. "Noble ideas that sprang from contorted truths. That is the history of Russia that Pyotr absorbed. One dictator goes and another takes his place." She let out an anguished sigh. "The men who killed my husband will be forgotten, but Pyotr will survive. Men die, but martyrs live on."

Matthews waited for her to say more. He removed his jacket and put it over her shoulders, earning her gratitude. She leaned forward on the balcony.

"We are cursed with cruel leaders. We defeated the Nazis in spite of Stalin's jealousies, lies, and paranoia. He worried about French and German invaders, but he worried more about his Jewish doctors and unhappy generals. He built an underground network of tunnels for evacuation in case of a coup. A train line runs fifty meters deep connecting Lubyanka and the Kremlin and then north to the train station."

Matthews turned to her. "How do you know?"

"You think the Americans are the only ones curious about Metro-2?" She smiled. "My husband wanted to investigate it for an article. We explored the underground tunnel that was built to divert seasonal flooding of the Neglinnaya River. The tunnel flows past the Bolshoy and curves around Red Square on its way to empty into the main channel of the Moscow River. It runs seven kilometers and there is a second underground rail system.

"We found white cockroaches that grow to eight centimeters, populations of bats, skeletons, rats the size of racoons, and the underground bunker Stalin built to survive a nuclear attack." She saw the expression on his face and laughed. "It's all true except for the rats and the skeletons." Olga dropped the flower stem. "And here we are, two almost acquaintances sharing state secrets."

They were quiet for a long time.

"Pyotr and I would talk about what Russia has become. He was an idealist, which I respected, but he was also a difficult person."

She looked off, but having started a thought, like a hive she had to itch. "There is no such thing as a perfect husband. Mine was imperfect." She looked at Matthews. "I was stupidly understanding of his idealism. He liked to call himself the curator of the museum of forgotten truths, which in a way he was. He said that in the midst of an anti-liberal government campaign against newspapers. We were in a crowd fleeing riot police and he said, 'This is how we live, but it doesn't have to be this way.'"

Olga turned away from Matthews. "He was wrong. Russia is that way and it always will be. In Russia, stories never have happy endings."

She stepped away from the railing. "We should go to bed."

❖

Matthews awoke the next morning. Bright light came through the half-closed curtains in the small bedroom. For a few moments, he struggled to remember where he was and what had brought him to the unfamiliar room. He sat up and realized that he'd fallen asleep in his clothes. He looked at his watch and saw it was past ten. How could that be? Then he remembered their long walk and the conversation on the roof. He put on his shoes and went to the living room.

"Hello? Olga?"

No answer. He looked in the kitchen and saw one teacup on the counter and, beside it, a dish with black bread and jam. There was a handwritten note, which he picked up.

I let you sleep so I could finish my article. There is jam in the cupboard and milk in the refrigerator. Please read it for errors. I tried to remember how you wanted to be quoted, but I made my own judgment about what serves your purpose best. My editor will publish it tomorrow or the day after. If my neighbor approaches when you leave, tell her you're my American cousin. Olga.

He pushed the note to the center of the table and looked at it from a distance. He read her three-page typed article twice, satisfied that she'd gotten most things right, and the details that she got wrong were wrong in the right way. It was good enough. It would buy time and shift attention from his real intentions. He had to take the next step.

17

The Plan

Matthews spent the next two days in Trinity Capital's offices putting his plan into motion. He held an all-hands meeting to announce a strategy to improve the fund's returns. He explained that minority positions in publicly traded companies would be sold and cash redeployed in one or two targets—prominent companies on the Moscow Exchange where Trinity Capital could use its significant share position to influence management, or oust it. Holdings he had accumulated over several years would be strategically repositioned, the phrase he used with his staff. There was no reason to hide the strategy from brokers. Rumors would alert markets and they'd take advantage of the uncertainty. Cash accumulating in Trinity Capital's bank account would be reinvested when the right target was picked. His employees were loyal, but he couldn't risk being forthcoming, and he needed their enthusiastic cooperation to pull off the plan. He lied that repositioning Trinity Capital would remove the fund's legal exposure to its tax audit. Separately, he had

Sorkin gather SWIFT routing numbers and banking details for the fund's shell companies in Cyprus, Malta, and the Cayman Islands.

There was a buzz in the room at the news and he sensed excitement at the mischief he proposed—and he said it all with a pious attitude. He was the owner, their benefactor, the architect of contrarianism, and he'd hired people drawn to that proposition. Educated Muscovites looking to the West. He saw enthusiasm in the room—pride and exhilaration on their faces. The receptionist beaming through her makeup; the thin IT guy gave a thumbs-up; his office manager, Anastasia, eager to fight back. All good people, all unaware they were being duped, but he would find a way to put money and exit visas in their pockets. They were loyal because he served them first and made sure that he ate last. How much of what happened in the room was his plan, how much his response to their spontaneous excitement? It didn't matter. They had their instructions.

❖

Matthews looked from his office window into the crowded street below, searching for his ride to the airport. Grigoryev was late. He squeezed, let go, and re-squeezed a tennis ball, working out his tension. Matthews suddenly stepped back from the window and turned off the overhead light, darkening the room except for the oblique light entering through the blinds. He pulled them back and again peered down at the busy street below, looking for the man he'd seen. Shoppers moved along storefronts and office workers on break smoked in the street. Lights in the apartment across the street were off, curtains closed.

Matthews saw the man again, emerging now from the darkened lobby doorway. A few minutes before, he'd leaned against a shop's display window pretending to read a newspaper, and then he approached a parked BMW. Matthews pulled back when the man raised his eyes to Trinity Capital's offices.

Grigoryev's text popped up on Matthews's cell. *I'm here.*

Matthews texted a different address. Matthews left via the building's rear freight entrance, passing through a back alley of dumpsters overflowing with garbage. He marched out of the alley and crossed the street, pulling his roll-on bag.

"You're late," he said, hopping into the parked car's passenger seat. "Surveillance was waiting in front."

"You'll make your plane," Grigoryev replied. "I had to make sure I wasn't followed. It is one thing to be ordered to pick you up at the airport and another thing to drive you to Sheremetyevo as if we are old friends. I had to take the Metro, then a bus to the car park where I keep this beater."

They had gone several blocks when Grigoryev handed Matthews a keychain having a Mul-T-Lock key with a black plastic top. "If you pull the plastic top, the key will separate. The bottom male is a USB drive with all the information for my new documents—name, photos, birthdate, all my home addresses from the beginning of time, etcetera, etcetera. Everything about Oleg Borodin that will become me."

He smiled at Matthews. "I told you I'd have it before you got on the plane."

"I never doubted it."

"Now you have to make sure you're not the unlucky bastard who is randomly pulled from the boarding lounge and searched. It would be my death sentence."

Matthews saw that the device had been expertly machined to appear like an ordinary key, and it took two strong yanks to separate the drive from the housing.

"We built the gadget to bring MI6 secrets from London. I kept a spare."

Matthews judged it. "Well done. In exchange, I have a request."

"A request for what?"

"For doing this."

"I'm doing *you* the favor," Grigoryev snapped.

"I don't work for the agency. I'm the courier here. To do this, I need your help."

"*Yob tvoyu mat*," Grigoryev cursed. *Fuck you.* He looked once at Matthews, clenching the steering wheel. "What help?"

"I need to get cash out of Russia."

"Don't press your luck."

Matthews handed back the keychain. "You can have this back."

"Your friends want what I have."

"Negotiate with them."

Grigoryev hit the steering wheel with his fist. "You haven't changed. The same friendly smile with a knife in your hand. I have a theory about people. People don't get better, they only get worse." He turned to Matthews. "How much money?"

"Ten billion rubles."

"Fuck me."

"Can you do it?"

They drove in silence for a few minutes and Matthews glanced at Grigoryev concentrating on the traffic on the Ring Road. He could see the Russian considering the implications of the request.

"I get what I want," Grigoryev said. "You get what you want. That's the favor?"

"It's not a favor."

"Favor, bargain, request. We have many euphemisms for the same blackmail."

Matthews handed Grigoryev an envelope with the details of Trinity Capital's bank accounts, SWIFT routing information, details of the shell companies. "The day after tomorrow Trinity Capital's account in Kreditbaank will be funded. I need you to move the funds to shell companies in the Cayman Islands, Cyprus, and Malta, which have depository relationships with Kreditbaank."

Grigoryev slipped the envelope into his breast pocket. "This will need to be approved by the bank supervisor. I will give him a story that I make up, which he will know is made up, but if he gets five percent he won't ask where the money came from."

They drove in silence for some time. Midday traffic on the Ring Road was heavy and Matthews saw Grigoryev glance in his side mirror.

"Are we being followed?"

"No." He looked at Matthews. "This game of ours is coming to an end. What I don't know is how it will end. Colonel Zhukov is a clever man. He's letting out rope to see if I'll hang myself. Yesterday, he asked me a question. It was clear that he had read my old reports on our first meetings. The records are stored in a remote warehouse, so it wasn't a simple matter of walking to a filing cabinet and pulling out a piece of paper."

Grigoryev nodded, thinking out loud, sharing his fears.

"I wrote up the intelligence that you gave me. Innocent stuff with a few bits of new intelligence to give our meetings the appearance of being productive. Colonel Zhukov called me into his office. He had the old files on his desk. He wanted to know when we first met and how I recruited you. I gave him vaguely specific answers. He interrupted me, lifting the stack of files and dropping them on his desk. He said, 'All those meetings. All these reports. Why nothing of value?'"

Grigoryev grasped the steering wheel, knuckles whitening. "I am being watched."

Matthews glanced behind to see if they were being followed.

"There's no surveillance. I made sure of that, but I am being watched at home. Three days ago a black Volga was parked outside my apartment block. It was there yesterday and today. My neighbors ask when Viktoria is coming home. Yesterday, I found the strand of hair I use on my door gone, so someone had entered. In my kitchen, I found a hidden microphone and another inside my television."

Grigoryev turned to Matthews. "Colonel Zhukov knew the day of your arrival. He knew your seat number. You have a problem in Washington. So far, only you know BYRON's face, but when this package gets into the hands of your technicians, others will know." His eyes narrowed. "Secrecy and speed. We need to cross the border when you return."

"I will give the drive to Technical Services."

"When?"

"When I get off the plane."

"When will they finish?"

"I don't know. They are careful. As soon as they can."

"There are many 'soons.' Soon tomorrow. Soon next week. Soon in a month. Whatever soon is, it's not soon enough."

Matthews knew the pressure that men like Grigoryev lived with. They drank too much, disobeyed orders, forgot details, and were bored by the political nuances of the work. They ran crazy, almost mind-boggling risks, but they survived because they knew how to live with fear.

Matthews heard fatigue in Grigoryev's voice.

"I'm good at this game. Zhukov is cautious because he knows my cousins are big shots in the FSB. But we are near the end."

Matthews was surprised to hear a wistful tone in his voice, and he thought him already nostalgic for the dangerous life he was about to abandon.

"Who was the woman in the restaurant with you and Sorkin?" Grigoryev asked.

"You were there?"

"I came but I left when I saw her. I don't sit with people I don't know."

"She is a journalist."

"She wrote this?" Grigoryev handed him a copy of the morning's *Novaya Gazeta* with Olga's byline on the article describing Trinity Capital's corporate raider strategy, accompanied with an unflattering photograph of Matthews.

"It is a bad picture. It makes you look like a troll."

"Can I have it?"

"Good plane reading. It is good that you're leaving, because this puts a target on your back. Now, I have to get your money to follow."

Grigoryev laughed. "Fuck me." He looked at Matthews. "If this ends badly, you go to jail. For me, it is different. I am zeroed." His index finger became a pistol and pointed behind his ear. "You know how I survive in Moscow? People don't know me, but they look at me in my uniform like I must be someone, so I act like I'm someone, and I get treated like I am someone. It is a good skill to have. No one doubts you're important if you act important. That's how I survive."

Matthews heard bluster in Grigoryev's comment. He had always been quick to give his opinion, which he offered as wisdom— always a curious mix of insistence and indifference—enjoying the risks that he flouted and then bragged about.

"In America no one will notice me," he said. "I will be the mysterious neighbor who is tolerated but never approached. It will be a difficult life for us, but better than *Genickschuss* in a basement cell. Do you remember when we met in high school? I saw the easy way you excelled with a light touch, as if good grades were effortless. You mixed easily with teenage girls. I was the awkward rhinoceros pushed by his father. Students thought I was a boneheaded Communist—a teenage apparatchik. I made jokes about it, but it was a show, and inside I envied you. You liked jazz and could recite Pushkin and Shelley. Do you remember?"

"We don't have time for this."

"Better now than in my retirement, or in a basement cell. At our age, we are only our past." Grigoryev glanced at Matthews. "Do you still live in Washington?"

"Outside the city. Watch out!"

Grigoryev had taken his eyes off the road and had not seen the car in front brake to avoid a sudden traffic slowdown.

"You'll kill us," Matthews shouted.

"*Mudak*," Grigoryev yelled out his window and honked twice as he passed the slow-moving car. Without turning to Matthews, he added, "We'll get there in time. The M10 is fast."

Silence settled between them again. Grigoryev was a compulsive talker, but the sudden braking had distracted him. His fingers tapped restlessly on the steering wheel and he turned on the radio to a Euro pop station. Traffic police waved cars past a gruesome car accident between a BMW and a truck. Two white-sheeted bodies lay on the roadway.

"How are your kids?" Grigoryev asked, when they were past the accident.

"My daughter died in a boating accident. My son blames me."

"I'm sorry. My deepest sympathies. I didn't know." His face softened with heartfelt condolence. "Viktoria and I don't have children. We didn't want to be responsible for bringing children into the world and having to explain the terrible shit. Now, sometimes, I think it would be better if we'd had children. Who knows? We've had a good life, except for my father. We have a dacha, friends, money. A good boring job." He looked at Matthews. "I missed our meetings after you left Moscow ten years ago."

Matthews wondered where the conversation was going.

"Tell your bosses in Langley there is a hotel video from his Moscow visit in 2013. It's grainy, but you can see the pimple on his fat ass."

"Hotel videos won't interest them."

"There are transcripts of the promises he gave Putin in Oslo. And records of money routed through Deutsche Bank to help finance his casinos and oil wells."

Grigoryev's face darkened. "Tell them they won't see the file until BYRON is out of Russia. There are other patrons for *dezinformatsiva* who will pay for BYRON's verses. Let's not play the silly game of 'show me something' or 'give me a taste' etcetera, etcetera. There is a loaded gun with a bullet for me."

"Keep driving," Matthews said. "Nothing will happen if I miss my flight."

Grigoryev was on the M10, driving at high speed in heavy traffic.

"I'm sorry about your daughter," he said. "I didn't know. It must be difficult for you. I had a sister who died too young." Grigoryev was silent. "You and I have done things that we regret. Hurt people we didn't mean to hurt. The business we're in thinks it's the most important job in the world, but it's not. If you made every one of us a bricklayer or an accountant, would the world be less safe?"

Grigoryev laughed nervously. "Think about that. What good have we done, you and me?"

He glanced at Matthews. "I'm sorry to hear about your son. Let me give you some advice. I grew up hating my father because he thought I should become like him—become who he was—but when I tried to explain that I wasn't him, he refused to listen. He's dead—God rest his soul—but I'm still angry. If only once he had asked: 'What is on your mind, Dmitry? How do you feel? Are you interested in joining the KGB, or would you prefer to be a poet?' *Bastard.*"

Grigoryev's curse startled Matthews and then he saw Grigoryev smile.

"I did want to be a poet. Remember how we daydreamed on the Moscow River. Vodka. Dreams of our futures. Sorkin, a terrible storyteller, thought he could become Tolstoy. I had verses in my Russian blood."

He looked at Matthews. "It was all crap. Then you came back with the CIA, and voila, you made me a poet." He said the word with bitter sarcasm. "I am BYRON. The last poet in Moscow. Mad, bad, and dangerous to know."

Grigoryev laughed quietly, unsettled. "Who knew this is how things would turn out?" He turned to Matthews with a grave face. "Talk to your son. Don't let him grow up like I did, hating his old man."

18

Sheremetyevo Airport

Terminal F was a colossal mass of passengers crowded together in the vaulted departure hall. Gates and times were announced over the public address system, and frantic passengers late for their flights pleaded to advance to the front of the line that snaked toward immigration control and security scanners. Plaintive cries of desperate passengers mixed with wailing babies and booming announcements and everywhere a sense of unease.

Matthews entered from the passenger drop-off zone shortly after 12:15 P.M., alert to the scene and scanning for airport police. By his calculation, the sea of people was a good cover and he proceeded with the casual demeanor of a business traveler accustomed to the indignities of international travel. Tall, purposeful, his roll-on bag in hand. To the trained eye of a border guard, he would be just another traveler patiently making his way through the crowd.

He had seen the border guard as he entered the pavilion, and he was there again near the queue moving slowly toward security, eyes vigilant. *A young officer*, Matthews thought. His uniform fit well on his trim body and he had the look of a new recruit who still took his job seriously. His hawk eyes observed the queue, looking for someone to pull out and question.

Matthews had placed the keychain in his pocket, where its discovery wouldn't raise questions. A casual glance at the keys wouldn't spot the seam, but rigorous scrutiny by a diligent officer might. Matthews wore a hat pulled down on his forehead and dark glasses. There was risk looking as if he were avoiding attention, but he had decided the greater risk was to be recognized from his photograph in the morning newspaper. FSB agents had his likeness—he was under surveillance, and the article added to the unwanted attention. It was reasonable to assume that border guards had been cautioned to look for him. Only an optimist or a fool would assume he was safe.

Nearby, the frantic wailing of a woman being pulled from the queue drew the crowd's attention. With an act of consummate self-control, he resisted the urge to push forward to the front of the line. He turned, following other passengers around him, and saw the hysterical woman. She had triggered an interest in the guards, who dragged her between them, indifferent to her pleas.

Interior Ministry police wearing body armor idled by a glass wall, automatic weapons slung casually around their necks. Matthews knew exactly how many times he'd traveled back to Washington, DC, from Terminal F, but the tension was always fresh. He kept track of his trips to remind himself that this part of his life would come to an end. Some departures went without incident, some had delays, but most, like his departure that afternoon, had the potential for an unforeseen catastrophe. There was a science to police surveillance—the Stasi had developed it and the FSB had mastered it—*gucken, narchen, greifen*. Watch, listen, nab.

Matthews overheard the man behind him tell another passenger that the yelling woman had tried to cut the line. Impatient people pushed forward and jockeyed for position. "Idiot," the man said.

Matthews stepped up to the immigration control booth and smiled at the agent sitting behind the glass barrier—a stern middle-aged woman with tired eyes and a loosened necktie. He slipped his passport through the slot. The agent turned toward her computer screen—matching passport photo to the screen's image.

"Crowded," Matthews said to connect, be casual. He watched her flip the pages. The public address system announced the departure of his flight, and behind, voice agitated, a man grumbled that he would miss his plane.

The agent looked at the complaining passenger and then directly at Matthews, pointing at his sunglasses. He removed them and made an effort to smile while the agent compared his face to the passport photo. She had the inscrutable expression of immigration agents everywhere, looking for a single reason to doubt the document. She brought her weighted stamp down on his passport.

"Next."

Matthews looked out the window of the Boeing 767. The plane had passed through a layer of scattered clouds on its way to cruising altitude. He allowed himself to relax into the feeling that he was finally safe.

A flight attendant had begun to serve drinks when the seat belt sign went off, moving her cart through the first-class cabin. He had heard of an Air France flight recalled to the gate from the runway, but he'd never heard of an airplane intercepted by Russian fighter jets and forced to return to Sheremetyevo.

His eyes came off the window and the regular pattern of farmland that was falling away as the airplane climbed. He turned to the flight attendant, who smiled at him.

"Two whiskies," he said. "No ice."

PART IV

19

Washington, DC—Red Notice

Matthews felt the chilly dawn air and he saw mist drifting across the smooth surface of the Mall's reflecting pool. Washington was waking, and there were few people out and the streets were empty. Early morning quiet lay a false peace on the sweep of lawn in front of him. He moved along the reflecting pool, taking his time, aware, too, of the distance he'd walked from the Lincoln Memorial. Early morning joggers ran under trees turned brown and yellow with the changing season. Ahead, beyond the Washington Monument, the bronze Statue of Freedom on the US Capitol was refulgent in the first light of day.

"Welcome home," the Director said. He stood on the grassy strip between the reflecting pool and the line of trees, and his knuckled hand casually held a long leash. "You remember Pooch." The Scottish terrier sniffed the grass, oblivious to Matthews's arrival. Matthews had been told to descend the Lincoln Memorial's steps and walk to the end of the reflecting pool.

"We watched to be certain you weren't followed." The Director nodded at a thin man in a worsted suit and black Homburg who approached.

"I asked James to join us. I hope you don't mind."

Linton allowed a vague smile to break across his face. It wasn't a smile, Matthews thought, but the expression of a man who felt obliged to be polite.

The Director's rangy eyebrow arched, his bow tie was tight on his neck, and his hands held the straining leash. His face was grave and he looked irritated and displeased.

"What happened in Moscow?"

Matthews recognized the accusatory tone in the Director's voice. On the flight, he had made cryptic notes on Grigoryev's mental state and he knew that the trickiest part of an exfiltration was to extract a person whose behavior put them both at risk.

"Where do you want me to start?"

"Start with this."

Linton removed a document from his leather portfolio and handed it to Matthews. Interpol's insignia was on the cover page, and below it, in alarming scarlet, the words "Red Notice." Matthews flipped through the three-page document and returned to the second page. His photograph filled the top of the page and underneath there were the details of his identity: age, physical description, language skills, known addresses, and at the bottom, the "Charge." The criminal act under Article 276 of the Russian Federation Criminal Code was listed: Espionage.

"This came in last night. The FBI deputy director called me at home."

Matthews lifted his eyes from the arrest warrant and looked from Linton to the Director. "This must have been issued while I was in the air. No one stopped me from boarding."

The Director's brow creased. "The FBI wants to take you into custody, but I told them I would handle it. The FBI can ignore this for a few days, but not a few weeks."

"You're being sought as a spy," Linton said, in a matter-of-fact tone, adding, "Espionage under Article 276 includes actions that threaten Russia's economic security. They don't like what you've done with Trinity Capital."

Matthews slapped the paper against his palm, voice sharp. "This is bullshit. I've made money. They don't like that." He waved the Red Notice theatrically. "You asked for a quick, easy favor." He strung out the vowels to underscore his irritation. "Now this extortion. They don't want me to go back."

"When did you discover you were being targeted?"

Matthews leaned forward. "Are you asking if this is related to BYRON? I don't know. It's possible, but it's also possible that it's a coincidence. Economic crimes come under Department K and BYRON is of interest to FSB counterintelligence. I have been targeted because I'm successful. You assumed Trinity Capital would be a good cover." He lifted the Red Notice. "You were wrong."

The Director looked at the other early morning dog walkers but then turned back to Matthews. "How was I wrong?"

Matthews answered calmly, face shadowed. "If you're part of the club of wealth in Moscow you can get away with anything, but if you shine a bright light on corrupt business practices you get noticed by powerful people."

"Putin?" the Director said.

"I've never met him, but he knows who I am."

"Does he know about BYRON?"

"FSB counterintelligence and the Sixth Service do. Putin probably does." Matthews paused. "They know because they have penetrated the agency. The FSB met me when I landed. They knew my flight number, seat assignment, and arrival date. They know about BYRON. They don't know his identity, but they know he's trying to leave Russia. I was questioned, released, and surveilled."

Matthews took out the keychain and displayed the thumb drive, pulling the male connection away from its casing. "This contains personal details that Technical Services will need to create the documents that will get BYRON out of Russia. He is on a restricted travel list and he needs an alias to cross the border. He will bring the *kompromat* with him."

"He trusts you?"

"No, no, but he doesn't have a choice."

Linton took the keychain. "We'll have the watermarks and paper stock in a few days."

Matthews lifted the Red Notice. "I can't go back."

"We haven't asked you to return."

"You'll be arrested when you land," the Director said. "One man in a Russian prison is enough. We're trying to organize an exchange for Birch."

"What happens to BYRON?" Matthews asked. "How does he get out?"

There was a long silence interrupted only by the yelping of two dogs playing together. Matthews looked at the two men staring at him. It was Matthews's great skill that allowed him to recognize the callousness of men who sent colleagues into harm's way from the safety of their air-conditioned offices on the seventh floor of headquarters. Proud speeches in support of duty, honor, and country to inspire men to take absurd risks.

"I can't go back," Matthews repeated.

"We wouldn't ask you to," the Director said.

Linton leaned forward. "They're looking for Alex Matthews. What if Alex Matthews is picked up by Interpol in Rome?"

"Fly to Rome?" Matthews looked at both men. "Get arrested?" His voice deepened with skepticism. "Why?"

"The real Alex Matthews returns to Moscow under a different name. New passport, new legend, non-official cover. You and BYRON drive across the Russian border and we'll have a team waiting for you."

Matthews saw Linton's pale face in the gray light. A beat of silence, but then Linton resumed describing his plan with the soothing reassurance of a salesman praising a customer's new ill-fitting suit.

"Interpol takes the false Alex Matthews into custody in Rome the day you arrive in Moscow. The FSB is informed that you've been apprehended. Interagency communications take time. Five days. Six. A week. By the time they discover they've arrested the wrong man, you and BYRON will have crossed Friendship Bridge."

It was the specific reference to the Estonian border that convinced Matthews that they had already assembled the plan and were waiting for the right moment to spring it.

"You don't have to do this," the Director said. "If you're caught, the charge will be espionage. You'll be convicted and jailed. You won't have diplomatic immunity."

"They won't catch you," Linton said.

Matthews listened to the short, spirited colloquy between the two senior men, talking about his life as if he wasn't present, each offering an assessment of the risk. He looked at the Director's big frame standing over the small terrier at his feet.

The Director's voice deepened and became grave. "I wouldn't be suggesting this if it wasn't important. It's risky, but given what's at stake, I need to ask. It's your call."

"I wish I had your confidence."

"You don't have to do this."

"I haven't said I would."

"If you do, we need to move quickly," Linton said. "The Red Notice will start to get attention." Linton lifted the keychain. "We'll get it done in a few days. No one outside of Technical Services will know."

A weak sun poked above the tree line and washed their faces in a warm glow. Among the three men there was the bond of secret work, which had held them together through long, difficult missions and made them tolerant of each other's foibles and uncomfortable convictions. Linton, the mole hunter, looked at Matthews with the patience of a confidence man who had offered an explanation that he hoped would vanquish Matthews's doubts. His face had an ascetic calm and his hands were clasped. For a moment, Matthews saw a stoic killer.

"We'll be indebted to you," the Director said. "We can't pay you, we can't acknowledge your work, but you'll know our debt. We are in a dark time."

Matthews took satisfaction in knowing that he could disappoint them, but he also knew he had to go back. Not for them. Trinity Capital's funds were at risk and all he had built was on the line. He had to take care of his employees and move his funds. His predicament was clear. He thought it was just like the Director to couch his request in terms of a greater good.

"I will need to tell Anna."

"If you must."

Matthews heard the cold concession. "I ruined one marriage serving the agency. I won't ruin another."

"How well do you know her?" Linton asked.

Matthews was startled and nonplussed. "She needs to know what's at stake."

"Secrecy is imperative."

Matthews considered the admonition and then he faced Linton, his voice implying that the problem was elsewhere. "Did you finish your investigation? Did you find the leak?"

"An official report was issued. It said what it needed to say to protect our suspicions and your work. There is no mention of BYRON. It's an exercise in obfuscation and it doesn't include any of the names on my short list."

"How short?"

"One."

"What are you waiting for?"

The Director raised his hand solemnly. "He's a suspect. We need to be certain. An innocent case officer's career doesn't recover from wrongful suspicions. We will keep him away from the operation."

"Who is it? Moscow station? D'Angelo?"

Linton leaned forward and whispered the name. "Wallace."

"I heard he's missing."

"Arrested for drunk driving." Linton added, "He was released on the condition that he undergo rehab, which keeps him safely away from the operation."

"How would he know my flight number? How does he communicate with Moscow?"

"We'll find out. We plan to keep him on the team, but he'll only know what we want him to know. He'll be quarantined."

"He's Anna's friend," the Director said.

"My friend," Matthews said, to quash the old canard. "She knows him through me. We served together in Iraq."

"Meet up with him. Give him a story that he is likely to believe."

28

BLT Prime Restaurant

A nna was in the mezzanine of the Old Post Office and she looked for her husband among the boisterous guests who had made the hotel a lively gathering spot for wealthy and powerful conservatives. The Romanesque Revival building had been transformed into a grand hotel that served Washington's Republican elite who gathered there to conspire, celebrate, drink, and to be seen in each other's company, taking note of who was there and who wasn't.

Anna enjoyed parties, but she wasn't sure she belonged at this one. No matter how boisterous or formal, gatherings of Washington's officialdom always made her apprehensive. She drew unwanted attention from older, single men and women. She felt the hustle and harassment that passed for conviviality. The same comments, the same naughty questions, the same boastful political loyalty, the latest election rumors, and the predictable invitations to a private suite upstairs. Her few years of Washington partygoing had trained her to slough off blandishments like dead skin.

"There you are," Jean said. They air kissed and Jean drew close, taking Anna's hand, whispering, "Isn't this the most disgusting display of Make America Great Again? I feel like a liberal spy among a room full of conservative Republicans. Can you believe the way they're dressed? Cowboy boots. MAGA hats. Red, white, and blue sequin dresses. Add a slot machine and you'd think we were in Las Vegas."

Jean had a big smile, pleased with herself. "I wouldn't have put this event together, but I need the money. I won't do another."

"You said that the last time."

Jean ignored the comment. "I did this to see for myself how BLT Prime has become the waiting room for the Oval Office. The hotel has become a safe haven from the federal government's liberal deep-state bureaucracy. I am here as a witness."

She winked. "I'm paid by Arab businessmen, Republican fat cats, and genuflecting diplomats who spend crazy money on his brand as a sign of filial piety or whatever you call it. I take their money. Why not?"

Jean pointed to a table in the middle of the restaurant. "He was here earlier, right there at table 12. POTUS, FLOTUS, and two Russians, or maybe they were Ukrainians. I can't tell them apart."

"Bayan and Kovalenko."

"I don't know their names." She smiled. "Rudy was with them. He had an unlit cigar in his mouth and his companion had a purse dog. POTUS received a few men who were allowed to approach and whisper in his ear. I swear. It was a scene out of *The Godfather.*

"I watched them eat. She had fish with white sauce, which she sent back. She hates sauces. He had a hamburger and a bourbon, but there was a cart of junk food by the table, which he ate. Lay's Potato Chips, Milky Ways."

Jean laughed, but quickly covered her mouth. "I would have paid to watch, but they were paying me. I've seen him on TV and in my dreams, but there he was in his glowing orange flesh. After eating, he schmoozed with donors and left with an entourage of advisors, handlers, and Secret Service."

Jean looked at Anna. "Is there anyone in the White House who doesn't kiss his ass?"

Anna didn't laugh. "Have you seen Alex?"

"Is he back from Moscow?"

She stared. "How did you know he was there?"

"Isn't he always there? I thought everyone knew. You look surprised."

"Who told you?"

"That he was back?"

"Yes."

Jean shrugged, startled by the question. "I didn't know it was confidential. My husband told me." She pointed across the restaurant. "Alex is there at the bar with Mark. He's waving at us."

Anna rushed to Alex, her long dress sweeping across the marble floor, drawing startled glances from guests. Without acknowledging Mark Driscoll, she embraced her husband and they held each other for a long moment and, as the excitement ended, she took his face in both hands and kissed him. "Thank God you're safe."

"You're crying," Matthews said.

"I'm just glad you're back."

"I heard you got home yesterday," Driscoll said, surprised. "Hugging like that you'd think you were just catching up."

"I was in London," she said briskly. "I got back this morning." She smiled as if it was none of Driscoll's business.

Driscoll raised an eyebrow. "Alex and I were just talking about how the CE Division is trying to find its footing in Putin's Russia."

"It's loud here," Matthews said. He pointed to the end of the long bar and urged them to move to a quieter spot. The restaurant's din followed them, but the absence of other drinkers nearby made it a private conversation. As they moved, Anna leaned into Matthews. "I said to meet here at seven and it's already eight. I was worried."

"Traffic was terrible." He made excuses for his lateness, blaming the Russian foreign minister, who was in town. Traffic throughout the city was clogged.

"Where's Wallace?" Matthews asked. "I thought he might be here."

"He's in rehab," Anna said. Her tone was casual, but concerned, and also brisk. "Jean said everyone knows, so it isn't gossip, but of course, she has a good ear for scandal."

Driscoll leaned forward, keen with interest. "The drunk driving arrest got Linton's attention. Wallace was told to deal with his addiction."

"He's a social drinker," Matthews said. "He's not an addict."

"He passed out and rear-ended a police car stopped at a light. A social drinker with a tendency to get drunk."

"How is Rose doing?"

"I'm surprised she hasn't left him. It's an open secret that he sleeps around. He's one of those handsome men whose good looks has contributed to his downfall."

Having had two drinks and being among friends, Driscoll lost his usual propriety, succumbing to gossip. "He always expected to have things be easy for him—thinking he deserved to become more than he is. I'm sure he's bent your ear about his family connections to Bill Casey."

Driscoll saw surprise on Matthews's face. "Maybe that came out after you left. Or maybe people kept it from you because they knew you were close." Driscoll paused. "We took him out of the loop on

BYRON. His drinking. His work habits. He resents the fact that he hasn't been promoted. He's always had this idea of himself that was at odds with how he's seen. You must know that? He's your friend."

"Friendly more than friends."

"He's always been seen as low rent. There was the scandal when he self-published a novel that wasn't cleared by agency censors. They almost shit-canned him for that, but he withdrew the book when he was told it was his career or his novel. He has always had the idea to turn his agency experience into thinly veiled fiction, but he's not a good writer. Some are born writers, some become writers, and some suckle the teat of hope. I read the book. It's pulpy prose with a ludicrous plot. It's not even as good as the terrible paperbacks that Howard Hunt wrote. Jesus," he exclaimed, "why in God's name do so many of us think we can take all the nasty shit we do and turn it into ripe, perfumed thrillers?"

Driscoll sipped his gin and tonic and added, "Our friends on the other side don't have that impulse."

The friends on the other side, Matthews thought: *the FSB.*

Driscoll set down his drink, lips smacking.

"I should visit him," Matthews said.

"Don't be noble with misplaced sympathy. He brought this on himself."

Anna put her beer on the bar. "That's a cold view. He's an intelligence officer with secrets in his head. He's a risk now, but he's a bigger risk if he's pushed out."

"He should gut out his time until early retirement." Driscoll set down his drink, centering it. "Visit him. Hold his grubby hand. He's got supporters even if I'm not one of them. I lay the Moscow debacle at his feet."

Matthews watched Driscoll stride toward Jean, a glamorous beacon of sculpted hair in a low-cut dress.

Anna stepped closer, ignoring Driscoll's comment, and kissed her husband's cheek. "I didn't hear from you for three days. I left voice messages. I was worried."

"It's loud in here." He took her arm. "Let's go outside."

Bronzed glass doors opened onto Pennsylvania Avenue, where gray-haired men in tuxedos and wives or girlfriends in gowns and shawls were arriving in black limousines. Doormen opened car doors for Washington's Republican elite and they passed cheering bystanders and paparazzi, camera flashes lighting the dusk. Across the street, a motley group held offensive placards and shouted insults at the arriving guests. One proper Washington dowager who arrived on the arm of a handsome male companion yelled back at the protestors, "You're all losers."

Sympathetic clapping from a few other arriving guests was met with harassing boos from the protestors, and in that moment, as Matthews crossed the street with Anna, he thought the Republican elite and their indignant liberal opposite formed a tarnished throng that was a reflection of what America had become.

Matthews saw a tall man emerge from the periphery of the rabble and he only noticed him because the man looked directly at him. It was startling. The man had a neck tattoo, gray hair pulled back in a ponytail, and a menacing expression as he advanced toward Matthews with quick strides, making no effort to hide his interest. His right hand held an object that glinted as it caught the glow of a police cruiser's rotating roof lights.

"He's got a knife," Anna said, clutching Matthews's arm.

Matthews, too, saw the blade and struggled for a moment with the idea that the man wasn't part of the protest. His clothes were wrong, his mood dark, and he had no interest in the well-dressed guests arriving for the evening gala. He had the grim determination of an assassin.

Jesus fuck. Matthews glanced around to see if the man was working alone or had companions, and he quickly assessed places where they could safely escape.

"Who is he?"

"I have no idea. But he sees me and he recognizes me."

A protestor threw a rock across the street, cracking the windshield of an arriving limousine, causing the car to swerve and collide with a streetlamp. The scene around the hotel's entrance erupted in a chaos of cries that shattered the fragile order. Metropolitan police, who were there to keep back protesters, swept in all at once. Other officers in parked cars jumped from their cruisers and the combined force created a human barrier dividing the groups. Guests waiting in the portico were hustled inside the hotel as another rock was hurled at a police car. Crackling police radios mixed with angry shouts from protestors and astonished cries from hotel guests. Police wielding plastic batons waded into the crowd, and nearby there were the shrieking sirens of approaching police vans.

"He's following us," Anna said.

The man had stepped away from the melee and approached them along the dark sidewalk.

"This way." Anna took Matthews's hand and directed him to the safety of the hotel, but police around the portico waved him off, and Matthews found himself stopped in the middle of the street—police in front, assailant behind. A speeding police van rounded the corner and Matthews was right in its path. He was momentarily blinded by headlights. Paralyzing fear fixed him where he stood. His mouth was dry. *Shit!*

He was pushed hard from behind and stumbled toward the curb, knees buckling. He didn't see the police van brake in a wild skid, but he heard the dull thud of steel on bone, and a cry of pain.

Anna was at his side, lifting him from where he'd fallen after her violent shove. His pants were torn at the knee and his palms bled with embedded pebbles.

Matthews resisted her urgent plea to leave and approached the assailant sprawled on the street, his right leg twisted at a terrible angle, his head cracked open. Blood, dark as oil in the night, pooled under his neck. Matthews saw the knife on the street by his palm, and he stepped closer to look at the face.

"Get back," the young police officer yelled, motioning him away.

❖

They watched paramedics lift the body into the ambulance from across the street. Its siren shrieked suddenly, as it slowly moved through the gathered crowd of onlookers.

"Who was he?"

"I have no idea."

"He was coming for you." She turned to him. "Did you see the tattoo on his neck?"

Matthews knew skull tattoos in Russian prisons marked convicted murderers. "I should report this to the police."

She shot him a look. "And say what? 'Oh, the man hit by the van was going to kill me.'" Her voice rose, harsh and mocking. "Mr. Matthews, what would a Russian want with you?" Anna paused. "The agency won't let you talk about this."

"You're jumping to conclusions."

"It's an easy leap to make." She stared at him.

Uneasy silence settled between them, and in a moment, they were moving along the sidewalk, certain about what had happened and uncertain what it meant. They moved quickly away from the chaotic, brightly lit scene. Anna took his hand and pressed it, comforting him. "Let's talk before you do anything. We should change the locks on the house."

The hulking Old Post Office was behind them and looming ahead in the next block stood the brightly illuminated White House. Night had fallen on the city, but the Georgian mansion glowed under the dark sky.

Matthews stopped at the black wrought iron fence that surrounded the White House. Beyond the mowed lawn and the security kiosk, he saw lights on in the second-floor family residence.

How had it come to this? he thought.

Anna was beside him, gazing at the graceful symbol of American power. Curtains were drawn, but then the fabric darkened as a ghostlike figure passed the window.

"What happened in Moscow?"

He'd felt safe in America when he got off the plane the day before—looking forward to a pleasant evening in Washington, removed from the dangers thousands of miles away in Moscow. Somehow a Russian agent had found him. Dread darkened his mood. If one agent knew how to find him, there would be others. He glanced back, but there was no one behind. He wanted to avoid her question, but he owed her an answer.

"Interpol issued a Red Notice for me." He saw her face blanch. "No one in the FBI is going to honor the order."

"They don't have to." She nodded back at the departing ambulance carrying the dead assailant.

They moved away from the fence and walked quietly toward Lafayette Park. She slipped her arm into his.

"What happens to Trinity Capital?"

"Its assets have been sold and the cash is being transferred to bank accounts in Malta and Cyprus. I have no reason to go back to Moscow." He said that he'd made adequate financial arrangements for the staff and that he would find a way to reward Sorkin. He put his arm around her shoulder. "It will work out."

"And BYRON?"

"He's on his own." He spoke without looking at her to avoid betraying his lie. "They'll find another way to exfiltrate him. I'm done." The first lie was the hardest, he thought.

Anna drew closer, taking his arm. "It's for the best. It's gotten too dangerous for you." She clutched his hand. "I know them, I know how the seventh floor works. If they can't find a way to get him out, they'll ask you. BYRON is too important."

The second lie was easier. "No one has asked me to do anything. If they did, I'd tell you. I don't want to live this way. I gave it up." He smiled. "Mikhail says hello. He invited us to spend New Year's with him and Veronica at his yacht in Martinique."

"Who's Olga Luchaninova?"

He looked at Anna, curious where the question came from.

"Mikhail mentioned her. When I couldn't reach you, I called him. He said you'd had dinner together, but when I called the hotel, they said you didn't come back that night."

"It was late. The Metro was closed and bridges were blocked because of protests."

"Did you sleep with her?"

"I slept on a bed in her house, but not with her. It was her apartment or a park bench."

They continued to walk in silence, but then he stopped and took her hands. "Her husband was assassinated for stories he wrote about FSB corruption. She had no interest in me. It wasn't like that."

21

Tranquility Woods

At a younger and more vulnerable age, Matthews had struggled
to find his confidence, but as he grew older and more accom-
plished, he found his confidence and with it came a different
struggle. He found it difficult to hear the truth about himself
when it was presented to him. He was told by an uncle that what
he wasn't good at, which he might not be aware of, by which he'd
be judged, was the thing he needed to address.

Friendship was one such thing. He was inclined to reserve
his judgment of people and he believed that each person stood
on his own two feet, and if he didn't, no amount of help would
prevent his failure. But for reasons that were only partly clear to
Matthews, he had made an exception with Tom Wallace. He was
prisoner of his loyalty to the man who found himself pushed into
a career in which he could never succeed. He was sympathetic to
Wallace's misery of being raised in an overbearing family with
his secret ambitions at odds with his parents' expectations.

Matthews's friendship with Tom Wallace was accidently forged in the Iraq War. Wallace's lead Humvee was struck by an IED as it entered a Fallujah suburb. Matthews pulled Wallace from the bombed vehicle and carried him to safety at great risk to himself. ISIS militants converged on the site of the attack and Matthews brought the wounded man to a nearby alley where he called in the attack and held off the better-armed militia until reinforcements arrived. Matthews bonded with the man whose life he had saved.

Matthews parked his old Volvo in the small lot at the rear of the sanitarium. It was Friday morning and there were few visitors. He thought it a pleasant prison for victims of crimes against themselves. At the front desk, a dour woman looked up from her computer screen with a slightly put-out expression.

"You're here for Mr. Wallace?"

"Yes."

"He told us to expect you. He's by the water, skipping rocks." She pointed down the hall where a French door gave a view of Chesapeake Bay.

Matthews strolled down the broad green lawn that sloped gently to the water. Outdoor furniture arranged in groups dotted the lawn and several chairs were occupied by patients enjoying the warm morning sun. Old and young, Black and White, wealthy and poor. Matthews's eyes drifted over them. Addiction, he thought, was an equal opportunity disease. He continued toward a pair of Adirondack chairs under a wide maple tree, facing a long pier that jutted into the bay, and looked at the seated man.

He recognized Tom Wallace's lanky frame, his dyed hair combed back on his head, and saw his preoccupation with a large yacht that made its way on the channel. Matthews had rehearsed what he'd say, and how to greet him, but then he saw Wallace wave him forward, and the suddenness of his smile, and the pleasant setting, made it hard to hold onto his lecture.

"You're late."

Matthews was at Wallace's side. They faced each other and then embraced.

"My first visitor and you're late."

"Five minutes late."

"There is nothing to do here except read and stare at the yachts. So I'm conscious of time. You're usually prompt, aren't you?"

"Five minutes."

"Five minutes is five minutes. If you'd been five minutes late in Fallujah, I'd be dead. Good to see you. Sit." He indicated the empty chair next to him. "Join me in my bucolic incarceration with the alcoholics, fentanyl abusers, and drug addicts. We are a merry bunch of lonely pleasure seekers."

"What are you reading?"

Wallace tossed the book he was reading at Matthews, who grabbed it midair. "You wouldn't like it. A shitty spy novel with no literary merit. *The Judas Hour.*"

Wallace pointed to other patients sitting in lawn chairs, faces raised to the sun, absorbed in the dull nothingness of their confinement. "We're called guests to make us feel that we're here voluntarily. Some are. Most aren't. I was told to commit myself."

He looked at Matthews. "Why are we here—them and me? Are we special? What is it about us that isn't in everyone? What? Where is the angry cop who cuffs a Black teenager at a traffic stop, or the film producer who demands sex from a starlet, or the senator accused of wife beating? They have their addictions—anger, sex, greed. My mistake and the mistake of my fellow guests is that we suffer from the gift of seeing the world for what it is and gild the ugliness with drugs."

Matthews clapped his hands slowly at Wallace's performance. "That attitude won't get you out of here."

"Why did you come?"

"To see how you're doing."

"You'll leave here and write up your assessment for Linton. A few bland observations sprinkled with the holy water of heartless sympathy."

"You're angry."

"Of course I am. Wouldn't you be? I drink. I'm not a drunk. I drink less than Driscoll, a divinely inspired jerk, if you don't mind my bilious dislike." He paused. "I failed a breathalyzer test and Linton said my career was over if I didn't admit myself. My career is already over."

Wallace looked at Matthews. "I was interviewed by Linton's grand inquisitors. They tried to make a thing out of my choosing Birch to be your driver. He's a kid. It was an easy job. Because the operation went south, they looked to place blame. Did they interview you?"

Matthews nodded. "Rose is worried."

"It's in her nature." Wallace looked off at the bay. "I haven't treated her well. You know, I wasn't her first choice. She should have stuck with her first choice."

"I thought it was the other way around."

Wallace grunted his reaction. His eyes came off the broad sweep of the shimmering bay where the sleek, gleaming yacht cruised toward the Atlantic.

"Someone in headquarters is against me. I am being set up. I've had time to think here. I led the team that brought in Anton Glok a year ago, but now half a dozen men claim that trophy. I hear he's going to be traded." Wallace shook his head and slumped in the wood chair.

Matthews appreciated Wallace's gimlet eye for the absurdities of their work. They sat together in silence, except for cawing gulls by the pier.

"Are you sailing?" Matthews pointed to the graceful sloop moored just beyond the end of the pier. "Is that the *Red Queen*?"

"It's approved therapy. I'm allowed out once a day and I check back in when I return. They've removed the liquor."

Wallace fixed Matthews with a skeptical expression. "Why are you here? You don't have better things to do?"

"I was encouraged to come."

"By who?"

"Driscoll."

Wallace shook his head. "He thinks I'm a government grifter."

"Anna is going to visit. She's worried too."

Wallace turned to Matthews. "There is gossip that we've been seen together at BLT Prime. Rose had heard it. It's not true. Anna works in the agency and so do I. We have reason to grab a drink together after work. You travel a lot, but a drink is all it is. Did I answer your question?"

"I didn't come to ask that."

"Why did you come? To feel good about yourself? To make sure that I didn't squander the life you saved?"

Matthews stiffened, irritated. "I can help you leave the agency if that's what you want."

"What's Anna's view?"

"She's concerned about you."

"You're lucky to have her. I was surprised when you married. She was the younger, exquisitely unobtainable interpreter and you a widowed intelligence officer."

"You said that before. Do you resent me? Are you jealous?"

He laughed. "A man your age with your dull humor?"

Matthews looked at Wallace. "Why did you pick Birch for Moscow?"

"You want me to say that I told Birch to wear a hoodie and be a rookie. That I compromised you to give up BYRON? That's what Linton wants to believe, but it's not true. He was your driver. Something unexpected happened. I had no idea you were there to meet BYRON."

"Linton thinks you knew."

"His mind is addled—it's a maze of paranoid suspicions. He sees treason in an expense report with a math error." Wallace shook his head. "Every morning he puts on his cloak of intelligence infallibility and ponders apostasy. He has convinced all of us that he doesn't make mistakes. He's caught up in the mole racket. I hear I'm on his wall chart."

Wallace stood and walked to the rocky shore. He picked up a flat, fist-sized stone and went to throw it at Matthews, who ducked. Instead, Wallace cocked his arm and made a strong toss, sending the rock over the cove's calm surface, where it skipped four times before sinking.

"If I had wanted to hit you, I would have. If I had wanted to betray BYRON, I would have succeeded. He would have been picked up by the FSB. There may be a Russian agent in headquarters. I suspect there is at least one among the thousands of employees. But it isn't me. I am the easy target. I fit their profile, but so do others."

Matthews joined Wallace as he strolled toward the end of the pier.

"It's not me," Wallace said emphatically. He turned to Matthews. "It might be no one. There might not be a malicious betrayal, just routine bungling."

They reached the end of the pier and faced the bay's shimmering water. Matthews wondered whether Wallace's comment was an honest protest or the dissembling suggestion of a man planting a seed of doubt.

22

The Red Queen

Matthews was awakened at midnight by the chiming of his cell phone. He reached over in the dark, fumbling for it on the bedside table, and grabbed his glasses, without which, by some vagary of concomitant senses, he couldn't answer the phone properly. He knew good news did not come at that hour. He glanced out the second-floor window looking for parked Russian surveillance. Instinct. There was nothing. He continued down the hall to David's room, fearing that his son might have been involved in a car accident.

"Hello," he whispered on the fifth ring, closing David's bedroom door.

"Alex, it's me. Jim Linton."

When the call ended, he returned to the bedroom and sat on the edge of the bed, clutching the phone. Anna was up and had turned on her bedside lamp. Her sleepy face was alive with concern.

"What is it?"

"They found Tom Wallace's boat on a sandbar a mile from the rehab clinic. He went for an afternoon sail and didn't return."

"What happened?"

"Jim doesn't know." He raised his phone like evidence. "He thinks Tom might have fled."

"Fled where?"

"Fled the clinic. Fled the country."

The next morning. Matthews joined Linton at the Kent Island marina. Federal agents in blue windbreakers stood inside yellow police tape strung across one section of the pier. The sloop was docked by itself at a far end of the marina, quarantined.

"He's with me," Linton said to the FBI agent keeping bystanders away. They ducked under the yellow tape and walked to the *Red Queen*. Matthews boarded after Linton and they were greeted by a burly man with an FBI cap and a holstered handgun.

"Gonzalez. Special agent in charge."

"James Linton. I spoke with you earlier. My colleague, Alex Matthews. Where was the boat found?"

"A Coast Guard cutter towed it off a sand bar opposite the Russian compound in Centreville. There was no distress signal. The Coast Guard was alerted by a boat returning from a cruise."

Gonzalez had the implacable expression of an experienced investigator who could see or hear anything without surprise, a man familiar with humanity's various dark impulses. He recited what he'd discovered since arriving. A call was placed to Tranquility Woods and the woman who answered confirmed the sloop had been moored there, but it had been taken out by the owner, who was not in his room. He had gone out for a sail that day, as he did every day, but he had not returned. He had been in good spirits when he went sailing, joking that it was a good day to sail around the world. The Coast Guard cutter that pulled the *Red Queen* off the sandbar found no evidence of anyone in the water or on the nearby shore.

Matthews listened to Gonzalez describe the chain of events that followed the discovery of the boat, including the call made to the local police.

"I understand the man who owns the boat works for the government."

"There is a national security issue," Linton said. "No one should talk to the press. The boat is off limits to everyone."

"National security" got the FBI agent's attention. He was skeptical. "I've heard that before. It's usually about a senator's wife or an unauthorized burglary. Why don't you enlighten me."

"Name is Tom Wallace. Intelligence officer with top security clearance. Talk to Burton Smythe, FBI counterintelligence, if you want more." He nodded. "What happened?"

"See for yourself."

Garbage was piled by the pier, and seagulls pecked at stinking fish skeletons spilling from a torn garbage bag. Matthews waved off an aggressive gull as he walked past, and then he was on board. In the cabin, Gonzalez lifted two plastic evidence bags.

"This was found on deck," the agent said, showing off the 9 mm Glock, and he pointed to the second bag. "The spent shell casing was found nearby. The Glock's magazine is full except for one bullet."

Gonzalez looked at Linton. "There was no sign of a struggle. We are looking for his body, but currents in the area are strong, so we haven't found it. If he committed suicide and fell overboard, his body may be miles away. A Coast Guard helicopter and two launches have joined the search."

"Why do you think he's dead?" Matthews asked.

Gonzalez paused. "It's one possibility. We know he wasn't on board when the boat was found. There is a bullet casing on deck and the gun was fired. Could he be alive? Sure, but let me show you something."

Gonzalez stretched a blue latex glove over his hand, moving Wallace's street shoes from in front of an unlocked cabinet, and then opened the door. Inside, there was another magazine, two thick stacks of one-hundred-dollar bills bound with elastic bands, a black diplomatic passport and two green passports all in different names. Two manila envelopes stamped CLASSIFIED in large red letters.

"A burglar wouldn't leave the money. Who has three passports in different names?"

Gonzalez moved to a cabinet that had been forced open. He pointed to the electronic equipment inside. "That is a burst radio transmitter that operates outside the frequencies used for civilian communication."

He stripped off the glove. "Who did he work for?"

"He worked for us."

"CIA?"

Linton nodded.

Gonzalez looked skeptically at Linton with the expression of an interrogator who had elicited a confession. His lip curled, but he became generous with what he knew. He described what had been found in the cabin—a water bottle in the refrigerator, saltines, a tin of tuna, and kidney beans in the pantry. Nothing on the boat suggested that it was prepared for a long cruise. Forensics had been on board earlier and they'd lifted prints and a saliva sample from a glass. There was very little to suggest what had happened except the gun, the shell casing, and the missing sailor.

"Do you know him?"

Linton touched Matthews's arm. Matthews had been looking around the cabin, pondering how orderly it was, as if it had been cleaned for a purpose, and he happened to see a pencil laid across typed pages. As he moved it aside, curious about an underlined reference to Russian political interference, he felt Linton's hand on his arm.

"He's asking you a question."

"I'm sorry," Matthews said, looking up. "You asked if I knew him?"

"Yes."

"I did." Matthews considered what more to say, what more he could say. "I saw him two days ago. He was upset, but he didn't look depressed to me." If it was a choice between friendship and justice, it had to be justice, but he wasn't asked to make that choice. "Angry? Unhappy? Yes. But he wasn't a man who was a risk to himself, not from what I saw or the man I knew."

"You don't know what's in a man's mind. He fits a suicide's profile—middle-aged professional white man and a heavy drinker."

Matthews hung back in the sloop's cabin when Linton followed Gonzalez up the stairs, and when he emerged on deck, he lingered while the other two stepped onto the dock. Matthews wasn't looking for anything in particular, but he didn't believe Gonzalez's assertion that Wallace had taken his own life. As he got ready to leave the sloop, he puzzled over the problem of Wallace. He was certain it wasn't suicide, but he had no intention of offering his proof. What man takes off his shoes, carefully aligns them, and then blows his head off? He wouldn't be believed and his protest would be put down to resentment at his wife's rumored infidelity. He had a better way of handling the matter, without a dramatic unveiling.

Matthews slipped under the police tape and approached a local police officer who had been kept away from the crime scene by the FBI. He wore a holstered pistol high on his hip and wiped his brow with a handkerchief. He motioned toward the FBI with the disdain of an officer whose authority had been usurped.

"This is your jurisdiction?" Matthews asked.

"It was."

"Alex Matthews," he said, offering his hand. "I didn't catch your name."

"I didn't give it."

Matthews pulled his hand back. "Did you find the boat?"

"We did. A lot of thanks we got for that."

"Did you look inside?"

"Until the Feds took over. No one tells me anything, so I don't offer."

"He worked for the CIA," Matthews said. He saw surprise on the officer's face and mild gratitude. "Call me if you hear something." He wrote his phone number on the back of a restaurant receipt.

"Why would I do that?"

"Maybe I can help you."

"You can help me by not asking questions I can't answer."

Matthews presented the receipt with two hands—smiling. "Call me if you want to know why you're being excluded. Call me if you find something and you want to know what it means. Call me for any reason." It was the old trick from when he'd recruited assets, offering help hoping to get information in return. Matthews smiled at the burly officer. "And you are?"

"Chief Whittle."

23
The Body

Matthews was at home with Anna, eating an early breakfast. David had thrown his backpack over his shoulder and headed out the kitchen door, late for school.

"Your dish," Matthews called out. "In the sink."

David paused, returned with a sullen expression, and dropped the bowl in the sink with a loud clatter. "Anything else before I miss the bus?"

When the screen door slammed shut on his way out, Anna put her hand on Matthews's arm. "That was uncalled for."

"Does he do that when I'm gone?"

She fixed her eyes on him. "He has one set of rules while you're gone and a different set when you're here that you feel compelled to enforce."

"Does he treat you that way too?"

"He's a teenager. You're not here as much as you should be. It's hard on him."

Matthews's phone chimed and he put up his finger to pause her question. "It's about Wallace," he said.

Anna stood abruptly. "I'm late. I'll see you tonight."

Matthews was put on hold by a woman who described herself as the assistant to Chief Whittle. "He'll be just a minute. He's finishing another call. We aren't usually this busy. We're a little town, but then something happens and, well, you know, we get busy."

Matthews looked out the kitchen window and watched Anna in the driveway. She backed her silver BMW out of the driveway, made a quick turn onto the state road, and drove off. He felt the scolding tone of her goodbye.

"I have Chief Whittle for you."

Matthews heard shouting in the background and then he heard Whittle yell at his assistant that he was on the phone, and he'd deal with the FBI when he was off.

"Alex?"

They exchanged a few pleasantries, but then Chief Whittle got to the point of the call. "You knew him. Better you than his wife. I'm not sure she could handle it, given the condition of the body. I need it identified."

Before going to his car, he considered whether the attempt on his life made the house vulnerable. Matthews confirmed that his phone received video images from the home security system's three cameras.

❖

Matthews glanced at the two FBI agents who stood by an unmarked sedan parked a short distance from the hospital's rear emergency entrance. They milled in a small group, frustrated at being excluded. The agent in charge yelled into his cell phone, pacing impatiently.

Chief Whittle led Matthews through the entrance, nodding at the FBI agent. "He's not happy that I'm keeping him out. They might have jurisdiction with a congressman caught in *flagrante delicto*, but murder is a local matter. They'll find a way to intervene, given who I believe the deceased is, but I will keep them out as long as I can."

Chief Whittle led Matthews into the morgue. The heavy-duty stainless-steel rolling cart stood in the middle of the brightly lit room. Formaldehyde and bleach tickled his nose and the refrigerated air cooled the sweat on his neck. A rusted drain sat in the concrete floor and a stainless-steel cabinet of body trays occupied one wall.

Matthews followed Chief Whittle to the green body bag on the cart. A mortuary assistant dressed in a sport jacket over a cardigan sweater responded to Chief Whittle's command and zipped the bag open with a gloved hand, stopping halfway.

He warned Matthews, "A floater usually doesn't resemble the person you knew. Keep that in mind. It was underwater three or four days and crabs did a job on it."

The article "it" implied a changed state and Matthews prepared himself.

Chief Whittle added, "A sailor called it in and I sent our cutter. We hauled it in with a wire basket. We haven't had any other missing persons reports, so I assume it's your friend. He's wearing a sock on his right foot that matches the left one we found on the boat."

Chief Whittle nodded at the assistant, who opened the zipper further and pulled aside the heavy plastic to reveal the head.

Matthews resisted the urge to look away.

"Bodies don't do well in warm water," the assistant said. "They're defenseless against crabs and decomposition. You can see that there is no skin color. Crabs worked on it at the bottom of the cove until decomposition set in and created the gases that floated it to the surface. It took several days because there was a five-pound dive belt on his waist."

Matthews looked hard. He nodded. "It's him."

"Look at the left side of his head, just behind the ear. There is a small wound."

Chief Whittle had the assistant use cotton gauze to remove oozing brain matter from the area.

"It's a bullet hole."

Matthews looked briefly at the entry wound and his eyes returned to the face, where he saw a grotesque resemblance to Wallace. The colorless skin had begun to slough off and there was only a vague likeness to the man he'd known. The body was a physical remnant of the spirit that lived in Matthews's memory.

"You're sure it's him?"

"His front tooth is capped. He chipped it in Iraq."

"DNA testing will confirm it's him, but I have what I need for now. Keep this to yourself. It's my investigation until this is a positive identification, then the Feds take over. I don't mind making the agents outside stew while I gather evidence."

Chief Whittle took Matthews aside, leaving the assistant to deal with the body. "Was he right-handed?"

Matthews considered the question. "He threw stones with his right arm."

Chief Whittle rubbed his chin hard. "Accident? Suicide? Murder? Those are my choices. We can rule out accident. How would a right-handed gun owner accidentally discharge a bullet into the back of his head behind his left ear?

"I'm skeptical of suicide. It would be the act of a contortionist to stand at the edge of the boat and put his gun behind his left ear, so when he fired, it dropped to the deck and he fell overboard. That's what the FBI would have me believe."

Chief Whittle added, "Does a suicide wear a five-pound weight belt?" He looked at Matthews with the satisfaction of a mathematician who'd solved a complex proof.

"Murder is the logical explanation. Logic guides me in my police work and here it also agrees with my instincts. The FBI doesn't want to consider it, or they've considered it but don't want to pursue it. Suicide might be the answer they're looking for, if they have to explain his death to the public. Suicide can close down an inquiry. Murder opens it up." Whittle considered Matthews grimly. "What did he do for the CIA?"

"I no longer work there, so I can't say what he's been doing, but he was in operations. You'll have to talk to the agency."

"Take a guess."

Matthews hesitated. "I don't know. I wish I did."

As he stood there, brooding on the old world of their acquaintance, he thought of Wallace's surprise in Fallujah, realizing that he had not died. Matthews didn't understand the look on his face until later, and he wondered if Wallace's look was the vague disappointment of a man who hadn't been allowed to die a hero's death.

"Can I look in the sailboat again?"

❖

The *Red Queen* was by itself at the end of the pier, away from other boats. The crowds of curious bystanders were gone and the FBI presence had been reduced to one agent who sat in an unmarked black sedan and his partner, a young woman, who was stationed at the pier's entrance, keeping locals from getting close. Rumors circulated about the sailboat and a small circus had gathered hoping to get a view of what had become a local sensation: "the spy boat."

Matthews heard the words from a bystander as he ducked under the police tape, held up by the agent.

"They don't talk to me," Chief Whittle said, following Matthews onto the pier. "You'd think they were investigating the Russians across the bay."

Matthews stepped onto the sloop.

"What are you looking for?"

"I'm not sure." Matthews answered honestly. He didn't know what he was looking for, but he hoped he would discover something that would answer his questions.

There was a beer can in the well of the wheel that Matthews poked with his pen. Had Wallace hidden it? Was it left over from the cruise to toss flowers in the bay? Had someone planted it?

The cabin was untouched from his last visit, but then he saw that the papers he'd seen were gone. Nothing else was removed. He stood at one end by the stairs and let his eyes drift across the cabin. He heard voices from a sailboat leaving the marina. Drinkers going out for a day cruise on a glorious day. "There it is," a woman yelled. "The *Red Queen*."

Matthews sat in the cabin. He tried to imagine what had happened. Wallace had not been depressed when they met at the clinic, nor had he been worried, beyond the usual concerns for his career and marriage. He remembered seeing an angry man exhausted by the unfair treatment from men he didn't respect.

His eyes moved across the cabin's orderliness—clothes folded, a glass still sprouting a straw, cabinet doors closed, no evidence of violence. Then he saw the ashtray with several cigarette butts. Wallace satisfied his need to smoke on the sloop away from his wife.

Matthews lifted the ashtray. Three butts, one with red lipstick. He placed it in an envelope that he took from a cabinet, flicking it in with the end of his pen, avoiding touching it. He slipped the envelope into his pocket. Inside a wastebasket, he found a crumpled tissue. He lifted it with his pen, sniffing it for scent, and then dropped it back into the basket.

24

Memorial

Chesapeake Bay stretched before the marina's patio like an ancient waterway disappearing between distant shores. Midday heat had brought oppressive humidity and, with it, severe thunderstorms that came suddenly and passed quickly. The sky was clear now. Dusk was a seam of brilliant orange on the horizon below a swatch of cobalt blue and the air had cooled with the promise of one season passing to the next.

Matthews stood near the front of the bar queue looking to see who he knew in the grieving crowd, when the woman behind him whispered a rumor about Wallace and pointed to the water. The *Red Queen*'s sails were stowed and it was at rest in the channel. The wind had picked up, causing her to swing slowly on her anchor. The sloop drew the woman's attention away from a clutch of middle-aged sailors in sockless loafers, white trousers, and forest-green sports coats, faces tan from a season of weekend sailing. They stood among women in floppy hats and colorful dresses. Everyone talked in respectful whispers about the man whose memorial service had concluded an hour earlier.

Rose Wallace stood with her husband's colleagues away from the bar, accepting condolences with a brave smile. D'Angelo was there beside Driscoll, whose wife, Jean, was talking to Margaret Linton at the patio's railing. Everywhere drinks were in hand and respectful conversation was punctuated by genteel laughter.

"It's the sort of send-off Wallace would have wanted," Linton said. The two men waited while the bartender mixed their drinks. "All his old enemies honoring him."

Matthews ignored the sarcasm. "He understood the job's politics even if he couldn't master them." He looked around. "I'm surprised he was buried so quickly."

"Rose let us handle it. It's better to not let these things linger."

The bartender presented Matthews with a chilled long-stem glass. "Gin martini. Three olives. No ice."

Matthews never drank gin martinis, but it was Wallace's preferred cocktail and he had ordered it to honor his friend. The first sip went straight to his head. He'd once been a big drinker, but age and his demanding travel between Moscow and Washington had diminished his tolerance for alcohol.

"Wallace could take four of those and still stand as straight as a fence post and look you in the eye with his speech intact. He liked his water under his boat, not in a glass." Linton raised his scotch and said loud enough for those standing nearby to hear. "To Tom Wallace. Friend. Colleague. Son of a bitch."

The two men moved out of the queue toward the mingling crowd. Matthews recognized a handful of men from the agency, but most were strangers—sailors in casual club attire who lived outside Washington's inbred intelligence community. Wallace's other world beyond the confines of his agency life. Knowing

Wallace, they knew each other, but they were strangers to Linton and Matthews.

"Respectable people," Linton said. "He lived a double life."

Matthews looked for the irony in Linton's comment but heard only vague humor.

"They're all here," Linton said, nodding at D'Angelo, Armstrong, Pierce, and Driscoll, who stood in a circle around Rose Wallace.

Anna, looking pretty in a strapless summer dress that matched the deepening blue of the sunset, held a drink in one hand and she adjusted a lace shawl with the other. The sun was falling and with it came a pleasant coolness.

"He was jealous of you," Linton said. "Wallace always had his eye on Anna, but he honored your friendship, so all I ever got were reports of innocent, work-related meetups. Drinks at BLT Prime. Coffee at Starbucks. Crap like that." He paused. "It's hard to lose one of our own. We have to wait for the FBI to do its work. They don't tell me what they're finding and I don't ask."

Anna had moved next to D'Angelo, who said something that made her laugh. Margaret Linton joined Anna in polite laughter that brought stern glances from quiet groups nearby, and both women lowered their voices.

"Gentlemen."

Matthews heard Driscoll before he saw him, and he stepped back to let the gray-haired senior intelligence officer join. Driscoll wore a dark business suit and starched shirt, and shunning a tie was his only concession to the casual event.

"We got a break with the weather," he said. "What a glorious sunset. The weather is on his side—one thing in his favor." He lifted his beer. "To Tom Wallace. Brilliant mind. Terrible doubles partner."

Matthews raised his glass, thinking: *God, they hate him.*

"I see Rose with Armstrong," Driscoll said. "She's handling this well, as well as anyone could. I'm surprised she brought these people together. I wouldn't have the courage. All the gossip and rumors. She seems to have risen above it. Good for her."

Driscoll looked at Matthews. "I think she appreciated your remarks at the service. I watched her in the front row. She was moved to tears when you told the story of how you worked together in Iraq. You were gracious."

Matthews nodded, acknowledging the compliment. He felt no need to respond, but then he did. "When honoring the dead, it's permissible to lie."

"Your compliments were thinly veiled barbs. Very clever."

Matthews nodded.

"I won't have you deliver my obituary," Linton said, laughing.

Matthews had been careful not to mention Wallace's employer. Their CIA colleagues knew who paid his salary, but the rest of the audience knew only that he was in government service in some vague colorless bureaucracy with an unrememberable name. Matthews remarks had deflected interest in Wallace's work by drawing attention to the mystery. Anyone listening to his light-hearted stories of how Wallace had been mistakenly identified as an agency employee might read the truth into his comments. He also put a lightly irreverent spin on the circumstances of the death, so by the end of his brief remarks, grim faces in the church were laughing in their tears. The spirit of his eulogy carried over to the marina. Complete strangers, who knew Wallace, greeted Matthews familiarly, thinking they knew him too. "Good to see you again." "Remember me? We sailed together." And, "You were funny and you got him just right." Matthews responded politely to the men he'd never met before, "Thank you. Good to see you too." The men then turned to their friends and carried on collegial conversations that avoided the gloom of Wallace's death.

"Does this change things?" Driscoll asked Linton.

"What do you mean?"

"What happens when your chief suspect dies? If it were me, I'd want to know if his death was a guilty man's act of conscience or a deliberate act to silence him."

Driscoll turned to Matthews. "Things are rarely what they seem, but in the seeming we can see."

Matthews raised his glass, remarking wryly, "So it would seem." He listened to Driscoll and Linton carry on a conversation that was a display of veiled conjecture, which made him feel like the outsider being pushed further away from their secrets. Shut out from anything he didn't already know. Matthews listened quietly to the wild speculation about Wallace's habits, his love of guns, and his desire to sail around the world in the *Red Queen* in retirement. Then Driscoll brought the conversation back to Matthews.

"There was excitement at BLT Prime after you left. A Russian was struck by a police van. The FBI identified him as part of GRU's 29155 unit. They're the ones who pricked the Russian defector Skripal in London with a nerve agent. No one knows why he was at the hotel."

Driscoll stepped closer to Matthews, suddenly confronting him. "What's your view? You haven't said a word, Alex."

"My view?" He felt their false candor provoking him to share an honest thought. "Jim would know better than I would. My view is that all this is hurtful to Rose."

"Poor Rose," Linton said.

"Everyone says 'Poor Rose,'" Driscoll said, adding, "She's handling herself well. Greeting guests, being gracious. She doesn't seem weighted down by grief. Tom didn't treat her well."

Mention of Rose directed Matthews's attention across the patio, where Rose begged leave from one conversation and approached Anna. The two tall, dignified women, one brunette, the other blonde, both in conservative dresses, regarded each other.

Matthews watched. They were close enough to hear each other without being heard by people nearby. Anna nodded respectfully when Rose spoke, nervously placing a second hand on her drink, holding it tightly. As Rose went on, Anna leaned back. There was no warmth in their expressions, nothing relaxed about their posture. Consumed by curiosity, Matthews didn't notice that Linton and Driscoll had stepped away and that D'Angelo was standing in front of him, nodding toward Anna and Rose.

"They seem to get along." He looked back at Matthews. "I understand that you were questioned by Linton's kangaroo court."

Probing. Matthews smiled. He saw in D'Angelo's face a nervous man trying not to be concerned. A target taking a measure of what others knew of the suspicions attached to him. D'Angelo was on Linton's list, but he was an unlikely culprit in Matthews's mind; he was too established in the agency and independently wealthy. But Moscow Station was an ongoing target of the opposition and sloppy oversight, careless security, and lax procedures could produce catastrophic failure and D'Angelo would be held accountable.

"I was interviewed early on," Matthews said.

D'Angelo threw back the last of his whiskey. "I told them what I know, which is shit. I was told to give Birch a car. They asked how I'd put an important mission in the hands of a rookie. Not my call. I inherited the kid. They asked the same questions over and over and you know, I'm still being asked questions. They think Moscow Station can run itself."

"Worried?" Matthews saw D'Angelo's eyes darken, a man rattled by the long, hidden process of the inquisition.

"Worried? No. Impatient. You left the agency when the knives came out." He smiled. "None of this looks good on a performance review. You know the place. Once you're under suspicion, it's hard to recover. I've had a good run, but I'll see what I do next. You got out with your reputation intact." He began to sip his drink, but then remembered the glass was empty. "When do you return to Moscow?"

"I'm headed to Rome."

"Not Moscow?"

It was the way D'Angelo said it. Matthews felt gripped by the dark forces of suspicion and even an innocent question excited his paranoia, fear looping back on itself. Reality was becoming a distorted reflection of doubt. He knew that paranoia could take on all the textures of real life, but at times this made it difficult to distinguish between a nervous man's innocent curiosity and the unconscious repetition of a man with an ulterior interest.

Then it happened. A cry. Heads turned. Everywhere the shocked gasps of witnesses to a violent act. A space opened around Anna and Rose. Anna's hand was on her cheek, fingers crimson. Nearby, Rose stood with her hand raised, like a boxer, glaring.

Matthews was at his wife's side with a handkerchief that he applied to her bloody nose and he placed a comforting arm around her shoulder. The shock of violence vanished with the restraint he brought to the moment. He led her away from the crowd, waving off offers of help. They left the patio and then were in his car.

He turned to her. "What happened?"

Anna removed the bloody handkerchief. "She accused me of ruining her marriage. I said I never slept with Tom. She insisted and she said she found cigarettes with my lipstick on the sailboat. I said they weren't mine, but she wasn't satisfied by anything that I said. She'd made up her mind, saying things that were wildly untrue. I lost it. I said something like 'Don't blame me for his hectic adultery; look in the mirror.' Then she slapped me."

Matthews drove home in an agitated state, and in the growing darkness of evening, a deep silence fell between them.

❖

Later that night, Anna slipped into bed naked beside Matthews. His eyes were closed when she lifted the covers, but he opened them when she placed a gentle hand on his shoulder. An invitation, he thought. To talk? To make love? He looked up at her, propped on an elbow, and their eyes met. Her hand played with his tufted chest hair, coaxing, but he removed it.

"What really happened with Rose?"

"Tom never loved her. He didn't keep that a secret. They had a private agreement to be cordial in public, but it was a show. He married her because her father was wealthy and prominent and he was tired of waiting for Jean. Rose wasn't his first choice."

Matthews sat up.

"Jean said she'd divorce Driscoll, but it didn't happen. They stuck it out for the children, and Tom moved on to marry Rose. So there you have it. He never loved Rose. He loved Jean."

Anna stared at Matthews. "Don't look so surprised. You never saw any of this. You were busy at work, or traveling, but I saw it every week. Tom confided in me, and Rose thought he was sleeping with me, but he needed advice, and I had the unfortunate habit of being a good listener—an interpreter of complaints." She crossed her arms. "Being Tom, he would have been happy to fuck me, but that never happened. I was his confidante. Rose saw more in our relationship than was there and became suspicious. It was a ter- rible mistake on my part. Tom and I would have coffee, go for a drink, he'd tell me things, but nothing in our intimate community is ever secret, is it?"

Anna said nothing more. Her eyes drifted away. The longer the silence lingered, the more her confession was an invisible object between them—a formless, tasteless, restless shape that divided them.

For a moment, Matthews thought he'd gotten the whole truth, but he began to think there was more. He looked into her eyes, trying to look into her mind. He saw only indignant anger that she'd been made to speak candidly. Not sure what to say, or even what to believe, he slumped against the bed's headboard.

"Why did you wait to tell me this?"

She tensed but was silent.

"It makes a difference," he said. "This doesn't look good. He's under suspicion and your little 'chats' will come out. You'll have to answer questions."

"It was all innocent."

"He's been accused of treason. Do you know how this looks? Do you know how it looks to me?"

"How?" she snapped. "Tell me. I want to know." Anger erupted suddenly, but no sooner had she spoken harshly than she recovered herself, aware that she'd lost her composure.

"I'm sorry," she said. "I don't mean it that way. I don't want to fight. I don't have the stamina for that." Her expression softened and she leaned toward him. "Of course I should have told you. It was wrong of me to meet him."

She moved closer and took the bed quilt in one hand, creating a canopy over their heads. Her face smoothed contritely into an apology.

"Oh, Alex, we're better than this. It was my fault. I should have told you."

Their faces were dark in the dim light of the sheltering quilt and she brought her face close, lips near his.

"Don't hold this against me. Kiss me."

Her performance weakened his resolve to hold onto his anger, and as he always did when she opened up to him, he was unable to resist her plea. He let her kiss him and he let go of his hard feelings.

"Let's talk in the morning."

Matthews felt bright sunlight on his eyes and it was only when he reached for the other side of the bed that he discovered Anna was gone. He'd slept deeply, forgetting the unfortunate incident, but her absence reminded him.

He dropped his bare feet to the floor and rose slowly, putting his arms through a bathrobe.

"Anna?"

When he got to the bottom of the stairs, he called her name again, and then again, louder, but she wasn't in the living room nor in the kitchen. She'd made coffee and had put out his cup by the carafe where he'd find it, as she usually did when she was the first out of the house—a consideration that had been a part of their life together.

Matthews poured his cup and then saw an envelope on the kitchen table in an obvious spot where he couldn't miss it. He lifted it like an unexpected gift. She had written "Alexander" in her graceful script. She used his full name when she wanted to get his attention, or was upset, or on a formal occasion. She had insisted that the priest use it in their marriage vows, and she'd called him Alexander a few times in bed with mock seriousness.

He carefully undid the envelope's seal, lifting the flap, and removed the note. He recognized the hint of lavender on her stationary: *Don't think badly of me. Some things are hard to explain. I wish the incident with Rose had never happened. I wish we could move away from the pettiness of life in Washington and make a new life for ourselves in the south of France, or Santa Fe, or Brussels, or wherever we can be happy together.*

When he finished reading, he refolded the note and placed it back in the envelope, as if that was where it belonged.

Matthews slid the envelope to the middle of the table where he'd found it. He pondered the words and the mystery of what she meant by "some things." What things? He felt their relationship had settled into an uncomfortable widening distance that left him wondering how they'd gotten there. Their marriage had been strained for a while and he couldn't precisely mark the moment that he'd sensed trouble. His travel was partly to blame, but he also felt the loss of her love.

Matthews stood at the sink and poured himself a glass of water, but his hand shook, and the glass fell into the porcelain sink, shattering. A shard pierced his palm and he quickly grabbed a paper towel to staunch the flow of blood, but his hand brought the whole roll off its holder and sent a stream of towels along the floor. *Shit.* He calmed himself and happened to see his face reflected in the window. He was a little rattled, a little tired, but there was no surprise on his face, and no joy. It was the worst feeling of all—to think of Anna making love to Tom.

25

Metropolitan Club

James Linton sat in a high-backed armchair in front of a large oil portrait of Allen Dulles. Linton's eyes were dark, like Dulles's, his face similarly pale, and he had the same impenetrable expression as the earlier director of central intelligence.

Matthews wasn't surprised by Linton's invitation to continue their marina conversation at the Metropolitan Club. A fastidious man, who patterned his week, habitually drank every Friday after work. Linton came to the Metropolitan Club to meet friends or sources whose company would remain private within the club's quiet rooms.

"You're looking at Dulles," Linton said, nodding at the portrait. He cleaned his glasses with the silk lining of his tie, leaving his red eyes naked and unfocused. "I've heard all the stories: slippers for his gout, his philandering, his dislike of Hoover. He tried to make spying a scientific business with Gottlieb's horrific LSD experiments but, above all, he understood that our job is to protect American interests by any means short of war."

Matthews thought that Linton was nostalgic for the measurable dangers of the Cold War, when the enemy was known and annihilation understood. The war on terror was stateless and the violence seemingly random, like a patrol lost in a dust storm.

Linton was dressed in a black worsted suit, white shirt with starched collar, and a tightly knotted tie, which made his eyes seem large. His English leather shoes were polished, his legs crossed, and his right arm was cocked at the elbow, holding a long-stemmed martini glass. His hair was brushed to the side, giving prominence to his forehead, age spots visible when he leaned forward, careful not to spill his drink.

"There will always be traitors," he said. "If there are secrets, there will be people who betray them. Taylor, Dowd, and Mercer were paid by their Russian connections, and we still don't know what the money bought. Dulles understood human nature, but he thought drugs could be used to rid a mind of free will—a distorted Catholic idea that you could carve sin out of the body, like a cancerous tumor. No one believes that anymore, but there are a few idealists who think that the radical solution to the secrecy problem in democracy is to be fully transparent—open about everything. Ludicrous and naïve. Like the claim you hear," his voice mocked theatrically: "If I had to choose between my country and my friend, I hope I would have the guts to betray my country." He laughed. "Romantic nonsense said by men who've never been in this business and have no clue what we're up against. Which brings me back to Wallace."

Linton lifted his glass. "To Tom Wallace. A nice memorial until you had to leave. Anna handled herself well. She's a professional. Rose was out of order, but she's had a lot to deal with, so it's understandable." He lowered his drink. "Will you join me? Gin martini, three olives."

Matthews gave his order to a waiter who had quietly appeared like a ghost.

"People get killed," Linton said. "It's a fact of the business we're in. I don't like it, but I don't fret over it. I don't lose sleep over Wallace's death. Rose will be taken care of."

Linton waved his hand in the air dismissively. "He's not on my conscience. We're not in the conscience business. The Russians didn't agonize when they pricked Skripal with Novichok."

Linton sipped his drink. "This place was more enjoyable before they admitted women and banned smoking." He paused. "At this hour we can have a private conversation in a public place so anyone who walks by won't say to themselves, 'Ah, there they are, two men from the CIA meeting secretly.' It's open enough here, but still private, and we can confide in each other." He looked at Matthews. "Any further thoughts about Wallace?"

Linton tossed out the question like a fly fisherman casting his lure into calm water.

"He never fit in."

The two men continued to talk casually about Wallace, and the conversation inevitably moved beyond their dead colleague to the agency's problem with the White House. The tone of the conversation turned querulous, opinions thrown out to provoke a response, and then the conversation shifted again to the question of loyalty. Two men trained in the art of obfuscation enjoying what they *weren't* saying. Linton said he favored private solutions to agency embarrassments. He raised the case of James Kronthal, who spared his family the disgrace of his treason by taking his own life.

"Wallace wasn't a good spy, but he was an honorable man. I would like to believe his death was a suicide. He took his life to spare us a scandal."

Linton smiled, but Matthews saw satisfaction on his face.

"Cheers," Linton said. "Dulles was old-school, Princeton, Wall Street, white, Episcopalian. He wouldn't be hired these days. He understood the existential threat posed by the Soviet Union, but that wouldn't qualify him to understand what's going on in Russia now, or in the White House. You do. You've made a fortune betting against the oligarchs."

Linton paused. "You should come back to work for us." He put down his drink and straightened the armchair's faded antimacassar, removing the offending wrinkle.

"Which brings me back to Wallace," he said. "Kronthal and Wallace. Are they the same type of traitor? Similar suicides?"

Matthews ate an olive, avoiding his drink. "You tell me."

"He always thought he was more important than he actually was."

Matthews heard in Linton's opinion the same sentiment that Driscoll had expressed and he wondered whether he was hearing an official line about the dead man—already a story was being written about him to satisfy the public's fascination with a dead spy.

"Why would he do it?"

Linton's eyebrow arched. "I think he did it because he could. Because he resented us and he wanted to get back at us. He was angry. Angry at you." Linton paused. "Frankly, I think he wanted to live out an experience that he could put into one of his novels."

Matthews almost laughed. He skeptically shook his head. "I don't buy that."

"Why did Philby do it?" Linton asked. "It wasn't about money. It was some distorted, noble idea he had of himself. The world changed, but he stuck with his ideology even as it became obsolete—like a steam engine in the gasoline age. And Aldrich Ames. A resentful man who thought he could get away with it. What drives men to betray their country? Who knows? Alex, there are more things in heaven and earth than flower in our imagination."

Linton leaned forward. "Here is what convinces me. *Red Queen*." From the bookshelf, he took a copy of *Through the Looking Glass* and gave it to Matthews. "*Red Queen* is an odd name for a sailboat, but it happens to be a character in Lewis Carroll's little book, along with the White Queen, and another minor character, Brillig, which John Paisley, another spy who died mysteriously on his boat in Chesapeake Bay, named his sloop. Wallace would have known that. Paisley was a complicated man like Wallace. Sometimes smart men get overconfident about their crimes. They make mistakes, leaving obvious clues of their treachery as part of the game. Wallace was echoing Paisley by naming his boat after a character in *Through the Looking Glass*."

Linton sat back with a look of satisfaction. "The Russians would see him as a problem—his drinking, his carelessness, and our suspicions. They murdered him in a way that made it look like a suicide—like Paisley."

"You don't really believe that," Matthews said forcefully. "He was peculiar and resentful, and an adulterer, but I don't believe for a moment that he was a traitor."

Linton leaned forward and spoke with a confidential hush. "Good God, Alex. I don't believe that either." He slumped in his chair and looked directly at Matthews. "I think he knew who the mole was and the Russians knew he knew. My bet is that he wanted to gift wrap the whole story of courtship, recruitment, clandestine meetings, and compromise with a neat bow and hand it over to us. Pats on the back all around and he'd finally have lunch with the DCI, or be invited to play golf with the national security advisor. Redeem himself in our eyes. Instead, he stepped on a land mine." Linton's cheeks puffed and his palms opened wide in a mock explosion.

Linton straightened the armchair's antimacassar again. "Russians in Unit 29155 work in teams. They lost one outside the hotel, but there were others. We've signaled to the Russians that we believe the suicide story. It'll be safer for you when you return to Moscow."

Matthews said nothing.

Linton pulled a black leather roll-on bag from behind his chair and presented it. The top was embossed with two gold letters: A. M.

"You will travel to Moscow under the name Alex Manners. That's the name on your false passport." He presented an envelope with travel documents. "The same initials, but a different name. It's a good mnemonic device. Think Alex M."

Linton unzipped the suitcase and lifted a cloth covering a seam disguised as stitching. "BYRON's new documents are in here. The material is a zinc meshing that blurs X-rays so the documents won't appear on a screen. There is a small danger a customs inspector will be curious, but it is a smaller danger than sending the documents through an embassy pouch. We'd have to inform D'Angelo. He'd alert his team. You'd have to collect the documents from the embassy and avoid surveillance leaving. Four risks versus one."

Matthews confirmed Grigoryev's documents. The internal passport, *Pasport Grazhdanina Rossiyskoy Federatsii*, the transborder passport, a birth certificate card marked with CCCP. The card had worn edges and the strike-throughs of a manual typewriter.

"Alex Manners's documents are in there along with a round-trip ticket. You won't be flying back, but a round-trip ticket is what immigration will expect."

Linton leaned forward. "You will fly to Moscow as Alex Manners, and another man, using the name Alex Matthews, will board a plane at Dulles International Airport at the same hour destined for Rome. He'll be staying at the Russie Hotel with a schedule of meetings with potential limited partners for his new fund. The hotel is booked to Trinity Capital. This is your new cell phone. Your old phone will be in Rome and the calls the other Alex Matthews makes will confirm to the authorities that he is the man Interpol wants."

"When do I leave?"

"Tomorrow evening. Here is an itinerary you can leave at home with all the false information."

26

Leaving Home

The most difficult conversations Matthews had with his son were the ones in which he had to lie about some detail of his secret life. He knew that David saw through the lie, feeding Matthews's guilt, and that was the case that afternoon as he prepared to leave for the airport. Matthews had packed his bag with five days' change of clothes. He didn't know how long he would be gone, but he needed to give the appearance that this was just another weeklong trip. He had ordered a car to arrive before David returned home from school, but when he came downstairs he saw his son standing at the fireplace mantel looking at the itinerary he'd left for Anna.

"Leaving again?"

"A few days. Rome."

"You never go to Rome."

"I'm moving Trinity Capital out of Moscow." Matthews wanted to say as little as possible to avoid giving the impression that he was being untruthful, but he also wanted to be open. The two opposing instincts conflicted and he noticed his son's confusion and his suspicion. He was a sullen teenager who resented Matthews's absences and his dissembling.

"You're home early," Matthews said.

David took a quart of milk from the refrigerator and drank straight from the carton.

"Can we talk?" Matthews asked.

"I have soccer practice. How long is this going to take?"

"Not long."

"What's up?" David sat on the sofa and then shot forward, placing the carton on the coffee table. He looked at his father with a mix of curiosity and impatience.

Matthews felt a desire to say more than he should, and the full scope of the fraught emotions between them made him a victim of his own reluctant reticence.

"I'm dealing with a difficult problem at work, but I want you to know that I love you."

He hadn't rehearsed the words, which came out quickly and unexpectedly, and he saw David's surprise. Love was not a word he used often with his son, but the coming trip, the danger, and their sudden encounter in the living room brought on an impulse to speak.

David sat back, a little confused, a little quiet. "What's in Rome?"

"Business."

"Why not Moscow?"

"Trinity Capital has a problem in Russia." He leaned forward, moving closer, and his voice deepened. Having said the word *love*, he felt a need to go on. "I haven't done everything the right way. I know you've been angry with me. I can see your feelings and some-times I get upset with you. No good comes from being angry with each other. No good comes from me not being understanding."

David nodded, surprised and skeptical. "Is that it?"

Matthews looked down to avoid showing his irritation. "Do you have anything you want to say to me?"

"What?" He drank again from the milk carton, but then set it down. "I'll get a glass. I know you want me to drink from a glass."

"You don't need a glass."

David looked at his father. "We can talk when you get back."

"I'll be gone longer than usual. It might be a long time."

David looked at his father, hearing the vague hint, and he drew a shallow breath. "They're all long."

"This one is dangerous."

"Are you worried?"

"No." He smiled through his lie. Was his lying to convince himself or his son?

"What do you want me to say? Take care of yourself. I'll say it. 'Take care of yourself.'" He looked at his father, voice deepening. "One day maybe you'll tell me what you do so I can understand who you are."

Honking in the driveway interrupted the conversation. It was the car that would take him to the airport. Matthews rose from his chair, glancing around the room to gather some measure of confidence that he would return to the house—wanting to believe it was worth taking the risk. Building a home for his family had been important to him. A safe place to return to. Books on the shelves waiting to be read, snapshots of David as a little boy, framed family photographs of a happier time. The garden beds of flowers, the dock, and the terror he felt leaving.

Father and son stood apart, facing each other, and he met David's eyes. He went to embrace David. He felt relief that his son returned the embrace, but the warm feeling was tempered by the fragile emotion. How had it taken him this long to say he loved his son, and he said it as he was leaving?

He pulled away and saw doubt and bewilderment on David's face.

"We'll talk more when I come back."

"When will you be home?"

"I'm not sure."

At 6:40 P.M. on September 19, a tall middle-aged man with graying hair combed to one side took a seat in the departure lounge at Dulles International Airport. He wore a dark worsted wool suit with a starched white shirt and knotted silk tie, slightly askew. A folded blue pocket square added a splash of color.

He sat alone with a black bag at his side and read the day's *Washington Post*, absorbed in his own thoughts, holding the paper upright to give the impression to anyone who looked that he was taking in the day's news. He crossed his legs, then reversed position, a tiny release of tension.

Across the lounge sat another man reading a different section of the *Post*. He was the same height, with the same graying hair combed to one side, and he wore a similar worsted suit. Anyone who happened to notice the two men would think that they looked remarkably alike. If they happened to glance at their black bags, the onlooker would notice that the embossed initials were the same: A. M.

The difference between the two men was their destination. At 7:10 P.M., the second man rose from his seat when the public address system announced the boarding of Delta Flight 38 to Rome. The first man rose a few minutes later and made his way from the lounge to gate 21, where Air France flight 104 to Moscow was boarding.

PART V

27

FSB Headquarters, Moscow

Colonel Viktor Petrovich Zhukov turned off the old radio behind his desk on the fifth floor of FSB headquarters, cutting off news reports of violent protests near Moscow State University. He walked to his office window and lit the last of his daily ration of Primas and gazed out at the wispy clouds of tear gas that were visible in the distance.

He drew on the cigarette and was glad that he was not responsible for the country's new political repressions. He thought the end of the Soviet Union had brought an end to intolerance, but the pendulum was swinging hard to the right again, crushing dissent. He was content with the job of finding the man inside the FSB who had betrayed Russia. As he considered the shifting political winds and rumors of conflict in the Kremlin, his desk telephone rang.

He answered, thinking it was his wife calling about their seaside vacation in two days.

"Viktor Petrovich?"

He listened to the excited voice of his second-in-command, who delivered the news in a burst of words.

"When did this happen?"

"I heard it from Department K an hour ago. The Italian carabinieri informed Interpol that Alexander Matthews arrived in Rome yesterday. He passed through a security screening without being arrested. It doesn't surprise me given what we know about the Italians, but later two officers took him into custody at the Russie Hotel."

"Shit." The curse slipped from his lips. He had objected to issuing the Red Notice, but his protest was ignored. He'd argued that arresting Matthews hurt his chances of finding the traitor in the FSB, but he had lost the argument. He had come to believe that there was a campaign against Matthews that went to the Kremlin.

He looked at his wall clock with different time zones and confirmed it was an hour earlier in Italy.

"Why would he go to Rome?" he asked. "Can you tell me that?"

"They don't know."

"Where is he now?"

"He was taken to carabinieri headquarters in Via di S. Vitali, booked, and released. Department K directed the carabinieri to find Matthews and hold him."

Colonel Zhukov shook his head. He knew that incompetence was an organizing principle in human affairs. Sometimes it worked in his favor and he saw its advantage in the current situation. He thanked his deputy and moved to the window, staring at nothing. He considered the reasons that a man whose business was in Moscow would travel to Rome. Was this a trick or was it possible Matthews had legitimate business in Italy? There was also the possibility that the carabinieri mistakenly took into custody an innocent man who had the misfortune of sharing his name with an American fugitive.

Colonel Zhukov was unlike his colleagues in most ways. He drank little, limited his smoking to half a dozen cigarettes a day, and rarely cursed—masking his emotions with an un-Russian-like reserve. He considered the news for a moment, letting the timing of Matthews's apprehension in Rome settle in. He understood that a development that was at odds with logic, and at odds with what he expected, required diligent scrutiny. Instinct told him there was a problem.

He returned to the files that he had requested, which provided details on Alexander Matthews during his time as Moscow station chief. He was a meticulous man and the papers were organized accordingly. Transcripts of debriefings of Russian nationals employed in the old American embassy at 21 Tchaikovsky were in the middle tray. They were mostly useful for understanding routines in the embassy, and didn't provide the deeper understanding that he needed. Active surveillance from those years sat in the lower tray, along with photographs of Matthews moving around Moscow. The photographs were flat, they didn't open up, and he could only guess why Matthews was caught buying lingerie in GUM, or who sat with him at dinner in the Metropol Hotel.

The top tray held intelligence reports extracted from US embassy typewriters secretly equipped with high frequency radio transmitters that captured and sent out each key stroke to a KGB listening station. He turned to these documents, which were as close as the KGB got to recording CIA conversations inside the seventh floor of the old American embassy.

He read through the files in the top tray again, looking for a clue from Matthews's old behavior—an unconscious act that betrayed a routine, or a mistake. The answer came to him just before noon.

He dismissed it at first, but he was drawn back to it and intrigued by the possibility. It was too compelling, too clever, too bold to be ignored. A man who knew Moscow as well as Matthews would know how to enter Russia and be invisible as he went about his business.

Colonel Zhukov's diligent approach to counterintelligence had been rewarded with regular promotions and the perks that often went to more highly ranked officers—a dacha outside Moscow, vacations with his wife at the FSB's Black Sea resort, an apartment in the CDSP Building on Bolshoy Tishinsky Lane, and complimentary season tickets to the Bolshoy Opera. Patience, diligence, and dedication to the job had elevated their modest lifestyle.

He called his deputy back, who gave an update on the Italian situation.

"Department K is sending a GRU team to Rome."

"Forget about Rome. Let them waste their time." He spoke sharply into the telephone. "Check if Matthews, or an American matching his description, passed through passport control at Sheremetyevo. Call me when you know something. I will be in the office."

He looked at his uneaten breakfast that his wife had packed. The coffee was cold and the sausage shriveled. His next call was the most difficult of the morning. His wife was not understanding when he said there was an urgent matter at work and he needed to postpone their vacation.

28

Kitay-Gorod District

Matthews stood across the street from the small, rose-colored Orthodox church on Staropanskiy Pereulok. The sad, cracked bell tower he remembered from his time as station chief was repaired, and the stucco façade freshly painted. Moscow's new prosperity had helped refurbish the old church, but with affluence came incivility, and the two taller apartment buildings that shadowed the humble church were spackled with spray-painted graffiti.

He continued along the narrow lane to the end of the block, where he glanced at his watch, saying loudly in Russian, "There's time for a prayer," and then he quickly returned to the church. He'd ended his hour-long surveillance detection route. He opened the heavy iron door and the cool air was a pleasant relief from the late afternoon heat. Dim light from the street revealed the domed space. A single flickering candle before the iconostasis illuminated an icon of Madonna and child. Incense burned somewhere.

So much had changed in Moscow, but the church was the same. An ancient oak cabinet that he'd used for dead drops years before still sat below icons of Saints Cosmas and Damian. The church was safe from casual scrutiny, a largely unvisited place in an increasingly secular city.

Matthews listened, ears tuned to danger, and then he looked at his watch. He was early. He moved to the icon—an old religious artifact for the faithful. He saw the silver frame, the faded oils, and he was drawn to the beautiful image. He placed his fingers on the frame, submitting to the urge to seek the relic's protective power.

"Are you religious now?"

Startled, Matthews turned. He saw Grigoryev step forward from the shadowed wall, his face alive with scorn.

"I didn't hear you come in."

"There was nothing to hear. I saw you enter." Grigoryev nodded at the delicate icon. "Your many sins won't be absolved by touching the icon and offering a shitty little prayer."

"How long were you standing there?"

"I waited to see if the man outside followed you in."

"I wasn't followed."

"You didn't see him. I saw you pass once and return. The man is in a car parked across the street. There are two entrances to the church and I came in the other, behind the sanctuary, through the priest's quarters."

Grigoryev put his hand on Matthews's shoulder. "He wasn't looking for you. Ukrainian mafia use an apartment in the building across the street. He wasn't watching for you, but now he'll make a report that at such and such hour on today's date, he witnessed a foreign-looking man enter the church. He'll have taken your photo that will be stapled to his report and submitted to his department head. We have to hope that it will be lost in the daily volume of surveillance traffic."

Grigoryev looked at Matthews's disguise—an ill-fitting wool suit, neck scarf, and wire-rimmed glasses. "It's not bad. You could pass for a Muscovite, maybe a technicum professor. Except for the shoes. How long have you been in Moscow?"

"Since Tuesday. Different name. I'm staying in a hostel in Arbat."

Grigoryev put his finger on his lips, silencing Matthews. He drew Matthews forward to stand facing the screen in front of the sanctuary.

"Pray with me," he said loudly, and then whispered, "The monk in the back is an old friend. I said I was meeting a widower who needed spiritual help. Stand close. He knows me, but the monks gossip and they talk to the FSB."

Matthews grew still, his eyes lowered as he listened.

"I came yesterday," Grigoryev said softly.

"You forgot the protocol." Matthews knew Grigoryev was unreliable. "One chalk and we meet two days later."

"It's good one of us remembers. I confused the sequence. Two marks two days is easy, but you made it hard—one is for two, two is for one. You always made things complicated."

Grigoryev nudged Matthews and he raised his eyes to a monk in a coarse ankle-length smock who stood quietly in the doorway, watching. Grigoryev ignored him. He pressed his hands together, bowed his head, and prayed in a deep, sonorous voice—a litany of pleas to God. When he was certain the monk had vanished, he turned to Matthews.

"Do you have my documents?"

"Yes."

Grigoryev approached the open door where the monk had stood, and closed it. "Show me."

Matthews removed an envelope from his jacket.

Grigoryev studied the worn paper of the birth certificate and expressed satisfaction at the strike-through indentations. He looked closely for defects in the faded red stamp covering the issuing official's cramped signature. "Good," he said.

Grigoryev flipped the pages of the internal passport, feeling the quality of the paper, and then bent the hologram watermark to confirm how light reflected on the embedded digital seal. He turned it over, inspecting it for a flaw that would excite the interest of a border guard. He turned to the photograph, taken eight years earlier, so the man who glanced at him would see the younger man in the photograph would align with the issue date of the document. He turned to the transborder passport's entry stamps, noting how the ink was faded giving the appearance of age and the paper worn as if repeatedly handled. Stamps had the varied pressure of indifferent agents processing another traveler.

"These will do," Grigoryev said. "They may question me, but they'll believe the documents."

He put the documents in his breast pocket. "We move forward."

"We're not done."

"Your money? It was sent. Check the accounts."

"It's not all there. A quarter was missing when I checked yesterday."

Grigoryev nodded. "I trust you, but I trust you more now that I have my passport. The missing money is in a numbered account. I will transfer it when I'm across the border."

Grigoryev looked at Matthews. "I have my documents. You'll have your money. I have the *kompromat*. What we don't have is time. The liquidation of Trinity Capital's assets and disappearance of the funds has gotten attention."

He paused. "Men in the Kremlin don't like you. The Fourth Service has begun a forensic audit of the bank's accounts. It will point to me. We have a few days, maybe less, to carry out my plan." He smiled. "We take the M1 to Ivangorod and the Estonia border, where my wife's cousin will be waiting on the east side of the Nava River. He'll be two hundred meters south of Friendship Bridge with his boat."

Grigoryev smiled. "Let's have a beer. We'll drink, talk, plan how to get a car."

"There's no time for a drink."

"There's always time for a drink between friends." He looked askance at Matthews. "We both have our worries. You got a Red Notice." Grigoryev put a cocked finger to his head. "I've got a zero."

Grigoryev's face had grim determination, a fugitive familiar with his bleak alternatives. "We are at the point of no return."

The quiet movement of leather sandals on the stone floor drew their attention, and then the wood door cracked open and a young monk appeared, eyes flitting from one man to the other.

"Father, my friend here is a sinner and his grief is deep. He tells me he will leave a generous gift for the church. I've told him that the order's orchard produces superb slivovitz. He asked to taste it. I wonder, Father, in his moment of need, if you could bring a bottle."

The monk brought the brandy and left. Grigoryev drank standing up, using the silver chalice when he found no glass, drinking from his generous pour.

"*Za nashe zdorovye*. To our health, what little is left of it." Grigoryev raised the chalice. "May God forgive two thirsty men in need of a cup."

Grigoryev savored the alcohol. "We'll cross the border together. Two men in a car will attract less attention. When they discover I've left my apartment, border guards will look for one Russian traveling alone."

He patted the documents in his pocket. "I have a new name but my ugly face will be visible to scanners at the airport or at train stations. Crossing overland is the only choice." He poured more brandy into the chalice. "Now, I can tell you the rest of my plan. Tomorrow I will buy a round-trip ticket at Belorussky Station for the overnight train to the south through the Ukraine to Uzhgorod at the Czech border. I will pay with a credit card and the FSB will be alerted, and they'll think I'm traveling by train. I will explain to my boss that I'm taking a train to Montenegro to join my wife. While Border Control police search train compartments at the Ukrainian border, you and I will be in a car crossing Friendship Bridge into Estonia."

Matthews thought the train diversion a terrible idea, but he didn't speak up. First rule of tradecraft: don't argue with the asset. Matthews tasted the brandy.

"Like this," Grigoryev said, taking the chalice, drinking the rest. "I will do my part, bringing the thumb drive. You will do your part."

"What's that?"

"You will find a car." Grigoryev waved off Matthews's surprise. "My car is not possible. When I go missing, they'll look for both my vehicles. Our car can't be stolen or rented. You asked what I haven't thought of. I haven't thought of how we'll get a car." He set down the chalice and looked directly at Matthews. "You'll come up with an idea. A solution appears when the problem is properly framed."

Matthews recognized the blustery optimism of a man who took chances and who enjoyed seeing Matthews become uncomfortable. His coarse language and sarcastic laughter belied an iron purpose. He didn't trust Grigoryev's stories and false confessions, but he trusted the man's desire to escape alive.

29

Truck Stop

At the far end of a small restaurant filled with loud, smoking truck drivers, Matthews recognized Sorkin sitting alone at a rear table. Savory smells wafting from the kitchen mixed with pilsner and somewhere a customer's raucous laughter became a coughing fit. A dog stood by one table, barking his demand for a scrap, and the buxom waitress threw off customers' clutching hands as she passed carrying heaping plates. Upon seeing Sorkin, Matthews made his way across the room, drawing attention.

Sorkin wore a business suit and had a glass of red wine, which he put down when Matthews took the chair opposite. There was no surprise on either man's face, no joy, and no greeting. Two men known to each other meeting among strangers in a restaurant—different social echelons ignoring each other.

"Is Olga coming?"

"On her way. Hungry? The blood sausage is good, if you like that sort of thing."

Matthews declined.

"My aunt owns the place and she will insist that you eat. She remembers that you liked her *tefteli*." Meatballs. He waved over a plump older woman with a colorful apron who arrived with a large plate of grilled meats and potatoes. She set the dish down and vigorously wiped her hands on her apron, encouraging them to eat. She smiled and revealed a gold tooth.

"*Yeshtye, yeshtye.*"

She left when Sorkin served Matthews. "I've offered her money to expand the place, but she refuses. She says she's too old to change and she is happy with her regulars. She is content to cook the same dishes with the same ingredients for the same truck drivers. She has little, but needs little. Happy with her one square meter of life—her one potato."

Sorkin nodded at Matthews. "You're dressed like a *muzhik* from the provinces. What's up? Tell me something that won't surprise me."

"Different clothes, new name. I need to get someone out of Russia."

"Do I know him?"

"Grigoryev."

Sorkin shook his head judgmentally and leaned forward. "You expect me to help your mission of mercy for him?"

A silence settled between them.

"Be careful. You know his tricks, so keep your eyes open." Sorkin vigorously cut his pork chop. "Whatever reason you have to help him must be important. Are you back with the CIA?"

"A small favor."

"Favors are never small if they fail. I thought you'd left spying behind to become a respectable businessman." He lifted his fork to his mouth and held a piece of black bread. "Grigoryev has his talents. He knows how to move money, so I'm sure he's helping. One favor deserves another."

"We're driving across the border. I need a car. No driver, just a car."

Sorkin's eyes narrowed and his lower lip quavered, irritated. "You'll have me arrested and I'll be brought down helping someone I dislike. You don't have another choice?"

"No."

"You're testing our friendship." He put down his fork. He was quiet for a moment, judging Matthews. "You can have my wife's blue Fiat. She'll report it stolen the day after you take it. By the time she makes her report you will be across the border. If you aren't, you're out of luck."

Sorkin looked at Matthews. "Does Anna know what you're doing? Is she aware you're in Moscow with a Red Notice against you, making escape plans in a truck stop?"

"She thinks I'm in Rome."

"You didn't have the courtesy to tell your wife. I'm sure she's crazy with worry. You ruined one marriage staying away from home. Don't repeat your mistake."

Matthews put a fork in his potato, slowly cutting it.

"What's so important you're risking arrest to exfiltrate a worthless son of a bitch like Grigoryev?" Sorkin leaned forward. "You don't owe me an explanation, but I'm curious. Did he agree to move your money?"

"Better that I don't explain."

Sorkin laughed. "I'm a friend, remember? Not some snitch. Go ahead, don't tell me something that might surprise me. It's your specialty."

Matthews lifted his beer, sipping, then slowly centered it on the table. "You asked me to tell you what you don't know." He paused, taking a measure of Sorkin's response. "The CIA believes there is a Russian penetration agent in Langley."

"Only one? They're optimistic." Sorkin smiled. "I said tell me something that I don't already know. I'm surprised we're even having this conversation." His voice deepened and he raised his misshapen finger. "He left me with this."

The mood between them tensed and unspoken rancor found its way into the silence.

"Maybe this is the end of things. I should stop being your lawyer and give up on you before my loyalty brings me down with your misplaced obligations to a shithead. It's a strange thing to see you get involved in a scheme that puts everything you care about at risk. For what? Because they appealed to your sense of duty?" Sorkin shook his head. "Bosses are the same in Langley and Lubyanka. They demand loyalty but reciprocate only when it costs them nothing. You're being used my friend."

Matthews's face reddened. "I don't have the time to argue the subtleties of my predicament. And you? Can I trust you?"

Sorkin put a calming hand on Matthews's arm. "You're not thinking clearly. Too much stress. Anxiety. You're becoming paranoid. Or delusional. You need to get your cash out of Russia and take a long vacation."

The proprietress put a plate of greasy fried fish on the table.

"Go ahead," Sorkin said, adding sarcastically, "It might be your last home-cooked meal." He forked a portion onto Matthews's plate. "You can have the car, but don't tell me any more. If I don't know, I can't use it against you. My ignorance protects both of us."

The two old friends ate, talked calmly, drank, shared a few stories, and lamented how principles languished in the face of Russian corruption and hopeful voices were silenced. The conversation was a surreal backdrop to Matthews's troubled thoughts about the danger he was in.

❖

Olga entered like an apparition, moving quietly through the restaurant in her raincoat, hair covered by a scarf. She approached their table, surprised to see glum faces.

"Did you just come from a funeral?" she asked.

"Sit," Sorkin said.

"What's the occasion?" She removed her raincoat, untying her scarf. Her hair fell to her shoulders and she stood before them in a long strapless gown and a pearl necklace. "The Bolshoi started late because of street protests and it ended late. This place is impossible to find."

"That's why we're here." Sorkin poured her a glass of wine.

"I'm sure you'll explain." She looked at Matthews. "Was the article helpful? Is your money safe?"

"The money is safe." He handed her a copy of an interview that she gave to Kommersant, pointing to a passage in which she explained how she tricked Alexander Matthews into disclosing his investment strategy.

She tossed it aside. "You don't like it? Does it surprise you I'm not a selfless journalist with only your problems to think about?" Her brow creased. "I have a career and you are a good story. I helped you, but I'm not Mother Theresa. This was good for me."

"There is a warrant for my arrest."

"Don't blame me. I'm not the one with the smell of scandal." She nodded. "Those thick lenses make you blind and you don't see clearly."

Matthews put the disguise glasses in his pocket. "I see what I need to see."

"He's leaving Moscow," Sorkin said, inserting himself. "But he needs a place to stay for a day or two." He looked at Matthews. "You can't risk a hotel. You registered under a different name, but your photo is in the newspapers."

Matthews reread the article that described him as a foreign swindler who bilked investors and fraudulently moved funds out of Russia. The photo made him look sinister. It was the one taken during the incident at the Hotel Baltschug Kempinski and it was published alongside Olga's smiling photograph.

"Why not? Stay with me," Olga said. "I require guests do two things, be polite and remove their shoes. The only danger is my neighbor, the snitch."

30

Near Tverskaya Square

Olga Luchaninova had not taken a lover since the death of her husband.

Matthews was not a total stranger, and she knew him well enough to find him attractive. He was also someone who would leave Moscow in a few days, and she wouldn't have to answer gossip of neighbors or friends who would want to know who the unfamiliar man was. He was slightly gray, mature, and married, and she didn't think that he would develop a syrupy romantic attachment after one night together. She didn't want anything to complicate her life, but she also missed sleeping with a man. A flame burned inside and waves of desire warmed her. One night, she knew, would quickly recede into memory, but one night with a man was better than none at all.

❖

They stood together on the roof balcony of her apartment building, looking out at the panorama of a darkened city. Low clouds hung over the sprawling metropolis and falling temperatures came with the cool evening breeze.

"Well," she said, drawing her arms around her chest. She stood beside him, feeling the awkward tug of her ambivalence. She saw him look off at Kudrinskaya Square, where mist obscured the top of the tallest tower.

He removed his jacket and gave it to her. "You're trembling."

"It's not from the cold." She met his eyes. "You were going to tell me your story."

"My story?" Nothing he could say would alter the danger he was in, and he had already put his safety in her hands, but his old habit of reticence was a reliable protection of unseen problems. *Where to start?* he thought. "You want to know why I'm in Moscow?"

"I want to know what you started to tell me the other night. We were standing here and you wanted to speak, but you didn't. Maybe it's why you're in Moscow. Maybe it's something personal." She finished her wine and poured more for both of them. "*In vino veritas.*"

Matthews drank his wine and leaned on the railing, looking off into the gloomy night, and considered her request. He spoke quietly, almost confessionally, and his doubts relaxed with a conscious act of forbearance against the urge to keep things to himself.

"It's complicated," he said.

Olga waited for him to go on, but when he didn't, she laughed. "That's it. That's your story, 'It's complicated'? Maybe you are duller than I imagined, but I don't think so." She sipped her wine and her voice lowered derisively. "Men." She continued to speak almost as if talking to herself, giving voice to troubled thoughts.

"There is more to my husband than I told you. The foreign press considered him a dissident celebrity and they gave him a public life that I didn't share. He also had another woman. When I learned about her, I was angry, but I also knew what kind of man he was. Vain, funny, a man with appetites. He had his life with me and another life with her, but when he was gone, she got nothing but her grief and I became the curator of his legacy. Living with his memory and the popular idea of who he was, and the private man I knew, has been lonely."

She looked at Matthews. "You are the first person I've told."

He went to speak, but she put her finger to his lips. "It's better not to say something you might regret."

"I've never met a woman like you."

She looked at him askance. "Introduce yourself to more people. You'll find me quite ordinary. I succumbed to the sorcery of my husband's affection."

Olga was pensive for a moment and looked at the red star above the Kremlin, partly hidden by the mist. "We're all different, but we're all alike. We enjoy the same wine, the same jealousies, take pleasure in talking, enjoy each other's company on a September evening looking out into the night, and we both want to escape this city—this life." Her arm swept across the panorama and came to rest gently over her heart.

She looked at Matthews and pointed at nearby apartment buildings. "Inside all the homes, what are there? Families or lovers, an old woman without friends. People arguing or laughing at comedy shows. They all have their problems—all have their unhappiness. Their loneliness. Their misery. Where it doesn't exist, they create it." She laughed. "In place of happy endings, we have Chekhov." Sarcasm rolled easily off her tongue.

A dark cloud moved overhead and the first drops of rain were followed by distant thunder. Suddenly, a cloudburst and then hail and dark driving rain. She ran hunched over to the bulkhead and threw herself inside the safety of the stairs, hair dripping wet, clothes soaked. He followed and the two of them stood close, panting. A moment of silence between them and then gasps of surprise.

"Look at you." She laughed. "A wet dog."

"You too. We left our drinks."

"This is Russia. There's always another bottle." She took his hand. "Come. It's warmer downstairs."

Olga let him pass into the apartment first, and quietly double locked the door, aware that her downstairs neighbor might be listening. They stood together by the breakfront for a moment, wet and hesitating.

"There is a towel in the bathroom to dry yourself. For breakfast, there is fruit on the table and water in the kettle if you get up before me." Her eyes lingered on him, searching his face. She turned to leave, but suddenly faced him. "You are a difficult man."

Her comment surprised him, and not knowing how to respond, he said nothing, but then he felt an urge to speak. "My wife has told me."

"Your wife isn't here. I am."

Matthews looked at her cautiously.

Somewhere outside, a piano struck up the melancholy notes of a nocturne and the pleasant music drifted in through the open window with a hint of fall's fragrances. The sensation of smells and the soft notes of the piano cast a momentary spell. Matthews took too long to react to Olga's proposal and she stepped away, but before doing so, she kissed him.

"Good night."

Matthews stood in the bathroom brushing his teeth and looked at himself in the mirror. He was as vain as any man, but he rarely studied himself in the mirror. Now he did. He had several days' growth of beard, his eyes were tired, and a pale, ghostlike face looked back. Age lines had formed on his face from years of stress. He wasn't a young man anymore. How had time passed so quickly?

He had never dyed his hair, as friends who resented getting older had. He kept fit by jogging and the exercise helped fight against the consequences of too many business dinners and too little sleep.

Standing there, looking at himself, he was flattered that Olga found him attractive. He pinched his abdomen, a crude measure of his weight gain, and mentally compared himself to the young man he'd been. Wallace came to mind, and with him, he thought of Anna. He wondered about their first adulterous night together. What had she seen in Wallace? He had no proof of her infidelity, but her denials were too angry and abrupt. Protesting too much.

It was a talent of Matthews to imagine things with a photographer's eye, and he'd put it to good use running assets in Moscow, but it became a curse when it came to imagining his wife's betrayal. The images came to him randomly, out of nowhere, as he crossed the street, or sat in a café eating lunch. Anna making love to Wallace. Hugging him, kissing his lips, wrapping her legs around his torso, as she had done so eagerly with Matthews in their first years of marriage. He saw her doing all the things they had done together. The images tormented him.

He hadn't called Anna, breaking their routine of speaking every night when he was away on business. He knew she'd ask how Rome was, and he didn't have the will to lie. Her denials echoed in his memory and they were impeached by his suspicions. The mysterious note she'd left referring to "some things." The gossip, her unexplained absences. He knew that their marriage was failing, but he didn't understand why.

He stood in front of the mirror for three minutes, but it seemed longer because of his thoughts. The whole of the sad state of his life weighed on him. Linton came to mind, brooding in front of his wall chart; he thought of Grigoryev and the absurd risks he was taking. He saw Wallace at the clinic skipping a rock on the water and being his rakish, funny self, and then, in his mind's eye, he was a grotesque corpse.

He never disliked him. Then he considered the odd phrasing, a sort of cover for ambiguous feelings. He didn't like him, but he didn't dislike him. He said this out loud to himself in the mirror—his reflection the only witness. The face that looked back at him was pale and familiar. He thought of Anna with Wallace, and hot adulterous rage welled up.

He wondered if Olga would consent to sleep with him. She'd been provocative when they'd returned from the roof, but then he remembered all the wine they'd drunk.

Matthews made his way to the narrow bed and pulled the covers over his head. His eyes closed, breathing calmed, and a peacefulness came over him. He wondered what thoughts were going through her mind. Perhaps another time, in a different life.

❖

Dawn's fingers tickled his closed eyes, waking him. Gray sunlight seeped around the edges of the drawn curtains and filled the small room. Temperatures had fallen during the night and the room was chilly, but under the covers he was warm. He turned over thinking that Olga was at his side, but the bed was empty.

Through the window, he heard the sounds of a waking city—rapid footsteps of office workers late to their desks, school children giggling through the soft patter of rain, and off in the distance the jackhammer of a construction crew. It started, then stopped, and then it began again with annoying persistence.

Matthews rolled onto his back, fully awake now. He folded his hands on his chest, fingers interwoven as if in prayer. He hung on to the peace of the night's sleep. He was glad he had not presumed upon Olga's hint that they sleep together. There was something satisfying about holding on to his faithfulness. In the wild dominion of his dreams, he'd seen a virtuous Anna come to his side asking why he doubted her. He was glad he hadn't acted impetuously. One adultery begat another and the journey of betrayal never had a good ending.

Resumption of the jackhammering brought him back to the moment. To what he needed to do. He slipped out of bed.

❖

He found Olga in the kitchen sitting at the table in a yellow silk kimono with butterfly sleeves. She buttered toast and looked at him when he sat opposite.

"It's good you slept alone," she said. "There's coffee, or tea if you prefer."

"Coffee," he said, rising to pour himself a cup.

"I don't know what I was thinking," she said. "The wine was talking."

"You're very attractive," he said.

"You can be honest," she said. "Or you can lie. Either one is fine with me." She pulled the kimono tighter on her pale chest. Her hair was uncombed and fell to her shoulders, which glistened with night sweat. They sat together without speaking. All their talking the night before had used up what they had to say and the morning's sobriety brought with it awkward silence.

Matthews was finishing a breakfast of scrambled eggs and black bread when he heard his cell phone ping with a text, and he saw it was from his son. He'd tried to reach David two days before, and when he didn't, he'd left a voicemail. The text read: *I'm fine. Don't worry. I spent the weekend sailing.*

"Everything okay?" Olga stood over Matthews with a fresh cup of coffee and then sat down across the table. "Do you need to answer? I can leave."

"My son." He shoved his phone in his pocket. "I left him a voicemail. He's fine. Enjoying my absence."

Her teacup clattered on its saucer and the joinery of her chair creaked when she leaned back, her eyes taking him in. "We're done with our eggs. This might be our last meal together."

"I'll help clean up."

"No, no, no. I like sitting with you. Who knows if we'll meet again, or under what circumstances. We can enjoy a moment in each other's company." She sipped her tea. "Do you know that you have a scar on the bridge of your nose?"

They both heard the cry outside in the street. A loud voice calling out urgently. A warning?

Olga moved to the window, pulling the corner of the curtain aside, and peered into the street. He joined her, looking over her shoulder.

Schoolchildren in blue uniforms and heavy backpacks walked in pairs toward the end of the block, enjoying the pleasant experience of having nothing to do but walk to school. One blonde boy of no more than ten years had stopped and shouted back with foolish courage at two policemen in black body armor emblazoned with ФСБ. Two others, across the street, were pressed against a doorway. Men and women on the sidewalk glanced quickly at the FSB but turned away and hustled along on their way to work.

Only the schoolboy yelled out, an insult or a cry of warning, but then he ran off.

"There," Olga said, pointing. Her neighbor huddled with an officer and pointed to Olga's apartment window. Olga turned to Matthews, frightened. "You have to leave."

Matthews gripped her shoulders. "Is there another way out. Across the roof?"

She shook her head, eyes tearing. "We are six stories and the building next door is three. You have to walk out the front door with your bag, just another man late for work."

He shook his head. "No one will mistake me for an ordinary Russian on his way to the office."

Olga disappeared down the hall.

Matthews lifted the corner of the curtain and he counted six FSB officers—two talking to the neighbor and four pressed against buildings along the street. He didn't see more, but he assumed more might be around the street corner, out of sight.

The neighbor talked excitedly, pointing. Matthews nervously pondered the armed men in black tactical uniforms waiting for instructions. It was out of the question to hide in the apartment, and equally dangerous to seek refuge in another apartment. His mind calibrated his bad options and an old, familiar fear settled in.

"Here, wear this."

Olga held up a Soviet captain's military uniform. Olga removed the dry cleaner's protective covering and put the gray wool jacket and trousers to his chest, confirming the fit. A medal was pinned to the chest.

"If you walk confidently, no one will ask questions of an Afghan war veteran wearing the Order of the Red Banner."

Matthews put his arms into the sleeves and worked the jacket's gold buttons through their slits. He shoved one leg and then the other into the coarse wool pants, tightening the belt. It was a snug fit, but comfortable enough. Her husband's old uniform bunched on his shoulders and Olga straightened the fabric, smoothing the lines.

She stepped back. "He was younger than you but your size, and he liked to eat. It fits well enough."

He placed the high-crown hat on his head, adjusting it to hide his hair.

"If you're lucky enough to get away you can keep it." She pushed him toward the apartment door, grabbing a worn leather bag from the front closet, which she pressed into his hand. She opened the door, looking to see if there was anyone. Her voice choked. "Now go. Get away while you can."

Matthews made his way down the wide circular staircase, taking the steps two at a time, glancing over the railing. He had gone two flights when he heard noise below. Three police officers confronted two people on their way out the front door. The woman was pushed aside, but her male companion was questioned, papers demanded, and when the abrupt interrogation ended, he was released.

Matthews saw the officers ascend the staircase. He couldn't retreat, so he proceeded down with grim determination. Overthinking the danger risked making him nervous or stiff, so he moved like a man who belonged where he was.

The officers arrived at the third floor just as Matthews entered the landing. They had climbed quickly, huffing out of breath, and blocked Matthews. There was a moment of hesitation when the young policemen saw the uniform and war medal. Matthews took advantage of their hesitation, brusquely using his hand to open a way past, and continued down the stairwell. He listened for a command to stop, but none came, and then a few steps further, he heard them continue upstairs.

Matthews paused at the building's front door before stepping into the damp morning air, rubbing his hands together for warmth, cursing loudly, so he'd be heard, "*Dissidenty.*"

Gray clouds had moved in and with them a light drizzle fell on the street. Fall was in the air and temperatures had dropped overnight.

He joined a small group of Soviet veterans in old military uniforms moving along the street, giving anyone who cared to look the impression that he was among friends. He didn't look left or right, and he didn't glance back. No innocent man making his way to a parade would be wary of being recognized. When he reached the end of the block, he separated from the others and became just another proud veteran minding his own business, moving through a city where people kept to themselves.

31

FSB Headquarters

At the same hour, across Moscow, a black Mercedes approached the headquarters of the Federal Security Service on Lubyanka Square. Pedestrians holding umbrellas passed in front of the entrance's hammer and sickle carved in stone, and a few glanced at the Mercedes, hoping to catch a glimpse of the arriving official.

Colonel Zhukov watched the driver open the rear door, and then he approached the passenger, nodding slightly, extending his hand.

"Colonel Zhukov," he said, introducing himself. "Welcome."

She shook his hand once and gazed up at the Neo-Baroque façade and its distinctive yellow color, deepened by the gray, misty morning. She wore a black pantsuit that had held its crease on the long flight from London, where she had stopped over before continuing to Moscow with a different passport. Her eyes were alert, her smile brisk and professional.

"Anna Kuschenko." She nodded at the facade. "It hasn't changed."

"When were you here last?"

"I was never here. There was a risk of being photographed by foreign agents posing as tourists in the square. I know it from pictures."

"We've been waiting for you."

"My flight out of Heathrow was delayed."

Colonel Zhukov presented a black-and-white police photograph. "This is the man arrested in Rome."

"I saw this in London. It's not Alex Matthews. He's here in Moscow."

❖

The windowless operations room was crowded with equipment. Technicians worked diligently, oblivious to tobacco smoke in the stale air. Overhead fluorescent light bleached color from their faces.

Anna stood in front of huge wall monitors and watched a uniformed FSB officer manage video surveillance footage projected onto the screens. Video streams came in from Red Square, entrances to Metro stops near the Hotel Baltschug Kempinski, and several busy street corners in the center of Moscow. Facial recognition technology scanned the crowds for a match to Alexander Matthews, and when a prospect was found, the face was enlarged. This routine had dragged on for several hours.

Behind Anna, two uniformed officers sat at computers that remotely controlled the surveillance cameras. She had been introduced to them, but even those who didn't know her name seemed to know who she was. When she looked, they quickly averted their eyes.

Too much time had gone by, she thought. So much wasted effort. What was the likelihood of finding one man in a city of twelve million people—a man who didn't want to be found. He would know how to avoid video surveillance, but it wasn't her place to criticize. She was surprised to see the computers were a generation older than the equipment in the CIA's secure counterterrorism facility in Virginia.

She moved to a large conference table where a young woman in a blue smock offered refreshments.

"*Shto by vam predlozhit.*"

"Coffee. Thank you."

Anna returned to the technician's station, thinking that it was useless to stare at monitors hoping to find a face in the crowd.

"How about him?" the technician asked, as a blinking red box pulsed on the face of a tall man who crossed a busy street.

"No," she said. "Wrong face. Too young. We've been here four hours. We're wasting our time."

Her voice was loud and irritated and quiet eyes looked up. Colonel Zhukov joined her, nodding politely. He explained they had intelligence that Matthews was in Moscow inside the large yellow circle circumscribing the city's center—and they needed patience. She leaned into him and spoke so that none of the technicians overheard, explaining that Matthews was a pebble in a quarry. It could take weeks, or fail entirely.

"Did you check on the woman I told you about? Olga Luchaninova?"

"We found her apartment. The neighbor thought it might be him, but he wasn't there. We arrested her."

Colonel Zhukov produced a pack of cigarettes and offered her one, which she took and allowed him to light. She drew deeply on the Prima, calming herself, and slowly released smoke from her mouth.

"What about him?" the technician yelled, pointing at a blinking box pulsing on the face of a tall man in a baseball cap leaving a hotel.

She turned to the monitor. "Enlarge it." She leaned forward and her brow knit, curious. "He has a hat like that." The video enlarged but the cap shadowed the man's face. "I can't tell. Zoom in on his wristwatch."

The camera resolved to a close-up of the man's right hand, and the dual-time-zone wristwatch cinched with a leather band.

"It's him," she whispered to herself. Then loudly, "It's him." She turned to Colonel Zhukov. "I gave him that watch. It's a Hermès. It has to be him." Her voice was alive with excitement.

Buzz filled the room and the hours of quiet were replaced with a new energy. The technician un-paused the video, zooming out, and Matthews continued to walk with his back to the camera. Colonel Zhukov was at her side with two other officers.

"Where was that taken?"

"By the Grafskiy Hotel."

The time stamp at the base of the video read 8:59 A.M. and the location was identified by an alphanumeric code.

Fifteen minutes later, a young officer came to Colonel Zhukov. "The hotel clerk says there is no one by that name registered. But there is another American, Alex Manners, who was registered for one night."

Anna returned to the wall of monitors where facial recognition technology processed hours of surveillance footage, speed increasing at the expense of accuracy. Possible matches were highlighted on a map of Moscow, red dots identifying where Matthews might have been. The technician called up images of the suspected sightings, looking at one, then another, dismissing the false positives while reserving a few possible matches for closer scrutiny. Sightings seemed to be random; there was no obvious pattern to his movements, only the confusion of contradictory evidence.

"He can't be here," she said, pointing to Arbatskaya Metro Station, "and a few minutes later here." She pointed to Donskoy Monastery. She turned to Colonel Zhukov. "We're wasting our time."

Anna's eyes narrowed. Fatigued from the long flight and the concentration required to review the hours of footage, her patience had worn thin. She knew of Colonel Zhukov's reputation for careful, deliberate investigations, but his approach was failing.

"He's in Moscow briefly. A few days. A week at most. When he leaves, his Russian asset will slip away. Or maybe he's already gone."

She turned away from the monitors and looked directly at the colonel. Her eyes were fierce but her voice was circumspect. "He left the CIA five years ago, but he hasn't forgotten his tradecraft. He will be doing what you don't expect. You'll waste time searching hotels. He knows that is what you'll do, so he'll avoid them. He'll do the opposite of what you expect. Check seminaries, hostels, the names of his employees, and anyone who might put him up for the night."

Her voice deepened with frustration, but it changed to a pleasant soprano to encourage the technicians. "Where does a prominent American businessman hide in Moscow? Who knew his movements when he was station chief? He is clever, but he is also a man of habit and routine. I *know* him. I know how he thinks."

Her question posed, she waited for an answer, grinding her cigarette in an ashtray, but there was only weary silence. Harsh fluorescent light paled her face and hardened her appearance. Her eyes settled on the men and her brusque confidence commanded their attention. She had trained for this moment and she had no patience for men who made a routine effort. In heels, she stood as tall as Colonel Zhukov and she knew that his career was at stake.

"Well?"

"We will find him," he said. "I'll have the records brought up."

Half an hour later, a technician directed their attention to the wall of monitors now displaying pictures of a younger Alex Matthews walking through a different Moscow—dirtier, older fashions, and fewer cars. In one, he was in front of the old American embassy. Surveillance photos showed him entering through the security barrier wearing a long coat; another telephoto shot showed him through a window in a café; and in another he walked along the Moscow River with a companion.

"That one," Colonel Zhukov said, pointing at a heavyset man in a tailored suit and scarf, wearing a fedora. "That man is a KGB asset who Matthews recruited." Another image appeared on the monitor and a man the same height and build sat beside Matthews in a café. In each, the man's face was turned away. The photos were taken with a telephoto lens from a distance. Different days, different men, different places, but the sense of the settings were similar. Two men meeting clandestinely, their conversation caught on film. In some, the men walked along the Moscow River; in others, they sat next to each other on a crowded bus.

"Who are they?" she asked.

Colonel Zhukov explained that the men were part of Matthews's network and all had been arrested and executed.

She looked at the faces projected on the monitors—middle-aged men, dull expressions, heavy drinkers. "What about BYRON?" She saw confusion on the men's faces. "That's the cryptonym the CIA gave the man we're looking for." She waved her hand across the wall of monitors. "He must be one of these men."

She used a laser pointer to highlight one man, his face in profile and partly hidden by a hat pulled down on his forehead. The photographer had captured him just as he looked away, face obscured, but the photo captured the moment when the two men exchanged a document. The brief handoff in a brush pass was caught and then they were gone.

"We think that's him," Colonel Zhukov said. "The others have been caught. It's our only photo of him and you can't see his face." He turned to Anna. "It's unfortunate. We can plan for everything, but we can't plan for him glancing at a young woman passing by."

Colonel Zhukov paced the room, hands behind his back, pondering. He stopped in front of her. "Dormant for ten years. Why would he come out now? Why end his hibernation?"

"The CIA is eager to get him out. That's all I know."

Colonel Zhukov tapped the laser pointer on his palm. "We know that he is a senior counterintelligence officer." He used the pointer to highlight an artist's sketch on a monitor. "This is what we have." The sketch showed a middle-aged man with receding hair, narrow, acne-scarred face, bushy eyebrows, and an aquiline nose.

"This is how he was described by the KGB officer who recruited Matthews. He claims to have seen the asset BYRON close up once. He gave these features to our sketch artist. He recruited Matthews but then dropped him when he discovered that Matthews was using their meetings to pass along *dezinformatsiya*. The game was called off. But he knew Matthews had other assets and his information helped us arrest the traitors you see on the monitors."

Colonel Zhukov met her eyes. "I asked him to join us. He is outside." He waved at the guard by the door.

Lieutenant Colonel Dmitry Grigoryev was led into the room.

He walked confidently and had a gruff expression. His big frame filled out his fawn-colored uniform, displaying a medal on his chest, his rank indicated by one gold star set on the green epaulet. He moved with the slight limp from an old injury, but he disguised the handicap with a slow, determined step.

"You made me wait. But I'm here." He nodded at Colonel Zhukov and the woman at his side. The sketch projected on the wall monitor caught his attention. "So, you're still looking for the traitor." Grigoryev studied the face that he'd described to the sketch artists—narrow face, acne, prominent eyes, large ears—so deliberately unlike himself.

He sat at the conference table, settling in like a bull lowering himself, and he nodded respectfully at the two people across the table, and then glanced around the room. "With all this technology, you'll catch the bastard soon enough."

He turned away from Matthews's photographs on the monitors. "What makes you think he's in Moscow?"

"That's him two days ago," Colonel Zhukov said, pointing to the man leaving the hotel.

"He'll make a mistake," Grigoryev said. "He is confident, but he won't see how his confidence can be used against him. What I know of him might help you, but it might not. I knew the side of him that he let me see, but it may not be the side that he is using."

Grigoryev sat back, patient smile on his face. He saw Colonel Zhukov's implacable expression. At that moment, he understood the predicament he was in. There was peril if he cooperated and there was danger if he didn't. But the consequences of refusing to help were immediate and the risks of being helpful were further away.

"I saw him a couple of weeks ago when he arrived in Moscow. I picked him up at the airport. The next day he said he needed help to get money out of Russia. I gave him some ideas. If he has returned to Moscow, he hasn't wanted me to know. And why would he?"

He looked at Anna's uniform and rank. "I haven't seen you before. Are you new?"

She didn't answer.

Grigoryev offered an observation. "If he is in Moscow, he'll use what he knows about the city to hide." He pointed at the hotel lobby surveillance video. "He knows where to look for cameras. You won't catch him walking into a hotel."

Anna stood and leaned across the table at Grigoryev. "Alex never mentioned you."

"Who are you?"

"Directorate S."

He paused, taking her in, judging the attractive woman staring at him. "His wife, then."

She didn't respond.

Grigoryev considered her. "He was married to a different woman when I knew him."

"If you were Alex, knowing what you know about him, where would you hide?"

"If I were Alex?" He laughed. "You know him better than I do, but hypothetically, I'd hide in plain sight. Somewhere he's stayed many times so the doorman or his neighbors won't ask questions. They'd know him as the American Matthews even if he's using an alias."

"We're checking passport photos of Americans who've arrived at Sheremetyevo in the past week," Colonel Zhukov said. "We'll find the name he entered under."

"You'll find him," Grigoryev said. "He doesn't think much of us. His overconfidence will force an error."

32

Kitay-Gorod District

Matthews entered the small Russian Orthodox church, closing the iron door behind him. He leaned against the door, listening for footsteps outside, but he heard none, confirming that the FSB officer texting in his parked car hadn't taken an interest in his arrival. His eyes adjusted to the dim light from the nave's flickering candles and he took in the familiar place—cool air, a mouse scurrying along the wall where someone had pissed.

Grigoryev stepped from behind a pilar by the iconostasis. He held a gym bag and wore a blue track suit with a zippered jacket, orange running shoes, and an angry expression.

"I ask to see you urgently, you arrive late, and now you're surprised to see me."

"I'm here."

"An hour late." Grigoryev cursed. "You're pretty casual for a man with half the FSB looking for him. Three hash marks. You forgot your own signal?"

"Protests against the military parade closed streets. I took a longer route."

"Look at you." Grigoryev nodded at the Soviet uniform. "You could be arrested if you're caught wearing that medal. A war hero impersonator." He opened his gym bag, pushing aside a pistol, and handed Matthews a second track suit. "Wear this." He waved off Matthews's look of concern. "Don't worry. We won't need it. When we leave here, we'll be two old friends enjoying our retirement with an afternoon jog."

Grigoryev offered his judgment as Matthews changed. "You never stop surprising me." He shut the arched wood door that led to the sanctuary. "I told the priest you left for Kiev so it wouldn't be good if he caught me in a lie. Have you got a car?"

"We go tomorrow," Matthews said.

"By tomorrow I will be in jail. There has been a development."

"Are you backing out?"

He raised his gym bag. "Does this look like I'm backing out? I left my apartment two hours ago with clothes and my documents. Everything else I left behind, the Meissen, my cell phone, uniforms, all our photos and keepsakes, my entire Moscow life closed up in the apartment. As I left, I bumped into my neighbor and I told him I was going to the gym. My car is parked where I always leave it—the spot is good for two days. Everything the same as always. Except I'm not returning."

He moved close to Matthews. "There is no tomorrow. It's today—or never. Let's walk."

Matthews let Grigoryev leave the church first and he glanced at the FSB officer, who was still on his phone. Schoolboys kicked a soccer ball in the street, but they dispersed when a garbage truck arrived, picking up the overflowing refuse. At the far end of the block, Matthews turned to Grigoryev. "What happened?"

"They know you're in Moscow." He looked hard at Matthews. "Zhukov called me to a meeting this morning to discuss you. Looking for you, wanting to catch me. Son of a bitch."

Grigoryev's hand trembled and his face lost color. "Zhukov's meeting was a test. I entered the room with photos of your dead poets projected on monitors. There was a photo of me, but my head was turned. They also had a shitty artist's sketch of me. There is a team organized to find you and they kept grilling me about BYRON. They used the name BYRON, so I know they got it from the CIA. The FSB doesn't call me BYRON. They have their own code name."

Grigoryev had begun to sweat profusely and his voice lowered. "I had to think quickly, trying to imagine what they knew. It might have been funny if it hadn't been frightening. Me looking at an artist sketch of myself while they cursed the photographs. One day I might laugh."

Grigoryev looked at Matthews. "There was a woman there from America. Directorate S. She didn't give her name."

Matthews had been walking quickly on the narrow sidewalk, police cars speeding past toward the protests. He took Grigoryev's arm, spinning him around.

"She knew all about you. Tall, blonde, attractive. American accent. Very determined."

Grigoryev threw off Matthews's arm. "Keep walking. We don't want to draw attention. I left the meeting, drew the chalk marks, and went home to pack. Two black Volgas were parked across the street. It's not unusual to see one, but never two. I found another listening device in the bedroom, which they must have planted while I was in the meeting."

Matthews contemplated what he heard, ignoring the rest of what Grigoryev said. Matthews's mind was a tangle of wild thoughts and he stopped on the sidewalk, heart beating in his chest. He breathed deeply and pondered the possibility.

"You don't look good," Grigoryev said. He wiped his brow, beaded with sweat from the afternoon heat. CS gas drifted down the street from police action somewhere in the distance.

"Let's go." Grigoryev pulled Matthews along, indifferent to his silence. "After I left the meeting, I thought how they judged my mood. Zhukov was suspicious, but he wasn't certain, so he watched me closely. Like a zoo animal."

Matthews looked behind at the sound of a siren.

"It's not for us. I got on the Metro at Tverskaya, changed at the next stop, hopping off on the next train. But I jumped off as the doors were closing and my surveillant was stuck on the train."

He turned to Matthews. "We have no time. We leave tonight so we reach Friendship Bridge by morning. From Moscow we drive to St. Petersburg and take the M1 to the border. My wife's cousin will pick us up in his boat that will be anchored two hundred meters south of the bridge. If we're lucky, we'll be out of Russia in twelve hours."

"I arranged a car for tomorrow."

"I can't go back to my apartment." He handed Matthews an old flip phone. "Call whoever you need to call. Tell them we're coming for the car now."

33

Near Tverskaya Square

D usk's light glowed orange on the fading day. Matthews passed
along the crowded sidewalk resenting the stares of ordinary
people going off to gulp a beer, devour dinner, or enter the cinema,
all with their insignificant and silly dreams, unaware of the danger
he was in. They trespassed on his thoughts and, in the moment, he
wished that he could trade places with them.

Matthews followed Grigoryev through a narrow alley to avoid
protestors gathering on a square, and he had the distinct impression
that Grigoryev had lost his way to Sorkin's apartment. An eerie
unease was everywhere—people moving quickly, voices speaking
urgently, and a rising cloud of acrid smoke. Rats scurried through
the alley's garbage and then Matthews followed Grigoryev onto
a tree-lined street with hints of CS gas in the air. Cars, motor
bikes, and belching trucks were knotted together in a traffic jam.
Sounds of throbbing engines mixed with exasperated drivers
who shouted out their windows at the invisible barrier impeding

their movement. In the distance, whistles blew. Further off, there was the growing din of an approaching crowd—the drumbeat of marching feet and a loud voice on a megaphone.

Matthews slammed against the wall, hiding from crouched riot police moving through the stalled traffic. He breathed hard and saw Grigoryev looking toward the approaching sound. The first protestors who appeared on the wide boulevard carried large banners and behind them came a raucous rabble. Students sang, older children marched beside parents, and a line of young women walked with arms interlocked, and above it all, an energetic man stood on a van yelling into a megaphone.

"Shame Tsar Putin!" And the crowd repeated the refrain, "*Putin khaiyla, la-la, la-la, la-la.*" The man with the bullhorn shouted, "Putin is a thief," and the crowd repeated, "*Putin khaiuyla, la-la, la-la, la-la.*" The call and response continued as the disorderly crowd moved slowly in front of the stalled cars. Fists were raised, placards waved back and forth, and the restive mass of protesters moved with a festive air.

Suddenly, somewhere in the rear of the crowd, the shock bang of an explosive device, followed in quick succession by two more explosions. The crowd heaved and swayed, as if hurricane-force winds had been unleashed, and frightened cries shouted a warning, "There! There!"

Interior Ministry troops with gas masks, shields, and black body armor pressed forward from side streets, squeezing protestors and cutting off escape routes. Ahead, a phalanx of helmeted troops wielding hard rubber truncheons moved forward in lockstep, shields raised. The line moved forward against the frightened crowd. Protesters scattered into the few side alleys, but those who fell slipped under the feet of the advancing troops and were dragged to waiting vans. They were set upon by FSB officers in black berets, who beat them fiercely. The vans, yellow lights flashing, devoured prisoners like whales swallowing krill.

Gray mists of acrid tear gas slowly spread down the street. The fumes reached Matthews and Grigoryev, who pressed into an apartment building's shallow entrance. Their noses stung, eyes itched, throats burned. Grigoryev handed Matthews a red bandana soaked with bottled water and they covered their faces.

Protestors ran between the stalled cars, provoking curses from drivers, some of whom threw punches at the fleeing men and women. Cries and shrieks from those unlucky enough to be gassed bent over, coughing and retching.

"I have another way," Grigoryev grunted, taking Matthews's arm. Grigoryev led Matthews toward the line of Interior Ministry troops. The street was littered with lost shoes and placards discarded in the rush to escape.

Grigoryev approached an officer in the front row and waved his Federal Security Service badge, cursing the protesters, and he put on a great show of holding Matthews in his firm grip.

"Let me pass," he shouted. "I'm taking this shithead for special treatment. He's a foreign provocateur."

Grigoryev was waved through the line with Matthews in tow, pushing his prisoner toward the van. But as they drew close, Grigoryev nudged him toward a narrow alley. It smelled of piss and garbage, but it was a safe place to wait until street activity ended. Dusk deepened and then the streetlights came on, one by one, revealing the detritus of the scene—knapsacks, water bottles, torn jackets, and pooled blood.

Grigoryev massaged his leg as he sat on a garbage can and breathed heavily. "I'm fine. An old injury resurrected by running." He nodded toward the alley's other end. "How far?"

"A few blocks more."

He took a Prima, offering one to Matthews. "I forgot. You don't smoke. Maybe you brought your Marlboro Reds for our boat rides to impress us." He lifted the cigarette and laughed bitterly. "We'll leave when the police have flushed all the scum from the streets."

Grigoryev drew on the cigarette, brightening the end. "They hate Putin and shout, *'Putin khaiylo, la-la, la-la, la-la'* in the streets and at the football matches. In Russia, we suspect the worst in our leaders and are surprised only when they are benevolent. In America, it's the opposite. You believe the best from your presidents and are surprised when they are corrupt and delusional. Evil is everywhere—here and in America. It's permanent."

Matthews turned to Grigoryev, amused by his urge to wax philosophical in the midst of the tear gas. He'd always thought him an odd person—one moment enjoying a bad joke, the next risking his life for an extra five percent on a currency transaction.

Grigoryev rose slowly. "Time to go." He followed Matthews through the alley, favoring his good leg.

Lingering haze cast a gloomy mood on the neighborhood. Residents, aware that the violence had passed, emerged from their doors or craned heads out windows. Rumors spread from one person to the next, mixing facts with speculation, and in short order the street confrontation took on exaggerated proportions.

"The car is two blocks in that direction," Matthews said. "It's waiting for us."

Upon turning the corner, they came to Petrovka Ulitsa and a small park with tended flower beds and groomed topiary. Mikhail Sorkin lived in a renovated Baroque apartment building in an elegant neighborhood close to center city. His five-story building faced the quiet park. They entered the park through a stand of young oak trees and moved through the foliage.

"That's Mikhail's building!" Grigoryev turned to Matthews, startled.

"We're taking his wife's car. A blue Fiat."

Grigoryev grunted a curse.

At that moment, Matthews spotted lights go on in Sorkin's third-floor apartment. The curtains were open, as Sorkin had said they would be in their earlier call, a signal. In the street, he saw Veronika's blue Fiat where Sorkin said it would be parked, but then he turned to a dark alley where tactical police in balaclavas were crouched.

"They're waiting for someone," Matthews said.

"They're not waiting for someone," Grigoryev said. "They're waiting for us."

Matthews glanced at Sorkin in the window, looking down into the street. His hand rose and fell in an unnatural gesture.

"He's waving us off," Matthews said. He saw two thuggish plainclothes police standing idly by the building's lobby on their cell phones.

"It's a trap," Grigoryev said. "I saw those men in the operations center."

❖

Grigoryev and Matthews sat on a park bench—two men unable to enjoy the pleasant warmth of a late summer evening. Matthews knew from Grigoryev's silence that he had grave doubts about the plan and he harbored deep suspicions. A cold mood gripped them and the unforeseen course of the evening was a catastrophe weighing them down.

"You never told me it was Sorkin's car."

Matthews waved off Grigoryev's complaint and aggressively defended himself. "I know him, trust him. You'd see betrayal in a dog wagging its tail."

"Fuck you." A grim reality darkened his mood. "It doesn't matter how we got here. We have no good choices, but of the bad choices, the worst is to take a train. We would fall into the trap I baited. They wouldn't know Borodin boarded a train, but they'd search the trains for Grigoryev. There is another not as bad choice. My wife's nephew lives on the other side of the Ring Road. He tapes a spare key under the hood. He will report it stolen in the morning, but by then we'll either be across the Nada River, or we'll be dead." He laughed grimly. "Either way, our problems will be solved."

He stood. "We'll taxi to his home."

"Where's the package?"

Grigoryev looked at him gravely. "I am the package. They want this, but it comes with me." He lifted the thick zipper pull of his blue track jacket. "We used the USB keyring to bring information from the UK, but this is more sophisticated." He touched the long metal zipper, pulling it up and down, proudly displaying its function. "If you separate the zipper, you'll find the male end of a USB drive. The *kompromat* is here, with me, five megabytes of data the CIA is risking your life to acquire."

Grigoryev zipped up the jacket. "Let's go."

Matthews didn't want to admit failure, but there were forces at work that reduced his hope that there was a reasonable way forward. Now he was in the hands of an erratic man whose long history of springing unwanted surprises put them both at risk.

34

Taxi

Y ou look like a big tipper," Grigoryev said, taking Matthews's arm and pushing him to the curb. Three taxis had slowed down when Grigoryev hailed them, but none had stopped. "Try that one," Grigoryev said.

Matthews vigorously waved his wallet at a silver Mercedes taxi speeding past on the other side of the street, shouting, "Taxi, taxi." The Mercedes did a quick U-turn, but the maneuver cut off a blue Audi, which honked violently. The Mercedes stopped abruptly in front of Matthews and the driver put his head out the window, yelling back at the Audi. *"Mudak."*

The driver looked at Matthews. "The idiot was gabbing on his cell phone and he should have been eyes on the road. Where are you going?" he said in the rapid guttural Russian of a man from the East.

"Grunatan Lane. Khoroshyovsky District."

"Mother of Christ." He looked Matthews up and down. "Two thousand rubles."

"On the meter."

"The meter is broken. I'll get you there fast. Safe too. There are street closures, but I know shortcuts." He twirled his index finger. "Get in."

Matthews got in the passenger side back seat, and coming from the other side, Grigoryev popped in behind the driver.

"Who are you?" The driver turned his head, eyes fierce.

"There are two of us."

"I stopped for one person. Two thousand rubles is the cost on a night like this for one passenger getting through the roadblocks. I charge another two thousand for the lughead who just got in."

"It's the law," Grigoryev said. "One person. Two people. It's the same price."

"What law is that?"

"Don't play dumb."

The driver had a thick neck, almond-shaped eyes, a few days' growth of a gray beard, and an ex-boxer's bent-out-of-shape nose. His expression had menace. "I drive my own car. I pick up passengers I want to pick up. I'm not an idiot Uber driver who needs an app to tell him when to turn left or right. I don't need a rude passenger who thinks he can jump into my car and I won't notice."

"That's okay." Matthews knew that a preposterous situation had the potential for danger. "The price is fine."

"You're smart." He turned around, his eyes narrowed in a moment of confusion. "I know you."

"You're mistaken," Grigoryev said. "He has the same ugly face as the shithead whose photo is in the papers. You're not the first to confuse them."

The driver looked closely at Matthews. "I drove you two weeks ago. A drunk walked in front of my car and I hit him. My car took a beating. You were my passenger. He got money out of me, but less because you spoke up for me." The driver looked at Grigoryev. "Listen to this *pendos*. He's a genius. And by the way, my name is Valentino. I have watched all his old movies. I'm a big fan of the black-and-white ones, especially the silent ones. I like the exaggerated faces—like the face of the shithead Audi driver. He can kiss my ass."

The Mercedes accelerated and Matthews settled into the back seat and, feeling the car's speed, he buckled his seatbelt.

Valentino turned on the radio and moved to the rhythm of the Euro pop tune.

"Do you like the music?" He looked in the rearview mirror. "It's an old Pussy Riot song. I like their music but I hate their politics. Russia needs a strong leader who can crush the weak, soft-hearted, jerk-off, liberal scum."

He turned to Matthews. "How about you? Do you like Pussy Riot?"

"Sure."

Valentino tapped the steering wheel in sync to the melody. "Police are everywhere looking for the cockroaches scattered by the gas. A twenty-minute ride will take an hour if we hit a roadblock, but don't worry if we're stopped. I know how much you'll have to put in their palm to get through." His eyes glanced at the mirror again. "What's that you've got?"

Grigoryev held up a cell phone he'd found on the back seat.

"Goose shit. It belongs to the last passenger. Motherfucker. He was an opera singer with his granddaughter. He treated me to an aria, so I gave him a break on the fare. Give me the phone. It's worth a bundle on the black market. New phones need to be registered so they can arrest you if you order porn. The old phones are worth a mint."

The driver laughed, but his smile disappeared when he looked at the mirror. "You don't think it's funny. You're quiet. Are you going to a funeral?"

Matthews looked at his wristwatch.

"You're late. That's it. Here we go."

The Mercedes accelerated into a turn onto Spiridonovka Street and slowed around the corner as it came onto a queue of cars at a roadblock.

"Police. This won't take long. It's the usual strip search, finger up your ass." He laughed.

Valentino cut the line of cars when he saw an opening and was next to pass through the yellow barrier blocking the street. Groups of Interior Ministry troops idled on either side of the street, arms resting on automatic weapons slung over their shoulders, faces hidden in black balaclavas. Two teams of FSB officers demanded papers from the first car in line.

"They're looking for dissidents," Valentino said. His hands tapped the steering wheel and he began to whistle a tune. "It's not far after this, a couple of kilometers."

Valentino had brought attention to them by cutting the line. Matthews stared nervously at the unfolding scene. One officer interrogated the driver of the lead car, while a second officer leaned into the passenger window, finger across his trigger guard.

"What's taking so long?" Valentino snapped. He put his head out the window. "Hey, I've got two passengers late for their mother's funeral."

Matthews leaned forward. "It's okay. We have time."

"I don't have time. I know a shortcut. This is taking too long."

Valentino had turned around in his seat and backed up the car, making two quick maneuvers so the car spun around and he proceeded where they had come from.

"*Ostanovish.* Halt."

Two FSB officers in black berets waved down the Mercedes.

"What are you doing?" Grigoryev shouted.

"Don't worry. It's a shortcut. You know how much money I lose by sitting in this shitty queue."

A tall FSB officer stood in the path of the car, blocking its escape, and he aimed his weapon. "*Stoy!*"

Valentino opened his window, smiling at the grim policeman, and pleaded his case. "These two gentlemen have an urgent appointment. I don't need to use the Ring Road. We'll just go a few blocks to the other side."

"Papers."

"Sure." He produced his license, registration, and internal passport.

Two other FSB officers joined the first and waited for the documents to be examined.

"Get out."

"What for? You've got my papers."

"Get out."

Grigoryev watched the driver step out of the car with visible annoyance. Then the driver's mood changed, mumbling to whichever policeman was willing to listen that he was an Afghan war veteran and a big supporter of the government, making a crude joke, but the police ignored his bonhomie.

Grigoryev whispered to Matthews. "We're next. My documents might pass scrutiny, but they'll recognize you."

Outside, an argument erupted between the driver and the three officers, who shouted down his indignant protests.

Grigoryev became nervous. A bead of sweat formed on his upper lip and he spoke softly. "It is time to walk away."

"You're out of your mind. Where do we go?"

"We've been here before. This exact spot." He pointed to the statue of Yuriy Dolgorukiy. "Do you remember? It's where we escaped from the KGB when we came out of the sewer." He nodded across the street. "Behind the statue is the tunnel entrance. We step out of the car slowly, look calm, waiting for the interrogation to go on, and make our way to the statue." He saw Matthews's confusion. "There is the manhole cover that we came out of. You, me, and Mikhail. We had to run fast to escape the police when they saw us climb out. Now we will do the reverse."

His face was pale and worried. "We can wait until they finish with the driver. Or get out and walk away. The manhole leads to the tunnels. There is a branch that leads under the Ring Road and will take us toward my wife's nephew's home." He looked at Matthews. "Understand?"

The driver had gotten into a heated argument with the tall officer. "Let me see your face. I'll report you." Valentino pulled down his balaclava.

Two officers grabbed Valentino's arms and threw him against the taxi's hood. He fought back, yelling a string of ripe curses, but two more men arrived to restrain him, and the scene quickly became chaotic.

"Now," Grigoryev whispered.

Matthews stepped out of the car first, pretending to distance himself from the unruly driver, and Grigoryev followed, stepping back from the altercation. Drivers and police in the immediate vicinity took great interest in the struggle, and watched fists strike the driver. A small crowd gathered. Matthews stepped back from the scene, slipping into the gathering crowd. More police arrived, and there was a brief moment of chaos when Valentino was thrown to the ground, cheek crushed against the asphalt.

Matthews and Grigoryev crossed the street. Two men in the dark night moving outside the perimeter of streetlights and they reached the huge bronze equestrian statue.

"Halt!" The voice came from behind.

"Run."

A whistle somewhere and then the world around them got very small. They slipped out of sight around the statue's stone base. Shouts in the night, flashlights carving arcs through the park's darkness revealing lovers, but the two men were still unseen. Matthews stood over the sidewalk manhole.

"Down here," Grigoryev said. Together they moved the cast iron cover and climbed down the ventilation shaft. Grigoryev went first and Matthews followed, pulling the cover back in place.

35

Underworld

Matthews held the ladder's top rung and took shallow breaths to quiet the clamor in his ears. Overhead, a gruff voice shouted commands and boots came to rest on the iron manhole cover. Curses, voices, the chaos of a search for missing fugitives, and then footsteps moved away.

Cold air from deep in the earth cooled Matthews's face as he climbed down the deep shaft. Light vanished as he descended, and then he was at the last rung and he let go, dropping to the floor. His cell phone screen went black and he was enveloped in primordial darkness. Water dripped nearby; a bat swooped past, and the quiet of the place was loud in his ears. He swiped his cell phone, excited a dim glow, and his eyes slowly adjusted to the dark world. He was still for a moment, seeking something to hold on to, and then the world began to take shape with echoes, smells, and vague surfaces. Old memories of Moscow's underground returned with a childhood fear of the dark.

He'd entered the tunnels with Grigoryev and Sorkin as adventurous teenagers hoping to find the Kremlin's rumored rail line, and he visited again as a young intelligence officer recruited by Moscow station chief George Mueller to look for underground communication cables. Mueller had been part of the team in 1955 that advised the CIA's effort to excavate a tunnel from Berlin's American sector to Altglienicke in the Soviet sector, where the Soviet armed forces were headquartered, hoping to locate and tap key communication cables. Mueller had supervised Matthews's underground reconnaissance, eager to reprise one of the CIA's boldest Cold War operations. Matthews had never found Stalin's bunker or high-capacity cables, but he found a few telephone wires, an ancient grotto with a skeleton, and one door that led to the wine cellar underneath the Metropol Hotel. He had drawn a map of the tunnel system that he submitted with his final report. The project was abandoned when senior White House officials feared that discovery of their phone tapping would jeopardize the thaw in Cold War hostilities.

"Grigoryev?"

Falling water could be heard somewhere, but sound had no provenance in the dark, and he couldn't locate the source. Cones of faint light traveled down the darkness where ventilation shafts penetrated the ceiling. Even his breathing was loud in the quiet place. Brick walls covered in moss rose to a vaulted roof, thick with bats. One passed close to his head, lifting his hair. A stream eddied over rocks in the center of the cavern and then he saw that they had entered at a fork in the main tunnel.

Louder. "Grigoryev!"

"Here."

Matthews shifted his cell phone and saw the Russian sitting on a large rock, massaging his leg.

"Remember this spot?" Grigoryev nodded toward the converged tunnels. "The bastards might have seen us enter, but they won't know which tunnel we take."

They walked for thirty minutes along the stream, moving carefully over rocks slick with moss, and paused frequently to orient themselves. Walked, listened, and then walked farther. They heard sirens on the street above, and at one point, they stopped to gauge the danger, but then continued, guided by the ventilation shafts' dim light. The tunnel sloped down and took them deeper underground. Matthews had forgotten the stress of making an escape from a hostile city, and he knew the price of failure was high. But if the trick was done well, the cost was unimportant. And he'd done it before, failing once, and that disaster came back to haunt him as they scrambled over slick stones. He felt his way forward, as if walking blindfolded. He'd never gotten used to mortal danger. Cold sweat, chills, and devouring fear took over his senses. More than once, he'd sworn off agency work to avoid moments like this—and now, like a bad dream, the feeling was back. The word *duty* came to him with a hollow ring.

Ahead, another tunnel intersected through a gaping hole blasted from rock, and from it came the sound of a waterfall. Matthews pointed his cell phone's light into the cavity and looked for features that he remembered from the maps he'd drawn. They moved through the ragged opening and had gone a short distance when they summited an iron trestle that carried a rail line over a stream that spilled into a shallow gorge.

Matthews stood on steps carved from bedrock. Grigoryev was at his side limping and favoring his good leg. His cell phone illuminated the rail tracks and then he pointed it in the opposite direction. The tunnel was wide enough for two train tracks, and signal lights disappeared in both directions—red one way, green the other.

They stood by the tracks, awed at coming upon what they'd missed years before. Below them, the stream passed through flood-control locks operated by giant rusted gears. Water flowed over the top of the sluice gate and dropped into a pool.

"This way," Grigoryev said. Then under his breath, "Shit." He pointed at a blinking red light high above the tracks. "Motion detector."

Matthews stood perfectly still.

"They know we're here." Grigoryev pondered which direction would take them north under the Ring Road and beyond the police encirclement. Across the tracks, a massive wood door was sprung open, rusted hinges pulling out from stone settings. "That leads to the street."

"You're sure."

"No, but more sure than you."

"Listen." Matthews put his hand on Grigoryev's shoulder, stopping him as he went to cross the tracks. In the deep silence of the underground, distant voices could be heard. Soft, but growing louder, men taking orders, but then the distant voices were gone. Exhaustion and the enveloping darkness played tricks on them. A dull, deep rumbling broke the quiet. Matthews turned his head and cupped his ear, listening. They were on the edge of the trestle and the rail beneath him began to hum and vibrate, and then the steel clicked and ached.

"There." He pointed.

A glowing beam of light appeared around a bend in the tunnel, its bright headlamp filling the darkness. The hot light came closer, moving slowly, and then the dark shape of a locomotive was visible behind the powerful beam. A shrill whistle pierced the quiet.

Matthews and Grigoryev scampered out of the path of the huge locomotive lumbering toward them with frightening menace.

"Here," Matthews said, taking refuge behind a boulder, but his voice was drowned by the screech of wheels scraping on curved iron rails. Blinding light filled the tunnel.

The locomotive, followed by a second, rumbled past slowly, its giant wheels clacking as it crossed the trestle, and beams underneath strained and groaned against the great weight. The boxy locomotives pulled sleek, silver passenger cars with red-and-white detailing. No identifying marks were painted on the sides of the locomotive, and window shades of passenger cars were drawn. The roof of one car had the white dome of a communication antenna, and the whole collection of cars and locomotives passed like a ghost train.

Grigoryev pointed at the last car, modified to include an anti-aircraft gun, muzzle lowered for the tunnel.

"Putin's armored train." Grigoryev spat. He hurled a stone at a window, but it bounced harmlessly off the safety glass. The train lumbered past and made its way slowly down the tunnel.

Across the tracks, the wooden door had been thrown open. Flashlight beams carved the darkness and settled on Matthews and Grigoryev, illuminating them like actors surprised to be caught on an empty stage. Cold light bathed them and for a moment they stood stunned and motionless.

A chorus of voices rose. The man in front shouted, "Halt!" In the rear another voice cried, "It's them," and then curses followed and an officer gave the order not to shoot.

Matthews couldn't see the figures through the blinding flash-light, but he recognized Colonel Zhukov's tenor voice. Matthews shined his light in their direction to even the score—each bright light an obvious target, but hiding the physical details of the person. He drew Grigoryev down to his side behind the boulder. Gruff voices ten meters away, alive with the excitement of hunters who'd cornered their prey.

Grigoryev's first shot came with a muzzle flash and an explosion of sound. Flashlights went out and then loud cries, shouted commands, and scattering police. One man stumbled and fell, cursing loudly. Darkness settled in the space—adversaries across the tracks invisible in a darkness punctuated only by the glow of red-and-green signal lights.

Matthews saw the lights blink as men crossed in front, approaching from both ends. A second man fell in the dark, cursing in pain, and then there was a splash in the river under the trestle. A voice somewhere closer, yelled, "There! There!"

Matthews ducked behind the boulder as a flashlight beam found him, and it was followed by a gunshot that whizzed by. The brief illumination revealed Colonel Zhukov waving his arms, pointing.

"You can't escape," he yelled. "This is over. For both of you. You'll be treated fairly."

"Fuck him," Grigoryev growled. Louder, so Zhukov heard. "Fuck off."

A second shot. A third. Brilliant flashes from one end of the tunnel and then a volley of gunfire erupted. It was impossible to know how many guns were discharged. Stray bullets ricocheted against the walls and several hit the iron gears, pinging loudly.

"Give up, Dmitry Ivanovich," Colonel Zhukov said in the silence that followed. "You'll be judged fairly. We know everything. Don't dishonor your father's name."

"Leave him out of this." Grigoryev reached around and fired his pistol.

"This way, come," Matthews whispered to Grigoryev, helping him to the stone steps, retracing the direction they'd come from.

Grigoryev resisted, clutching his leg. Matthews saw the wetness on Grigoryev's trousers and felt warm blood. Matthews couldn't tell how serious the wound was.

"You go," Grigoryev said. "Maybe you'll get lucky. I won't make it." He sat against the rock and lifted his pistol. "I'm a good shot even in the dark. Ten bullets. Seven left. Six for them. One for me. Better to die here than in a basement cell. It's the same death, but here I get the pleasure of shooting a few of the bastards."

Matthews heard boots crunch the gravel between the tracks. He saw Grigoryev's face, shadowed in the meager light, eyes alive with grim determination. Voices louder now, closer, two flashlight beams in the darkness.

"They're here," Grigoryev said. "Go." Grigoryev slipped off his track jacket and handed it to Matthews. "It has what you want if you're lucky enough to escape. It's no use to me."

Grigoryev pulled Matthews close and whispered. "You've been a terrible friend. Look what our acquaintance has gotten me." His sarcasm became a plea. "Tell Viktoria not to expect a pension from the shitheads I worked for."

Another gunshot, closer, and voices approaching.

Matthews slid down the first two stone steps and then carefully took the next few in a crouch, holding the rock wall and feeling his way down. Dim light from the ventilation shafts guided his steps to the river. He kept to the sides of the tunnel, attuned to the sounds around him. Water flowing around rocks, his nervous breathing, a bat passing close by. He proceeded that way for a short time, guided by light from the widely spaced shafts, and he saw a ladder that led to the street.

Behind him, bursts of gunfire. Muzzle flashes that briefly illuminated the walls of the tunnel. Automatic fire came in volleys and was returned by pistol fire. Then a brief silence followed by a single shot.

❖

Matthews's memory of the tunnel system they'd entered helped him retrace his steps to the iron ladder that led up to the street. He paused under the iron manhole cover, listening for voices. The only sound he heard was from within the tunnel, where men were approaching. When he was satisfied that he could risk climbing out, he moved the heavy manhole cover aside.

He emerged from the underground wearing the blue track jacket and stood to his full height. It was dark and no one took notice. He shoved the cover back in place and turned to find two FSB officers pointing pistols at him.

"Well done," Colonel Zhukov said. "You almost made it."

Matthews recognized the colonel's false tone of friendliness that he remembered from their first encounter—a man whose victory could make him generous with his compliments.

"The motion detectors work in both directions. There was no escape for you."

Matthews felt exhausted, the excitement of the attempted escape extinguished, and there was also the terrible knowledge of what was coming next. He'd been in a Russian prison cell before.

"I have questions for you," Colonel Zhukov said, "and if you provide answers, things between us will be friendly." He pointed in the direction of the Bolshoy Moskvoretsky Bridge and the Moscow River. "We'll drive there. You'll tell me what Grigoryev can't."

Matthews got into the blue-and-white BMW with rotating roof lights, and they drove a short way to the Moscow River.

Matthews followed the colonel to the stone esplanade that overlooked the wide mouth of the Neglinnaya tributary, which emptied into the Moscow River. A gray Interior Ministry patrol boat sat in the channel, churning against the modest current. A body being pulled from the murky river water drew a crowd of curious bystanders.

Matthews knew it was Grigoryev. His blue track pants matched the jacket Matthews now wore, and he recognized the one orange running shoe. The other foot was bare and muddied.

As the patrol boat approached, Matthews got a better view of the uncovered body on deck. Grigoryev's damp hair flat on his head, his eyes vacant in death, and his chest had a gaping exit wound.

"He wanted to die a hero," Colonel Zhukov said, "but he was a coward who lived an outrageous lie. He called out that he was surrendering with information against you—to betray you. I didn't believe him. Why would I?"

Colonel Zhukov looked with contempt at the body sprawled on the patrol boat's deck.

"He jumped into the river thinking the current would carry him to an escape. I yelled he was a bloody fool. The marksman fired one shot before I could stop him."

He turned to Matthews. "I had questions for him, but now you're the one who will have to give me answers."

36

Lefortovo Prison

Fall arrived fiercely that week and all over Moscow, but particularly in the basement cell of Lefortovo Prison, the cold made sleep difficult. Matthews lay on a thin mattress in the green prison garb he had been issued when he was processed into the old jail—relinquishing his watch, wallet, and his clothes, which were placed in a plastic bag with his name. His personal belongings were sent off to a storeroom, awaiting return upon his uncertain release.

He'd been allowed to keep his wedding ring, but he'd have been happier if they'd removed it. He'd tried to get it off, but his knuckles had thickened, and the guard, seeing the difficulty, told him to forget about the ring. Matthews tried to remove it again to rid himself of a different incarceration, but it wouldn't budge.

He lay on the bed under the cotton sheet, shivering. He had grown accustomed to the subtle ailments of age, but he felt his aches more acutely in the cold. Chilly air came through the small fortochka pane at the top of the high window, open to the night air. He had stood on the bed reaching through the iron bars, but the wall was too thick, and the window out of reach. He'd pounded on his cell door, but the guard who answered had left and not returned.

He'd fallen asleep in the early morning—exhausted, cold, weary, curled in a ball.

❖

"Wake up."

Matthews's hands were stuffed between his thighs for warmth and he'd used his cloth slippers as a makeshift pillow. He opened his eyes and saw the guard's polished black boots. He did as he was told, sitting up, and he shifted his legs over the side of the bed. Sleep had been nearly impossible with the pain of mistreatment and itching lice, but now he was awake, groggy, unready for the day's punishment. Cold air in the room fogged his breath and he rubbed his hands together.

The guard had a beefy face, narrow eyes, and a sharp nose, giving him a menacing look. He held a hard rubber cudgel that he repeatedly slapped in his palm, impatient to get on with his work. His black hair was trimmed and matched the sharp cut of his chevron moustache.

"Stand up."

Matthews rubbed his numb legs, massaging his muscles to regain feeling. As he did, the guard struck his ears painfully.

"Quickly, fuckhead. They want you."

Matthews stood unsteadily, trying to feel the floor with his right foot, numb and tingling. His cell door had opened without him hearing. Other cells on his corridor might hold prisoners, but he couldn't tell. Prisons always had systems for cruelty and he had become familiar with Lefortovo's. The pretrial detention center held prisoners who were being kept away from the outside world—dissidents and foreigners accused of espionage. Padded cell doors closed noiselessly, carpets covered corridors to muffle footsteps. Quiet was broken only when guards banged on pipes to alert colleagues a prisoner was being escorted. No calls. No visitors. No newspapers. Nothing but the enduring torture of silence.

All this came to mind as he was led down a bleach-smelling corridor and then taken up a narrow flight of stairs. He mapped the path for no good reason, but it kept his mind alert, and he knew that staying sane required making a continuous game of the indignities of incarceration. He counted the steps up, remembering the turns of the walk, the cells that were empty and those that were occupied, preparing himself for the hardship that lay ahead.

"In here."

The small room had tall windows that admitted natural light, a welcome change from the cell's cold fluorescent glare. There was a lumpy sofa and two wood chairs across from each other at a gray metal table.

"Did you sleep well?"

Colonel Zhukov rose from a high-backed wood chair in one corner of the room. Tall, alert, uniform perfectly creased, his dark eyes gave him a severe look that softened with a waxy smile.

"I've slept better."

"Sit." He pointed to the table.

Matthews did as instructed. He folded his hands and looked across the table at the colonel, who removed his high-crown hat and placed it carefully to one side. A precise man, he moved deliberately, like a choreographed dancer. His long hair was brushed back on his head and he rolled his thumb across his fingers, a tic.

Matthews thought he saw a new attitude in the officer—a jailer confident in their new relationship.

Colonel Zhukov produced a pack of Primas, tapping it on his arm, but didn't bother to offer one to Matthews.

He drew on the cigarette, brightening the end, and then stood. He paced the room, one hand behind his back, the other holding the cigarette between his fingers. He walked slowly, eyes alert, moving around the table like a wolf circling his prey. Long strides, a puff or two from the cigarette, and the sound of his leather boots on the wood floor.

This went on for a short time and then he sat opposite Matthews, placing his half-smoked cigarette on the table's edge.

"You are a difficult case. There is much interest in you, as you can imagine. A man who was Moscow station chief, who ran a spy network against us, who is now a wealthy investor defrauding our tax authorities."

Matthews heard a prosecutor's indictment being presented in the colonel's casual observation, pretending to be concerned. He didn't respond in any way.

"You're a big prize," he said. "But we live in a complex world and not everything we want to happen comes to pass. Or it is worse than we expect."

Colonel Zhukov leaned toward the guard, who whispered in his ear.

Matthews turned to the view outside where a giant oak tree was bursting in russet brown with the changing season, thinking this might be his only view of the fall colors. The room was bare, walls a yellowed white. There was no comfort, nothing to gaze at or contemplate. Nothing at all. Nothing to hold on to except his calm.

The guard opened the cell door and stepped away to allow a visitor to enter.

"I believe you know Captain Anna Kuschenko," the colonel said.

Matthews turned to Anna. She crossed the room in a smart, forest-green FSB uniform, gold star on a red epaulet. Her straw-blonde hair was hidden under a high-crown cap with a black visor. She stood militarily erect behind Colonel Zhukov, who rose, and she briskly saluted him and then rested her hand on her holstered 9 mm pistol. Two interrogators enjoying the misery of a prisoner's happenstance, mindful of his fall.

"Hello, Alex."

Matthews met Anna's eyes. He knew her face, but there was something unfamiliar in her demeanor. A different person stood before him. She looked like his wife, or someone with her mannerisms, but she wasn't the woman he'd slept beside, laughed with, and affectionately hugged. She was a double.

"I don't expect you to say anything," she said. "We have business to discuss."

He nodded, his mind a tangle of wild thoughts that he held on to because they were dangerous. He was her prisoner and their past was rewritten.

Colonel Zhukov sat at the table and Anna moved to the chair, where she sat, crossing her legs, and watched intently. The colonel took a pad of paper and a sharpened pencil, pressing the red record button on a small audio device that the guard placed on the table.

"My name is Colonel Viktor Petrovich Zhukov, deputy head of Department M of the Federal Security Service. Today is September 30, 2018, at 8:30 in the morning. This meeting is being held in Lefortovo Prison and I am here with Captain Kuschenko and the prisoner, Alexander Matthews." He looked at Matthews. "Can we begin?"

Matthews nodded, an old instinct to be courteous, but there was nothing voluntary in his cooperation.

"Speak up. The recorder needs to hear your answer."

"Yes."

"You were arrested as you climbed from a ventilation shaft. You had entered a tunnel with Lieutenant Colonel Dmitry Grigoryev, who was shot when he tried to escape."

Matthews listened to a long recitation of the circumstances of his capture, imprisonment, the history of his involvement with the CIA from the refracted perspective of the other side, and then came a list of supposed tax fraud charges, with details he knew could only have been developed with information stolen from Trinity Capital's office. He heard nothing that he didn't know, but he saw that the arguments against him were being shaped into what would become his indictment—and he wasn't sure if the meeting was going to be an interrogation, a mock trial, or something else.

"At the time of your arrest you carried a false passport. Under Article 276 of the Russian Federation Criminal Code, you can be charged as a foreign agent working against the security interests of the state. An arrest warrant was outstanding at the time you were taken into custody. You are now accused of entering Russia under false documents with the purpose of undermining state security, conspiracy to attack social order under the Russian Espionage Act, and abetting the theft of state secrets."

He looked up. "These are serious charges. If convicted, you could be sentenced to many years in prison. Our prisons are not so pleasant as the ones in America. Do you understand?"

"I would like to speak with my embassy."

"Perhaps."

"Perhaps what?"

"Perhaps if you cooperate."

"I am entitled to a lawyer."

"What you think you're entitled to and when we permit those privileges depend on your cooperation."

Colonel Zhukov twirled the pencil between his fingers and then tapped the air, an orchestra conductor waving his baton. Matthews realized that the colonel didn't intend to write anything down. Zhukov withdrew his hands to remove them from striking distance.

"Was Grigoryev the traitor who the CIA called BYRON?"

Matthews met the colonel's gaze but said nothing.

"You recruited Dmitry Grigoryev. And there were others. Who else is there working for the CIA?"

"He was the last one."

"I don't believe you."

"That's not my problem. I can only tell you what I know."

Colonel Zhukov held the pencil in his fist like a dagger. He smiled with contempt. "You left the CIA, but you came back to Moscow with Trinity Capital. Why did you return? Who have you tried to recruit? Why did you make contact with Grigoryev? How long was this operation planned? Who authorized it?"

Matthews scowled at the numbing progression of questions, but only answered two. "It came from the top. Grigoryev had something Langley wanted."

"What?"

"I don't know. I was the courier."

"You didn't act like an errand boy."

Matthews met the colonel's eyes, irritated, but he didn't respond.

"What was so important for BYRON to crawl out of his hole?"

"I don't know. I was doing a favor."

The colonel leaned forward, eyes fierce. "I don't believe you."

"I didn't want to know. They didn't want me to know. It was to be one meeting—in and out. Over. Done with." Matthews felt hot anger flush his face. "She knows." He looked at Anna. "Ask her. Is that enough cooperation? I want to speak with my embassy."

"Shithead." Colonel Zhukov slammed the pencil on the table, splintering it. He rose abruptly and spoke rapidly in Russian to Anna, his tone harsh and upset. He walked with long strides to the door and motioned for the guard to follow him out.

Matthews called after him. "I give you my word. I don't know what he had. I would tell you if I knew, but I don't."

Colonel Zhukov turned and contemplated Matthews. "Convince her if you can."

❖

Matthews waited for the door to close. He saw Anna rise from her chair and move to the table, where she sat opposite him. Their eyes were averted and then they looked at each other. He was aware of her perfume's fragrance, a lavender eau de cologne he'd bought for her birthday. The familiar scent mixed with the hint of cleaning agents and the stench of human suffering that lived in the room.

Matthews looked at her. *Why?* He didn't want to contend with a lie, so he said nothing. How odd, he thought, to be with her in the room, she wearing the crisp uniform of the enemy. Her blue eyes were warm, but also cold.

He was familiar with how the spy lived apart, alone, burdened with the psychological dangers of difficult work. The practice of deception was not hard, but it required stamina to live continuously in danger. A professional trained to live two lives at the same time, holding one apart from the other, each carried forward with confidence, sincerity, and cunning. Like a nesting doll—a *matryoshka*—inside one person was a second, and maybe a third. But he also knew how the heart suffered in isolation.

Matthews studied her expression, wondering about their marriage. He saw the whole of their suburban Washington life together like a fragile artifice—her restless socializing and his guilty jealousy.

"I'm here to talk," she said. She nodded at the surveillance camera in the ceiling, where the blinking red light had gone dark. She'd pressed the recording device's stop button.

"It's just us. No one is listening. Nothing will be recorded."

"You're in charge?"

"He's in charge. I'm looking out for you."

Matthews stifled an urge to laugh, as if now, after all her lying, he would believe her. "Why do you think I would tell you something I wouldn't tell him?"

She shook her head. "The other way around. I might confide something I don't want them to hear."

He raised his arms theatrically. "Good. We'll be honest with each other. Try something different in this marriage."

"You weren't surprised when I walked in."

Matthews looked at the view out the window where autumn trees were a pleasant momentary distraction. He turned back to her. "Should I have been?" He observed her face, hoping to read her expression, but he saw only her trained composure. "I suspected a lie, but I made a big mistake."

Neither spoke for a moment.

He looked at her. "How did you know I was in Moscow?"

"I knew you weren't in Rome. I didn't believe you'd go to Rome."

"Why?"

"We had a pact. It's the only European city neither of us has visited and we agreed to go together. You don't remember, but it's not a thing a woman forgets."

A beat of silence. He pointed at the medal on her uniform. "I've made you a hero." He added almost as an aside, "When did you turn?"

"I was never turned. Russia is in my blood. I came into the world this way." She looked at him for a moment. "Where is your loyalty? To an idea, an ideology, an accident of birth?"

He pressed her for details of her life, but she declined to discuss her training or her deployment. He asked when it started and who her parents were, suspecting that the whole tapestry of her past was false.

She crossed her arms and gave no indication that she would answer. "It doesn't matter."

"It does to me." He leaned forward. "It doesn't have to be this way."

She laughed. "Which way is that? Groveling for a favor from an ambitious Washington bureaucrat who thinks nothing of sacrificing you?"

She looked at him skeptically. "You would have us live together in a cottage on Chesapeake Bay—a couple living their crummy lives with barbecues and dinner parties among friends we don't particularly like. We would be horribly unhappy. Cocktail parties, boastful politics, shallow patriotism. It's not something I want, nor have you the power to grant."

She looked at him with intense belligerence and patted her breast. "I am Russian. The West believes it's superior, but it underestimates the Russian soul. Russian blood defeated the French and the Germans, not Stalin. Now wise men in Washington puff up their chests, ignoring their own hypocrisy, and export so-called democracy around the world. How well did it work in Vietnam, Chile, Iraq, Afghanistan? Russia will prevail because she knows how to suffer."

She measured America's political health by the raucous clamor of a deeply divided electorate. "America will defeat itself without much help from us." Her eyes were hard, face calm. Opinions she'd kept to herself were coming out.

"Do you really believe that shit?" he snapped. He waited for her answer, but none came. His words were casualties of her unwillingness to listen. An obstinate woman. It was a waste of time to slip into a debate about abstract principles.

"What happened to Wallace?"

"He should have left the agency like you did."

"Linton thinks the Washington *rezident* ordered his murder."

She stood and moved to the window, looking out at the giant oak and beyond, across the street, flower beds dying with the changing season. Quiet for a moment. She turned to him. "It's convenient to blame Wallace's death on us, but his silence serves the CIA."

He nodded at her holstered pistol. "Did you kill him?"

Her eyes were incredulous, expression defiant. "That's who you think I am?"

"I don't know who you are."

Silence lingered between them. He searched for words for her: funny, loving, clever, cruel. Matthews leaned forward. "What went on between you and him?"

"He wanted advice about his wife and sometimes he talked carelessly about work, which he began to regret. He invited me to his boat that day. Others arrived. I wasn't there when it happened." She returned to the table and sat across from him, folding her hands. Their eyes met in a sort of acknowledgment.

"What did BYRON have that was so important?" she asked.

"I don't know."

"Dormant for ten years. Why was he resurrected?"

"He lacked your faith in Mother Russia." He rounded the syllables to deepen his sarcasm.

"Alex, I am on your side. Don't make this difficult."

"Difficult for you? For me? For us?"

"You're in prison. You chose to work with the Director. Did they offer money, or were you eager to get back in the game?" She leaned forward. "I don't think you know who you are. Too many days of living in the dark tunnel of espionage—overdosing on suspicion."

Matthews recognized the technique. The interrogator trying to get under his skin. "I didn't know. I didn't ask. They didn't offer. It was a favor."

"I don't believe you. You're too smart, too clever, too cunning not to have asked the question before you put your life at risk. I know you. I know how you think."

Matthews had the strange feeling of being the victim of her careful observation. He had run assets and he knew how to slip into an asymmetrical pattern of thoughts and behaviors that defined the connective tissue between handler and target. He had learned to skillfully balance giving information about himself to encourage the other person to open up with secrets and trust. He had done it, but never had it done to him. He sank in his chair, feeling the tyranny of her betrayal and the helplessness of his situation.

"*Kompromat*," he said.

"Against us?"

"You can guess."

"What's in the file?"

"I have no idea."

"Where is the file?"

He raised his hands in mock surrender. "I was searched. Grigoryev was searched. I don't have it. The deal was that he'd hand it over once he was over the border."

Matthews felt a sense of relief that he'd told her what he knew, and he saw her pause hearing the convincing calm in his voice. He had no state secrets to divulge, no compromising facts, but offering one honest detail allowed him to hold on to another.

They looked at each other. All the complex feelings of a strange marriage filleted by the knife edge of truth.

"Why did you save my life at the hotel?"

She considered the question. "We needed you to return to Moscow. I could say that and it would be the truth, but it might not be the whole truth." Anna leaned forward. "How did the woman, Olga, get involved?"

"Through Sorkin. She had nothing to do with Grigoryev and knows nothing. She wrote an article, that's all."

"Did you sleep with her?"

Startled. Matthews looked at her. He thought he detected a beat of jealousy. He remembered their evening together at the NATO conference in Vienna in the hotel bar. Her performance at the piano was a little too easy, a little too brilliant. It would not have been possible without training in a counterintelligence charm school.

"I have been regretfully faithful to you," he said. He expected to see satisfaction on her face, but instead he saw gratitude.

She stood. The meeting was over. Anna put on her cap, folding her hair underneath, and assumed the rigid posture of an FSB officer. At the door, she turned to Matthews and said casually, "Putin has taken a personal interest in your case. It's good for you that he wants Anton Glok freed more than he wants the satisfaction of having you suffer in a Russian prison."

37

Vienna International Airport

Two Months Later

Matthews exited the forward door of the Sukhoi military aircraft and paused on top of the disembarkation stand. Winter held the day in its grip and he zipped up his blue track jacket, returned to him when he left prison. No one had offered him a coat when he stepped from the warm plane into the cold.

The late afternoon sun was obscured by low clouds and sleeting rain. Vienna's staggered skyline was barely visible through the coming dusk, and the remote section of Vienna International Airport was largely empty. An old aerodrome stood nearby and a sturdy biplane plodded across the tarmac headed to the hangar where two obsolete military aircraft were being harvested for spare parts. In the distance, commercial passenger jets took off with a roar and vanished into the clouds.

Not more than fifty meters away stood a gleaming white Gulfstream executive jet, its tail numbers masked. A marksman in Marine fatigues stood in the G5's open door with a scoped rifle. Four men from the Gulfstream walked to a point halfway between the Russian and American aircraft. It was too far for Matthews to make out their faces, but he could see that the lead man was tall, wearing a Homburg, and an aide held a black umbrella against rain that was turning to snow. On the other side, there was a bald, husky man whose hands were bound behind his back. He was pushed forward by one of the Americans.

Where is the press? Matthews thought. He expected to see a media circus waiting to capture the newsworthy prisoner exchange—vans with parabolic antenna sending a live feed to an eager audience, and he had fretted what his son would think seeing his handcuffed father led by armed Russians. But he saw only two planes parked on the airfield.

Matthews was nudged forward and he took one step down the airstair, holding the handrail, moving cautiously. Behind him, Olga emerged from the aircraft's door. Her red hair was shorn, her scalp was bruised, and her bandaged forearm was covered by a coat thrown over her shoulders. The FSB officer at her side cut zip ties from her wrists, and then he did the same for Matthews and Simon Birch, who stretched his arms overhead, testing the movement. He wore the Harvard hoodie from the night of his arrest at the hotel, but his face was thinner, his mood uncertain, and he looked around with the defeated expression of a long-held prisoner unfamiliar with freedom.

Olga's face showed the hardship of her two months in prison: sad eyes, weight loss, a dull desperation in her hollow cheeks that even the prospect of release didn't assuage. Prison had not been kind to Matthews, but he'd suffered less. He didn't have diplomatic immunity, but he was a prominent American businessman whose cause in the world's press spared him from the worst hardships of the Russian penal system. His eyes came off Olga and Birch and looked around. A Russian sniper in body armor and a black balaclava stood in the Sukhoi's rear door. His scoped rifle was cradled in his arms, muzzle down, index finger poised on the trigger guard. He withdrew into the plane when Matthews stared, disappearing from view, but his boots were visible in the dying light.

"Ready?" Anna asked, urging Matthews forward.

"Where are the television cameras?"

"They aren't needed."

"Better with cameras."

He stepped off the stand and stood to one side of three Russians conferring at the bottom of the airstair. Colonel Zhukov took his eyes off Matthews and turned to the two FSB officers who fidgeted as the weather rolled in, cell phone pressed to his ear. Colonel Zhukov wore a greatcoat, and leather gloves were pulled tight on his hands. The start of wet snow made him restless—a man hoping to conclude the prisoner exchange before the storm delayed a return to Moscow.

Matthews rubbed his wrists, massaging away the pain, and looked at the other two. Olga's face was pale and he saw her eagerly look at the Gulfstream. Birch fidgeted, glancing around. There was a long wait while Colonel Zhukov conferred with an absent authority, and then the call ended.

Anna joined Colonel Zhukov in a short conference, talking in urgent whispers. She wore her smart forest-green uniform, but her hat remained on the Sukhoi, so her hair was lifted by a breeze that whipped across the tarmac. Her hand rested on her holstered 9 mm pistol. At the conclusion of the conference, she approached Matthews.

"There's a problem."

"What?"

"I don't know. We're getting back on the aircraft to wait."

"No," Olga cried.

The lead American at the halfway point between the planes called out, "Are we doing this?"

Matthews squinted through the weather, wiping snow from his eyes, and he saw the American's overcoat and his black Homburg. He recognized the deep concentration of a man charged with an urgent mission, and he knew it was James Linton. Linton stepped forward, followed by his aide, who kept a wide umbrella over his head.

"Walk with me," Matthews said, taking Olga's arm. "Let them try to stop us. Keep walking."

Colonel Zhukov confronted Matthews, blocking his way. "Stay here. This isn't agreed."

Anna intervened, pointing at the bald Russian prisoner held by the Americans, who stamped his feet nervously. "He's our prize." She pointed at the American prisoners. "They are nothing. If we return to Moscow without him, you'll have to answer why you sacrificed Anton Glok."

Matthews sensed a change in the mood, darkened by the blowing wind and dropping temperature. Everyone's eyes converged on Anna staring down Colonel Zhukov. The American aide had dropped his umbrella and slowly moved his hand to his holstered pistol. The Marine marksman in the Gulfstream's door lifted his rifle in response to the Russian sniper stepping forward to the edge of the plane's door.

"What's the holdup?" Linton yelled.

Colonel Zhukov walked briskly across the tarmac and joined Linton—two men, American and Russian, conferred in the invisible neutral zone.

Matthews saw them argue, but the roar of departing jets kept him from hearing what was said. He looked for an encouraging sign of an acceptable outcome, but the two men gesticulated angrily. Snow fell more heavily, drifting across the tarmac, and it landed on their heads and faces, melting on their cheeks. Matthews peered through the blur of white and the brisk wind swept the snow here and there, making it hard to see. All the rigorous planning, he thought, all the hours of preparation, the endless discussions of contingencies for the unforeseen, but no one had thought to plan for the snow, the cold, and the effect on their growing impatience.

What was the problem? Matthews couldn't believe they didn't care about Glok. He looked for another reason for the delay. The exchange had been agreed, documents read and reread, vetted, approved, but still the two adversaries leaned into each other, aides holding umbrellas over the two men.

Glok grew agitated, stomping his feet, and he glanced toward the Russian sniper. He gestured at the two negotiators.

The pilot of the Sukhoi emerged from the plane's door and called the Russians to the base of the airstair, motioning also at Colonel Zhukov. The Russians convened in a tight group, leaning into the pilot. Matthews glanced around, his guards a few yards away, thinking they could dash toward the Gulfstream, but he knew his chances of making it to the plane were poor. Matthews heard them talk with agitated voices and he heard Anna's indignant protest.

Glok shook off his American guard's restraining hand, cursing loudly. "What is taking so fucking long?"

Colonel Zhukov stepped away from the others, raising his arms, giving a thumbs-up, and motioned for the prisoners to be released. Matthews let Olga follow Birch in single file, and he went last.

Matthews had gone a few yards when he felt someone come from behind and walk at his side. Anna squeezed his hand.

"The sniper is for you," she whispered, looking straight ahead.

Matthews glanced back at the Russian in the plane's rear door, rifle raised.

"When Glok is released, he will shoot you. That's what the pilot said. Those are the orders from Moscow."

Her voice was nervous, but firm. "I didn't know about this."

She was quiet and momentarily lost in thought, a troubled look on her face. Her forehead creased with anger and she mumbled, "Why are they doing this?" She shook her head and her eyes were fierce with incomprehension, but indignant too. She turned to Matthews. "I will walk with you to the Americans. Walk normally. Don't stop. Don't turn. I will be behind you. When I say to, you must run. They'll know something is wrong, so you will have to be fast."

Matthews looked at her. "Why are you doing this?"

"It's not obvious? You need to ask?"

"Yes, I need to ask."

She stared. "David doesn't deserve to be an orphan."

Exchanged documents were getting wet in the snow and diligent aides placed them in envelopes when the momentary delay passed. Arrangements agreed, Linton had the prisoner released and Colonel Zhukov motioned Glok forward, waving brusquely.

When Glok crossed the invisible boundary, he raised his fist in a little show of victory and emotionally embraced the Russian guard. He lifted his arms triumphantly, did a little jig, and an ebullient smile broke across his face.

"*Spasibo*," he said to the Russians around him. To the Americans, he raised a middle finger, but as he passed Matthews he said, "Good luck."

"Walk," Anna said to Matthews, nudging him forward, moving behind the other two. "Don't run."

"What's the problem?" Linton called out.

Matthews felt weak in his knees, knowing there was a target on his back. A prayer slipped from his lips as he looked ahead to the Gulfstream. He was nervous, but another part of him was calm—comfortable that this was his time to die. It had always been that way—a dangerous border crossing, or the solitary man on the run in a hostile city. He was there again with his fear. His eyes closed and he stilled himself to receive the sniper's bullet. He knew that precautions were useless against fate.

"Walk," she urged.

He felt her hand grip his arm, pushing him forward so that she was between him and the sniper, denying him a clean shot.

"*Ostervorni.*" Halt.

"Keep walking."

More shouts and tension charged the air. The opposing groups sensed a new danger and with the confusion came caution. Matthews saw Birch hustle toward the Gulfstream, taking long, quick strides, half a step ahead of Olga.

Snow fell harder and covered the tarmac in a soft blanket of white. Footprints left a confusing pattern in the snow.

"Now," she said, looking back at the Russian sniper. "Run."

Matthews had sprinted a few yards when the first shot rang out. The bullet was close enough that he felt the sharp snap of the projectile's sonic wave. The second shot was further off the mark and it was followed by loud cries of men who threw themselves to the tarmac or ran hunched over to an airplane. The small patch of earth exploded in chaos.

Matthews stumbled from an old pain in his leg and he fell forward on his knees. Anna was at his side helping him to his feet, shouting to move, and turned to calibrate the danger of the delay.

The Russian sniper pointed his rifle at Matthews, and in the corner of his eye, Matthews saw the muzzle flash of the Marine's weapon. The muted sound of the shot was followed by the dull groan of the Russian sniper, who staggered and fell backward.

There was a moment of stunned silence. Matthews turned to Anna, who stared at the Russian fallen in the aircraft's door. She waved her arms at the FSB officers, a peacekeeper hoping to quell further violence. Another shot rang out. Matthews heard Anna's cry. And then a second shot. The Marine sniper's first bullet had struck her in the upper body, sending her onto her back, where she lay motionless on the tarmac. The bullet had entered just below her breast pocket, leaving a small circular hole in the fabric, and the second exited through her shoulder, taking off part of her uniform. Scarlet blood mixed with virgin snow.

"No," Matthews gasped, dropping to her side. For one long moment he stared at her quiet face and the growing pool of crimson under her shoulder.

The shock of death sank in with uncertain consequence. Colonel Zhukov rose to his feet and advanced toward Matthews with his pistol in two hands, aiming. Linton rose from his crouched position, waving wildly to bring an end to the shooting.

Matthews saw Colonel Zhukov approach through the snow and his old training kicked in. He grabbed Anna's holstered 9 mm pistol, flicked off the safety, and assumed a crouch, pointing the weapon at Zhukov. Matthews's hand shook and snow melting on his forehead blurred his vision. He blinked and wiped his eyes with the back of his hand. Zhukov's first shot was wide, but he kept moving forward like a wolf stalking prey. Matthews carefully sighted his weapon and squeezed the trigger. His shot missed but he fired twice more in rapid succession. One shot harmlessly passed through the fabric of Zhukov's flapping coat, but the second tore into his forearm, dropping him to one knee, weapon skidding out of reach.

Matthews crossed the tarmac toward Zhukov, pistol raised. He didn't hate the wounded Russian, but his mood was cold as he advanced on the man who had conspired to kill him. He charged the pistol, lifting it to fire.

"Enough." Linton took Matthews's arm, holding him back, and the two men confronted each other, and in the brief pause, the opportunity to strike was lost.

An FSB officer was at Zhukov's side, shielding him, and led him to the Sukhoi, where Glok scampered up the airstair. When they were on board, another Russian pushed the stand away from the plane's fuselage and grabbed a dropped rope ladder. He swung in a wide arc as the plane moved slowly, but once he was hauled inside, the pilot powered up the engines and the plane lumbered toward the main runway.

❖

Matthews knelt by Anna's body. Linton was at his side and put his hand on Matthews's shoulder.

"She's gone. We don't have time here."

Matthews hesitated but rose slowly.

"We suspected something like this might happen."

Matthews looked at Linton, searching for an answer, but getting no satisfaction, he turned again to Anna. Her face was still, a mask he couldn't see past, hiding her further from him. "She was a good spy."

"They're all good."

"Not like her."

The snow had changed to a weeping mist and the crimson dusk was gathering up the dying light of day. Rain to snow to rain again.

"We can't leave her," Matthews said.

"She doesn't belong to us."

"They left her."

"The Austrians will deal with this."

"And do what? We should take her. She saved my life."

"After she betrayed us." Linton's eyes came off the sight of approaching emergency vehicles. "This is a crime scene. She is a Russian national. We have to leave."

Matthews felt the oppressive frustration of agency rules playing against him again.

"This mission is over," Linton said. "Not every mission succeeds."

"This one didn't."

"You're alive. That's enough."

Matthews stood over Anna. A stranger with a familiar face. The misting rain had stopped the same way it had begun—suddenly, quickly, unexpectedly. Her face had lost color and was ghostly pale in the deepening dusk. Moisture darkened the green of her uniform and blood from the wound became black in the snow.

Matthews was unwilling to let the moment go until he found some solace or understanding. His feelings were raw as he looked for an answer in her face, believing—hoping—he could answer his nagging questions. He gazed at her for what seemed like the eternity of death, but it was only a moment or two. He felt Linton's hand on his shoulder.

"I'll be on the plane." In the distance, one siren was joined by another. "It's time to go."

Matthews looked down. Her legs were splayed awkwardly and he thought he should adjust them, to make her comfortable. It made no difference to her, but he did it anyway. He gazed at her, repelled by her and feeling contempt, but other feelings stirred as well. He searched her face, but it held her secrets. He touched her cheek, still warm, but cooling from the melting snow. Tears came to his eyes and fell to his cheeks. He brushed them away.

"Rain," he said to no one in particular, eyes welling up. "Shit." He shook off the emotion.

It was a short walk to the Gulfstream, but he knew it would be a long journey home. He passed Linton at the top of the stairs. As he moved inside, Linton said, "She must have known it could end this way."

❖

Matthews slept during the dull, gloomy flight home, but halfway through the trip he was awakened by severe turbulence. Outside the window, he saw impenetrable night and could only imagine the weather they were going through. He knew his son would be at the airport to meet him, and he rehearsed what he might say to explain everything David would have read in the press, but then he thought it better not to prepare too much. Better to let the emotion of the moment bring them together.

Across the aisle, Birch was asleep, mouth open, an empty whisky glass resting in his hand. Olga was in her seat beside him, head against the window, sleeping. She'd cushioned her face with a pillow and pulled a blanket up to her neck, lost in her restless dreams. In sleep, she held his hand.

His thoughts turned to Anna. He saw her in his mind's eye, but he realized that what he saw was only a small part of her, the edge of her ear, her nose, a burst of sunlight that shadowed her face. He knew consciously that his memory was shaped by what he wanted to see, and yet he was startled when he forced the issue and really looked at her. The best things he'd seen—fingers dancing on the piano, wind in her hair on the sailboat, her laughter, the canopy she pulled over their heads in bed—couldn't be experienced. He couldn't relive those moments, but he could summon memories that had the sharp point of a moment. Even now, knowing what he knew, it was hard to believe that they hadn't shared some happiness.

Matthews was unsettled and in need of human companionship, but seeing the other two asleep, he removed Olga's hand and joined Linton in the front of the plane, taking the track jacket.

Linton looked up from the after-action report he was typing on his laptop.

"How do I prettify this shit show? We got you and Birch, but Glok will be back at work selling guns to African dictators." Linton nodded at Olga. "How did she get involved?"

"Bad luck to know me. Collateral damage."

"You're a cynical son of a bitch."

"Keeps me hopeful."

Linton laughed. "We lost BYRON. Maybe that's a good thing. We won't have to deal with the child in the White House."

"Try this."

Matthews held the thick zipper of Grigoryev's track jacket. He pulled with his right hand to separate the USB drive. He pulled once and nothing happened, then he yanked harder, but the zipper remained intact. He lifted it, looking closely for the seam in the tricked-out device, but there was none. He stared, brought it close to his eyes, and then dropped it. There was no concealed USB drive. There was only an aluminum pull.

Matthews was appalled. Everything Grigoryev had told him was true. His wife left for Montenegro fearing for her safety. His father disowned him for his corruption. His fraud attracted the attention of Department K. His name was on a restricted travel list. He'd become a suspect in the FSB's mole search. Only one thing was false. The thought struck him like a punch line in one of Grigoryev's absurd jokes. Sometimes a zipper is just a zipper.

Matthews saw it all at once—the full scope of the colossal deception and how the agency had been taken in—duped. Grigoryev had offered up a rich prize that he knew the agency was desperate to get its hands on, and in return, he demanded to be exfiltrated.

Matthews didn't know if he should laugh or groan, but a part of him was impressed by the sheer audacity of Grigoryev's scheme to escape Russia. He remembered how Grigoryev had described parts of the file with its seductive details. So brilliant. So breathtaking. Dangling a prize so attractive that it blinded them all. The best lie was the one you hoped was true. All of it, he thought, for nothing. Lives wasted.

Matthews sat back in the seat, stunned and quiet. He dropped the zipper and slowly, but with the full knowledge of what he knew had happened, he shook his head, laughing quietly to himself.

Linton leaned forward. "What's so funny?"

He tossed the jacket at Linton. "Here's your *kompromat*."

Linton took the jacket and tried the zipper once and then placed the jacket on the companion seat, like an unwanted gift.

"That's it?" Matthews asked. "No interest?"

Linton nodded at the jacket. "I would have been surprised if there had been a USB device."

An awkward silence settled between them and the jet's hum was black noise in the cabin.

"I never trusted Grigoryev and I never supported the Director· on this mission. I was the skeptic and I was right. Our investigation into Dowd's and Mercer's involvement with Russian election interference is ongoing and we'll see where it leads." He leaned forward. "I had a bigger prize. I wanted to find the FSB's penetration agent in Langley."

Linton leaned back and looked at Matthews. "I found her with your help, but I couldn't read you in on my suspicions." Linton lifted an invisible fishing rod and cast an imaginary lure.

"I was the bait?"

"You were never at risk. We're still trying to establish how much damage she caused, agents compromised, and how much information she passed along. We can connect her to the loss of the GRU general last year, and her fingerprints are on the arrest last year of the Russian Foreign Affairs officer. It's likely she's connected to KEATS's and BLAKE's disappearances. I suspect she used you to get to them. We're reviewing what she did, or knew—everything she touched. It will be a long process. She was in meetings where classified matters were discussed and missions planned. She had pieces of things that would help them complete several puzzles, and accessing her knowledge would have been an ongoing threat to the lives of several assets."

"The sniper was for her, wasn't he?"

Linton returned Matthews's gaze calmly but said nothing.

"You killed her."

Linton folded his hands on his lap and the look on his face expressed regret and satisfaction in equal measure. He raised his hand slightly, like a pope blessing his audience, exercising his claim to infallibility.

Matthews was quietly outraged. He listened to what Linton had to say as he went on spouting all the usual empty appreciation for his part in the mission, adding that nothing that happened in Vienna would be public. "We gave medals for bravery on D-Day and the Battle of the Bulge, but there was no recognition for valor when Saigon fell. No matter how brave the men and women who risked their lives, we don't want to remind ourselves of our failures."

He added that the agency, the Director, and he—Linton—were grateful for Matthews's help. Russia House was cleansed, men's lives were safer, and Trinity Capital would get support, if it wanted to rebuild. The agency would consider using it as a vehicle to channel funds to sensitive clandestine operations in Saudi Arabia, Iran, or Syria.

Linton was rambling. Finally able to say everything that was on his mind, he gave more than he needed to, almost as an apology. Not knowing where to go once he began, he didn't know how to stop.

"I discussed with the Director how much you should be read in, and we agreed that keeping you in the dark was the safest way to proceed. It wasn't a matter of trust. We trust you. It was to minimize the operation of chance, and we knew, well, that you had feelings for her."

Matthews listened to Linton. He had the story, or the story they wanted him to have, and while he knew there were things not said, he was confident that he had received a reasonable accounting. He was surprised by how little anger he felt. There was no point in being angry. It took energy to be angry, and he had none left to give. He was exhausted. Spent. When he was imprisoned in Lefortovo weeks after his arrest, he had imagined a scene like this—answers to his questions coming in an orderly fashion confirming his vague suspicions, and now he was exhausted by the truth. He looked at Linton thinking, *You killed her. For what?*

Matthews took the drink Linton offered like a sacrament. His calm expression, his cold eyes.

Matthews turned to the window, avoiding Linton, and he saw brilliant lightning flashes that left a residual black image in his mind. In the darkness outside, he saw Anna's face reflected in the window. Looking at him. It was the expression he'd seen on her face when she lay on the tarmac, only her eyes were open, looking at him, and for one moment, he thought she was trying to speak. Then another lightning flash and her face was gone.

He turned back to Linton and resisted an impulse to throw his drink in Linton's face, but then he did.

"I understand," Linton said, dabbing his face with a handkerchief.

For an instant, there was a flash of anger in Matthews's heart, but he quelled it, knowing that it would do no good to go down that path. He was too tired to rise up and fight the world he'd grown up in, that had trained him and made him who he was. He was alive, he thought. That was enough. He wasn't content with what had happened, but he knew that he was powerless against the agency.

Acknowledgments

Principle characters in *The Poet's Game* are fictional, as are most of the events that are depicted, and the novel's imaginary world unfolds around invented events in Washington and Moscow. Dialogue attributed to historical figures is made up.

My agent, Will Roberts, read several drafts of the novel and his wise editorial suggestions strengthened the book. Beth Parker, my publicist, worked her magic to bring the novel into the world with grace and finesse. I am indebted to my US and UK publishers for their support, particularly Virginia Wenzel, editor, Pegasus Books, whose keen insights helped shape the novel. I also want to express my gratitude to Claiborne Hancock, publisher, and the marketing team under Jessica Case. Jamie Hodder-Williams, No Exit Press's publisher, has been a staunch supporter.

Michael Pietsch graciously commented on an advanced version of the manuscript and suggested several changes that significantly improved the novel. John Beryle, US ambassador to the Russian Federation 2008-2012, corrected Russian words in the manuscript and made invaluable suggestions on Russian culture that only someone who had lived in Moscow could provide. Other helpful insights came from Dan Hoffman, former Moscow station chief, and David Aufhauser, former US Treasury Department general counsel. Among the book's early readers were my fellow writers in the Neumann Leathers Writers Group—Mauro Altamura, Amy Kiger-Williams, Aimee Rinehart, Dawn Ryan, Michael Liska, Erin McMillan, and Brett Duquette. Bill Raduchel, Shane Whaley, Tim Shipman, Andrew Feinstein, Rae Edelson, Bruce Dow, Matthew Palmer, Fred Wistow, Dwyer Murphy, Joseph Kanon, Kevin Larimer, Elizabeth Kostova, Polly Flonder, Mary Knox, Mark Sitley, and Nahid Rachlin have been generous with their support and encouragement over the years.

Many books and journalistic accounts were indispensable sources of information about Moscow during the first decades of the twenty-first century. Books that particularly helped me understand the Kremlin's attitudes toward American investors were Bill Browder's *Red Notice* and *Freezing Order*. Mark Leibovich's *Thank You For Your Servitude* provided insights into Washington's political zeitgeist during the novel's time period. An Atlantic Council's report, *Lubyanka Federation*, was a source for understanding the byzantine rivalries among different FSB directorates. I owe a literary debt to Josip Novakovich's novel, *Rubble of Rubles*, which inspired one scene, and to Len Deighton's oeuvre. Journalistic accounts of FSB and Russian mafia involvement in bank fraud and money laundering provided helpful details, particularly an interview with an FSB defector who now goes by the name Janosh Newmann. The Cosmos Club conversation among couples on how they met was inspired by a memorable dinner I co-hosted at Union Square Café among Otto, Joe, Dan, Charles, and Mick and Jo.

I owe special thanks to my wife, Linda, to whom this book is dedicated—teacher, mother, loving partner, and grandparent extraordinaire.